The Exploding Fete

Benjamin Obler

Also by Benjamin Obler

Javascotia

*Animals in the Yard
and Other Circumspections*

The Mombaccus Expansion

Aqua Fox Press

Mombaccus, NY

Aqua Fox Press is a division of Aspiring Writer Syndrome.
www.aquafoxpress.com

Exploding Fete, The / Benjamin Obler —1st ed.
ISBN 979-8-9856091-0-3

Technical Note

This work employs Outcome Branch Narrative Technology™. At designated points in the narrative, you as a reader may select a storyline that pleases you most; that most aligns with your conception of the world; that offers you the most satisfying array of moral outcomes and stylistically presents featured brands to your liking. Outcome Branch Narrative Technology™ transforms an otherwise stagnant and prescriptive reading product into a robustly pleasing customized *experience*, the prime feature of which is not having or being or doing but *choosing*. That is, choosing again and again and thereby eternally *becoming*. Becoming more like yourself with every choice.

To get the most out of your OBNT-enabled device, simply look for the appearance of Outcome Branch options printed at the bottom of a page. For example:

**If you think Lois should pursue a career
as a social-media influencer, turn to page 18.**

**If you think Lois should start a tech company,
turn to page 19.**

The page number printed in gray is your ticket to total immersion in personalized narrative experience and guarantees a plot arc that harmonizes with your existing viewpoints. Our tastes and preferences are precious—let's not corrupt them! Enjoy!

If this doesn't make you free
It doesn't mean you're tied
If this doesn't take you down
It doesn't mean you're high

If this doesn't make you smile
Yeah, you don't have to cry
If this isn't making sense
It doesn't make it lies

—"Superunknown"
Chris Cornell / Kim Thayil

The
Exploding
Fete

Part 1

The Fete

—1—

Petra Barnhouse was the first to arrive at the Winslow's fourth floor townhome on Washington Avenue. She set a pineapple torte atop the credenza and was taking off her navy blue trench coat when she heard the hostess's clacking heels.

"And is the trophy put away where I said?" Mrs. Winslow asked.

Jerome Ardizzone walked beside her. "Yes, it's up in the att—" The fastidious head of the catering staff, was an lean, clean-shaven man with a bony nose in a trim-cut suit.

"Ah, ah," Mrs. Winslow scolded. "Mrs. Barnhouse!" She drew together her yellow cardigan and forcing a smile, touched her cheek to Petra's.

"Good evening, Mrs. Winslow."

"Hello, and welcome."

Petra understood that the gathering would be large and that Mrs. Winslow's evening would be a marathon of hugs, kisses, hellos, thank yous, congratulations, and, hopefully, congratulatory good-byes. "Candace, you look magnificent. Just point me to a quiet corner," Petra said. She lowered her head as if seeking absolution. Pentecostals pride themselves on displays of mercy and expect to be appreciated for this quality. And yet it was her mercilessness that had earned Petra the nomination that brought her here tonight.

They spoke of the torte, which she didn't have to do. Then Mrs. Winslow gestured towards the massive parlor and said, "Well, by all means, dear." She ordered Jerome to take the torte, and ran her hand over the surface of the credenza, testing for moisture.

Petra did not know whether the hostess was cruel or humane, only that she was an illustrious socialite and philanthropist. She was recognizable as the face of the Foundation, from its messages of national outreach. Mrs. Winslow's bore a sense of high standing, which kept Petra from daring an obsequious smile. She entered the parlor in a state of somber reverence, the very first guest.

Early summer, early evening. A room as impeccable as those featured in *Architectural Digest*. There was something quite unlike rural Pennsylvania here. She circled a table of lustrous wood and sat in a Louis quatorze chair, crossing her legs to make a smaller impression on the cushion, tucking her hair behind her ears, flattening a crease in her wool skirt. The room was utterly silent and draftless behind the sturdy seals of the huge windows, which looked high-tech. The snug comfort that the rich enjoy. The rest of the place seemed neo-Gothic, perhaps—or Baroque? Petra couldn't be sure.

Petra Barnhouse completely embodied the supplicant air of a candidate waiting in hope of having a redemptive prize awarded to her. She had sat exactly like this before many piano recitals and Christmas mass concerts in her younger years. When the doorbell rang, she didn't flinch and watched the foyer with twinkling openness and expectation. Her teeth, like xylophone keys, expanded the welcoming aspect of her visage. Mentally she labored to let go of any apparent selfish desires.

Hermann Donskoy stepped in, a man of stature and 76 years, hearty, ruddy as from labor or a blood condition, yet over six foot and pure gentry meat. Mrs. Winslow appeared shortly.

"Hermann Donskoy. I smell lavender," Herman said, shaking Mrs. Winslow's hand.

"Oh."

"I hope it's a synthetic candle. The real stuff will have me in a storm of sneezing."

"Essential oils in a diffuser, I believe. Jerome?" Mrs. Winslow turned her entire torso, neck stiff as if to suggest some nascent inflexibility.

Jerome's air, Petra thought, was of an aide-de-camp, standing close at Mrs. Winslow's elbow. "That's correct. Nature's Bounty. Do you know the brand?"

"I certainly don't," Herman said. "You should be more mindful of people's sensitivities. I would have thought you of all people..."

Petra, looking on from afar, turned away.

"I'm terribly sorry, Mr. Donskoy. Jerome, turn the thing off, for god's sake."

"Well, we'll know in a matter of minutes just how potent it is. Nevertheless, I'm delighted to be here," Donskoy grumbled.

Mrs. Winslow held a palm in the direction of the parlor, in the manner that dog handlers hold their palms on the plastic turf of the Westminster Kennel club during exhibitions.

"The red Chinese," Donskoy said, dropping into the chair beside Petra Barnhouse. It only took him a moment to turn a minuscule dial on his hearing aid, which he'd removed. Then he replaced it in his right ear, the side near to Barnhouse. "For three years, I listened to Morse code on US-Army-issued headphones, broadcast by the red Chinese. If that doesn't mangle your hearing, I don't know what will."

Petra sank. Her hardships were not nearly so historical in scope. When one's suffering is connected to history, recognition comes that much easier.

Introductions.

"I wasn't aware they'd be confiscating our prized possessions," Donskoy said.

"You mean the cell phones? It's an understandable precaution."

"Is it?"

At the ground level, near the front gate, both Barnhouse and Donskoy's mobile phones had been taken away by a duo of men dressed in security black. Donskoy had watched as his ancient Motorola—and device he barely tolerated, and seldom used—was place placed in a locking pouch. In return he'd been given an electronic chip with an ID number on it.

"I have a sick wife at home. If she drops, she can't very well reach me on this, can she?" He held up the chip like it was a dog turd.

Petra, incredibly impressionable of arising opportunities and seeming downturns of fate, brightened. Here, she could engage her tact and also her helpfulness. She could begin to spread her reputation throughout the gathering. They didn't have their phones but this was the original thing—schmoozing. Face-to-face talk (which, around the world, would soon cease).

"I'm terribly sorry about your wife. But they take phones because of social media, you understand. People will try to sway the results, or be swayed."

"I don't care about that," Donskoy said with a wave of his hand.

"No, but plenty others do, and Mrs. Winslow and the foundation cannot have a breach."

"Mmm," Donskoy groaned. "It takes very little to create controversy these days, if you ask me."

Barnhouse smiled. To be beleaguered by technological advancements didn't count for anything. Technology had advanced on us all equally, like a heedless stampede of ...mmm, bison perhaps.

The doorbell rang again.

—2—

The chime was nearly ceaseless now, as it should be, being just past 6.

In the kitchen, Mrs. Winslow said, "Darling, just in time," to her daughter Joyce, who entered through the door that came directly from the underground parking garage.

"Take over door duty, will you? I have Jerome and the starters..."

"Let me take my coat off, for God's sake," Joyce said. Thirty-nine years old, Caucasian, a woman who served as executive director of a foundation out of familial obligation. Her true joy was marathons, kettle bell workouts, road cycling, whole foods and the raw food movement—anything strict that contributed to the intensity and extremity of life, that added an unpredictable contour to people's presumption that, as a member of a millionaire family, she enjoyed sloth, gluttony, rich food, boozing, etc. Joyce draped her belted double-faced camelhair coat over some furniture, out of the way.

"Jerome! Jerome!" Mrs. Winslow yelled.

The room was hot and smelled of rising bread, browning pork and rosemary. Four members of the catering team shuffled around the ovens, the Viking range and the ten-by-six island topped with 1200 pounds of quartz. They bent over cutting boards, tossed the sizzling contents of pans over dancing orange flames, and uncorked bottle after bottle of Sonoma cab, decanting glugging, bloodlike quarts into carafes.

Jerome emerged from the pantry, where he had retreated to make calls and stand a chance of hearing and being heard.

"Yes?"

"Did you check the inscription, like I asked?"

"I did, I did. They got it right."

"What about polish? Couldn't you run over it with a cloth. I think there's a bottle of something around here for the stainless steel. That would be okay, wouldn't it, on brass?"

"Mrs. Winslow, it's spotless already, I assure you. It came

wrapped several times over. Bubble wrap, packing paper. You know, it was *just* made."

"Yes, but it's been handled. Find time to wipe it down, for me, please."

"Of course, Mrs. Winslow."

She began to eye a browned spinach leaf in a salad bowl. Seeing her distraction, Jerome began to move away.

"And Jerome."

"Yes?" He demurely spun on his heels.

She pulled him close by the elbow and turned both their backs to the staircase leading to the attic. "Be discrete, won't you? No one must know the whereabouts, you see. This is a coveted award, and really ...shall we say, passionate people cannot be counted on to act fairly. You understand."

"I understand." As Event Coordinator for one of the premier outfits in the city, Jerome was very well practiced in authentically yessing. Clients like Mrs. Winslow must never feel patronized, and they never did, with Jerome at the helm. Boondoggles happen; things go wrong; sous chefs have meth addictions and flip out, leaving Brussels sprouts to burn; freezer delivery trucks have failing refrigerant systems and liver pate spoils; inexperienced servers trip—on and on. But Jerome's face was freshly shaven, minus the soul patch; he weighed 121 pounds and looked tremendous his slate-gray Kenneth Cole, single-breasted suit, with cloud-white oxford beneath, no tie. Looks mattered. Event Coordination was a game of impressions. The impression of infallible leadership. Modelling the impossible: perfection. Execution of a dream. So far things were flawless, and in about four hours, he'd be smoking on the veranda, and if he had his way, clinking his flute of prosecco against that of the young and uberhot Joyce Winslow, perhaps stealing a glance down her million dollar cleavage.

—3—

In the parlor, Evonne Sorenstam-Finch was nearly in tears already, though she'd just arrived, and this made her feel disappointed in herself, because she had chastised herself so eagerly in advance, made such preparations and plans, issued declarations that she wouldn't cry, at least not right away. But she couldn't help it. Around her already were such *amazing* and worthy people, like Petra whom she'd just met, the dearest little woman, obviously a woman wronged in many ways, short-shrifted in terms of height and beauty and who knew what else, but her small saggy face revealed much disappointment, surely a life lived in the shadows of larger presences, washed this way and that by uninvited forces. Then there was this esteemed gentleman Hermann who'd selflessly deposited his life on the line in service of his country back when there were no Facebook groups where appreciation could publicly accrue and memes capture the gratitude of a nation, and it had obliterated his senses, literally, his hearing. And we all know how these heroes were welcomed home—with a shovel and, Here you go, set down your rifle, and head on down to the steel mill and shovel bitumen into the blast furnace 45 hours a week, at the end of which we'll give you thirty dollars or so. It was all so devastating and beautiful and Evonne was just besotted with awe and humility and gratitude. She moved from person to person, shaking hands, her spine bowing into a more complete circle at each guest she met—such that she nearly forgot they were really co-candidates, fellow applicants—competition! A fact that cast Evonne into a conflicted state where her humility plummeted so low she didn't know how she would recover her own deservingness, something that the abjuring of which threatened her stability, for how many nights now, since receiving the announcement of the fete, her invitation, had she imagined being called up to Mrs. Winslow's side and standing before a throng of the worthiest people like herself, hugging Mrs. Winslow and being hugged by all the foundation's committee members, or panelists, or board members or delegates or whatever they were, one after the other, taking the podium, if there was a podium....

Evonne wore an eggshell colored linen skirt and blazer combination and wore her auburn hair tied back in a bun, which she felt was appropriately austere, the hairstyle that a person might adopt waking up in a refugee camp, where there were no showers or electricity. She was 27 years old and worked in Pittsburgh as a design director for the advertising firm Janklow & Janklow. Having settled on a divan across the room from the others, she was saying to the man beside her, "...just the many assaults, of course, and a kind of unrelenting experience of lingering pain. That has driven me back from life. Doubt too. Doubt, I think, is the invisible factor in cases such as mine. One doubts that it is safe to participate in society. One doubts the point of trying. One doubts that justice will prevail. And then with the events of the week, this whole testimony of Mr. Kavanaugh..." A tear barreled down her cheek.

Joseph Hector Depace was the recipient of Evonne's confidences. An apparent Caucasian of Brazilian and German descent, his body swam in an overlarge department store suit. Inexperienced at wearing a suit, he kept the blazer buttoned as he sat, and the lapels and collar rode up near his ears. One thing Depace was experienced in was presenting himself as if he were ignorant of his infirmities. Fifty-three years old, with large ears, dark eyes, and short-shorn hair, graying at the temples. Listening to Sorenstam-Finch, he worked to release strain in his sinuses and brow that had taken up permanent residency there since the death of his infant daughter Gloria to S.I.D.S and the later death of his wife, Valerie, to acute thrombosis, blood clots, diabetic complications, heart murmurs, and the hazards of surgical fistulae. His life was absurd, and his duty now was to survive it with dignity until he could lie back and close the lid on it, shielding him from the world's gaze.

The fete and the award offered Joseph little in the way of hope. His expectations were low. Only in the furthest rear alcove of his consciousness could he lay a cognitive hand on a parcel containing the remote and unlikely gift that he might be selected and arrive home yet tonight with statuary in his hands that somehow relieved the bleakness of his condition. He felt about it the same way that one feels about hitting the Mega-Millions: you know the surer thing would be to flush the ten dollar bill down the toilet. At least then you're positive of where you stand.

Joseph's stomach growled, and as he listened to Evonne—closely listened, nodding, eyes locked on hers—he also listened for the squeak of a door hinge. Coming in, he had spotted the caterers in their vests at work in the kitchen, when a very sexy woman had passed through the swinging door. Also his eye had alit on the empty heating trays and lamps in the room adjacent to the foyer, which awaited, as he did, the arrival of buckets and buckets of sumptuous cuisine. He smelled the rosemary and the pork and even the red wine. His mouth watered.

Joseph owned a little corner store in South Minneapolis—e-cigarettes and lotto tickets were the big money items. After that, his life revolved around potato chips, beef jerky, energy drinks, rolling papers and blunts. He netted about 15K a year after rent and insurance. He'd flown to the U.S. from El Salvador in the 1960s with his wife, Valerie. Thirty years they'd lived and worked here, paying taxes, but never obtaining citizenship. When Valerie became ill, they didn't have the medical coverage they needed to get proper treatment. Her emphysema and COPD advanced quickly, with many debilitating side-effects. She left the world less than a year after the diagnosis.

"You still carry much grief," Joseph said, seeing Evonne's tear. One of the enduring—and last-remaining—assets of his life was the cultural inheritance of observational powers and truth-telling. The romance of gypsy psychics. Witchcraft, voodoo. Cultural legacy. Bloodline stuff that you couldn't set in a bin going through TSA security. His grandmother had been that way, reading tea leaves and palms, communing with ancestors in her mind. Joseph had never forgotten and would never forget the day he'd come in the house, about 8 years old, after running all the way home from the new shopping mall built in his little town. "You've stolen something!" his Grandmother correctly observed, taking one look at him.

"Mr. Depace, I don't know that I'll ever be free from the

bonds of grief," Evonne mused. She was enlivened to this kind of grandiloquence in this moment. Though she wasn't southern, it was a southern-sounding litany. That charmed her. She felt elevated. Mr. Depace, pitiful though he was, had suffered mere loss of life. He was a touch brownish, which was wonderful, but his story didn't have the complexity, the layers, that anyone with a read on the situation would expect in a recipient of an award of this caliber. Depace's was a case of straight-up misfortune. Medical misfortune. Cells mutate. Viruses infect the system. Hardly something we can rally against. This was an age of powerful injustices. We cannot squander this opportunity. Evonne saw Mr. Depace as a kind of padding of the roster, not a true contender, and that invigorated her spirits.

Joseph and Evonne's close conversational contact was then pried apart, as if by a mothering chaperone looking to cool romantic fires. They both helplessly looked up and around the parlor to comprehend the general commotion that harassed the periphery of their vision and other senses. A half dozen people stood about the carpet, in shiny shoes and dresses, making introductions: a burbling of appreciative hellos and how-do-you-dos flying. A Rachmaninoff symphony had begun playing as well, from some quarter of the townhome, and the door chime continued to strike, even while Joyce Winslow loudly welcomed the new faces emerging from behind the door, peering curiously into the room. All in all, a dozen or fifteen people occupied the space, and though the massive parlor could hold many, many more, the character of a party had suddenly been established. That electric exchange of identities. Not raucous, for the occasion was solemnly professional. But appropriately celebratory. Invitations had gone out months ago, and the peaking of so much anticipation filled the room like a heavy fume, almost as one sees fog over certain lakes and streams in the morning, when the atmospheric conditions are right. It is at times such as these that the realization is brought forward that so much more than oxygen occupies the invisible areas of a given space that we're all entitled to inhabit.

—4—

New to the party, and feeling the heft of the carpet beneath her feet, was the depressive Asian-American theater director Christine Wong, an extremely dignified and accomplished lesbian, who had heroically survived many severe bouts of suicidal ideation and morbid lethargy after giving her all to a production of *The Vagina Monologues* at the Charles Lerwick Playhouse in Mossley, CT. Also the graduate student Merrill Roselli, 22, a stand-out for his youthful appearance, toothy vibrancy, and the bulkiness of his argyle sweater, to which several pins and medallions were affixed, symbolizing his support of causes. When a greenhorn wishes to appear more beset by age, he dons a sweater, the heavier the better. A homosexual and former class president, Roselli's reputation was that of a stunningly erudite and eloquent speaker on issues of equality, civil rights, and the importance of representation in local government. He had organized an Occupy movement in Chicago during the summer of 2011; and throughout his college years, and continuing to the present, he had authored dozens of articles at a popular online publishing platform, articles that guided readers towards the correct attitudes and behaviors in regards to many sensitive social situations, topics such as why it's important to be mindful of offensive adages and idioms alive in our American dialect, and why not to buy Happy Meals with giveaways of figurines that embody gender stereotypes, and how to organize a boycott of local businesses that discriminate, such as the Coloradan cake decorator famously did.

These newcomers were observed by the hulking Hermann Donskoy, who had risen from the seat beside Petra Barnhouse to mingle. Donskoy, despite his curmudgeonly bent, liked to be in the know, part of the action. Roselli was a highly problematic figure, Donskoy felt, with his exuberant activism and easy proximity, via college campus, to the all the latest concerns. The contender had arrived in the ring. Let him dance around in his boxer shorts, swiping at the air. But the threat of Roselli was dampened, Donskoy felt, by the very thing that gave him an advantage: his youth. Roselli would have a lifetime to garner awards, and surely Mrs. Winslow and the committee members recognized the importance of serving someone more distinguished upon whose door opportunity was less frequently heard knocking.

We go through life with a portfolio of diminishing enthusiasms, a great man once quoted a great man as saying. Donskoy had experienced this diminishment directly, keenly.

"This place is huge," Wong remarked to Donskoy, looking around.

"I've seen bigger. Goebbel's summer home was twice this size, and wall to wall antiquities."

"Well, if you're going to play that card," Wong muttered, noticing Donskoy's hearing aid—in the din, he wouldn't hear. She faced him directly—which required her to look upwards—when issuing the challenge, "What's troubling about this whole affair is the privilege, don't you think, Mr. Donskoy?"

"Privilege?"

"Like the way history is always written by the victors. Why should the Winslows be the arbiters in this? They're old money, whites, imperialists. Who gave them the power to ascribe value?"

"Honey, that's the way the ball bounces," Donskoy said, looking across the room.

Wong gasped. "I'm not your honey!" Then she blushed, and searched the others to see if anyone had overheard.

"About time," Donskoy quipped. Though his hearing was shoddy, he knew what it looked like when a man in tux undraped a tablecloth, to reveal a row of booze bottles atop a high counter. He headed starboard without saying excuse me.

Wong was self-described "tough as nails" though her wife Julie believed Wong took much abuse, such as the abuse she'd taken from the lead actress in The Vagina Monologues, leading to her post-run exhaustive stupor. This amounted to a kind of resiliency. "Yeah, a drink" Wong said, following Donskoy. He was harmless anyhow; this was the year of the woman, rightly so, and no way would the foundation select a member of the male species. She'd bet a year's salary, a hundred and twenty thousand dollars, on it.

—5—

Across the room, Petra Barnhouse spoke to Andrew Knuthe, a middle school Biology teacher in Tulsa, Oklahoma, and cancer widower. Knuthe, a bearded ginger of Welsh lineage with an easygoing manner, had been, up until 18 months ago, happily married but now he was enjoying (not literally) life as a single man and single father. He had not dated yet or sought female companionship in any way other than professionally, though he had received and not refused the company of neighbors and colleagues, who brought casseroles and brought their chatty, good-willed selves into his home. Increased participation and vigilance in various causes and campaigns had been the chief distractors for Knuthe from his grief.

"It's ironic," Knuthe said, "that just when we had this anti-bullying campaign, what was it, in 2014 I think, you know, this *It gets better* number... they did commercials, billboards, magazine ads, right?"

"*It gets easier*, I think it was," Petra said. She remembered the movement, texting YouTube URLs to her nephew, who had valiantly come out to his family (Barnhouse's sister Dorothy being his mother) in the previous year.

"Oh, you're right! You're right! *It gets easier.* That's what it was," Knuthe said. Knuthe was an evolved man who'd never mansplained anything in his life, had no problem admitting his errors, never assumed the superiority of anyone over anyone else. He was a very uncommon type who was paid just over fifty thousand a year by the Osage County School District.

Barnhouse smiled.

"But we were making such progress. Then who do we elect but the biggest bully the country has ever seen. Bullying is literally his go-to diplomatic approach. He bullies people online. I mean, the irony of that, the hypocrisy, is not lost on the media. You know, the first lady's *supposed* cause."

"Yeah," Barnhouse knowingly groaned.

"So it's not just politically that we've regressed."

"Oh, for sure, for sure."

Knuthe sighed.

"You must see a lot of bullying in your job," Barnhouse said.

"Oh god."

"Middle school. That's when it can be the most prevalent."

"Every day."

"Tsk."

"Horrific stuff. The kids are my passion, you know. They're why I do it." Knuthe was never one to dwell on the negative. It was habitual. He wasn't just a guy to say that he didn't dwell on the negative, or who robotically utters that directive, *Well, no point dwelling on the negative*. No. Just as soon as he felt the weight of negativity in any conversation, positive words came out of his mouth. This is what made him an inspiring role model and someone so healthily rebounding that it aroused suspicion and garnered him awe. "The rest is gravy. Some teachers play the martyr. Oh, the grading, oh I'm exhausted."

"I taught two years. It *was* exhausting."

"You know the tennis player Roger Federer? The guy hardly sweats. When you love what you do, it's easy. You have to love it."

To Knuthe, most things were reducible this way, could be stated simply, were not complex, were nothing to make a fuss about. His own children, Dean and Lucy, he had parroting his mottos like, *It is what it is*. And *Que sera whatever* and *Life goes on* and *Meanwhile, in reality...* It was true, the world was swamped with people belabored and beset by tragedies and government conscriptions that in just times would not even exist. The fete was the right thing to do, an appropriate token, a veritable symbol, a worthy cause. But its main appeal to Knuthe was that when school boards review salaries, they look at awards, credentials, additional certifications, etc. If he ever had a few extra bucks, he wanted to get a new black lab. The hunting dog he had, Trevor, was getting on in years. Eleven years old now. When Trevor pointed, he looked like a drunk doing a line test on the side of the highway. Highly unsteady on arthritic legs. Knuthe wanted a new lab. Chocolate or white—it didn't matter.

"Is there a stipend with this award?" Knuthe asked.

Barnhouse had been gazing out the window to Washington Avenue four stories below, noticing how from this perspective on a developed urban boulevard the sidewalk-planted trees and the pedestrians and the marquee signs looked just like they do in architectural drawings.

"It's a cash prize," she said, turning back. "Twenty-five thousand."

"Mmm." Knuthe hummed along to the Rachmaninoff. He had played French horn in high school and college and recognized Concerto No. 2, Opus 40.

"This sucker's filling up," Knuthe said. "Here, let's, uh..." He stepped back to make room for the cluster of six or so people easing into the parlor. Just barely, he touched Barnhouse's elbow to draw her back. She understood and sidled with him.

Her face brightened. "What a wonderful group! It's marvelous to have these people gathered here."

"It is. It really is," Knuthe said. Maybe a white lab would be better than chocolate? Is that possible? "Well, I tell ya," Knuthe said, for the dream of a new dog, a new era in his life, just didn't seem likely to leave his mind unless he spoke of it. "If I get this prize, I'm getting a new hunting dog. That's what I'll do with the money. And pay down the kids' school loans, of course."

"You hunt?" Barnhouse said.

"*Love* to hunt. Grouse, pheasant, duck."

"I'm vegan."

Knuthe pursed his lips and nodded—not entirely regretfully. Just acknowledging, dwelling in the fact of difference, which was entirely natural.

"The bar seems to be open. I think I'll get a glass of wine."

"O! kaaaay," Knuthe said tightening a smile, stuffing his hands in his pockets and peering at the black wingtips he hadn't worn since someone's funeral. Whose was it?

Oh, right, his wife's. How could he forget? Because he'd blocked it out, that's why. Because his mottos didn't sufficiently apply on the matter of his wife Shari's rapid contraction of breast cancer, its insanely virulent advancement, wildfire-like spread to her internal organs, and her abrupt departure from this world, from Andrew's life, and from the Knuthe family, where she held a prominent leadership position of wife and mother.

Knuthe was of the disposition that it was best not to dwell, and then along came an incident that he felt obliged to become active in, and did become active in, so much so that it kept his mind occupied to the point that he didn't really feel the grief of his recent loss anymore. Precisely the point. What happened was that the Oklahoma school board began to meddle in the Biology curriculum used in its schools, holding advisory panel meetings with the consortium who farmed out the authoring of criteria delivered to publishers of classroom instructional materials. Knuthe, hearing about the alteration of some language around fossil fuels vs. wind, solar, and other green energy technologies, requested transcripts of the advisory panel meetings, and inferred that the changes were driven by their state representative, a Republican. Knuthe took a meeting with the man in his capitol building office, and found out that it all began when the Honorable Representative Kirtz saw a multiple-choice question on his son's homework asking:

What contributes to climate change? Gas, oil, or all of the above?

The right honorable representative thought the correct answer should be None of the Above. From there, the rep brought together a Natural Gas advocacy group, paired them up with some science professors from Oklahoma University, and had them author revised curricula painting fossil fuels in an ever-so-rosy light, actually going so far as to say their use benefits the environment.

Knuthe raised holy hell. Got himself interviewed on the news. Colleagues made a hashtag. He refused to teach the curriculum and for that he was fired, until protests led to a governor's order, and he was reinstated. He grew comfortable, but not arrogant, in his status as a *cause célèbre*, using his notoriety and the synergy (in a way, he was bullied by the state representative and the school board) to create an anti-bullying after-school group and draw attention to the importance of kind treatment of others, no matter their differences, which was gratifying and an important part of his character, despite the fact that one of his favorite hobbies was killing animals with firearms.

—6—

Jerome leaned over the kitchen island and addressed Tara Voss, a wiry woman with black hair gelled high, shaved above the ears, pierced eyebrow, inked forearms, which were bare for the task of carving radishes. Jerome's employer, Premier Events Management (PEM, or "Premier"), was a financially distinct entity from the catering division that employed Tara ("Grand Soir Gourmands"), but the two companies were owned by the same parent company, Malone Enterprises, Gabe Malone CEO and Founder, and the companies were in essence frequent partners. Jerome and Tara had worked together for several years. "When can you step away? I need a hand upstairs," Jerome said.

"Gimme five to finish these," she said, gesturing to the bowl of washed, unpared radishes.

Jerome went away and came back. When she was ready, Jerome said, "Leave your phone. Put it in a drawer or something."

She did so.

"Sorry—protocol. We also need a clean towel." Tara peeled one off a stack of white linen towels. "Ah, gloves." Tara fished out a pair from a dispenser pack. "And this." He handed her a bottle of polishing agent. "Follow me."

They ascended the wrought iron staircase to the attic. Jerome shouldered open the door, which was sticky in the frame.

"In here."

The attic smelled of moth balls and moist cardboard. Finished in dull brown paneling, it had an A-frame celling. The bannisters and fixtures were cobwebbed, and dusty light shone on an old rolltop desk, some lamps, and sagging boxes. "Over here," Jerome said, crossing to a dormer window, under which he'd set the trophy.

"So what's up?" Tara asked.

"Mrs. Winslow wants this polished." Jerome said, standing clear of the trophy, letting Tara approach it. "It's brand-spanking new. But that's her wish."

"You're the boss. Use this stuff?"

"Yeah, yeah," Jerome took up his phone to answer texts from his boss, Gabe, an antiques dealer by blood who was too dyspeptic to work on-site with clients. He'd offended too many in the past, lost Premier too much business. Gabe oversaw all client relation matters, finances, staffing, advertising, and the all-important social media. It was his company. He was a control freak. It was annoying for Jerome to have his phone buzzing all night, but he was used to it. Not often, but sometimes Gabe even had a good idea when a jam came up. Right now he was just being nosy about how everything was going. Gabe tended to assume there'd always be a crisis. He wasn't necessarily wrong.

Candace wants the trophy polished, that's all, Ardizzone hammered out with his hummingbird-fast thumbs.

Tara's thumbs were being jammed into surgical gloves, same with her fingertips, which stretched the rubber until it snapped into place. The trophy was three-feet tall, and though elaborate and even artistic, not that different from something a softball team would win at season's end. The topmost figure greeted Tara first: a female cherubic sort in the realistic vein—curvaceous, breasted, unnaturally sleek—raising an ivy ring above her head. Victorious, but nondescript. What had she won, exactly? Arranged shrubbery. Tara crouched down, set the polish on the floor and the rag on her knee. She tilted the trophy back to study it. Tri-pillared with fluted Roman Doric columns set on a single footing of some kind of fake alabaster. It had heft. Lead perhaps, with brass coating. At the bottom, a gold inscribed plate.

"The Foundation for the Advancement of Inclusivity and Recognition?" Tara said, looking up to Jerome.

Jerome kept thumb-typing, eyes locked on his mobile. "F.A.I.R." he stated, diplomatically.

These two were professionals. They'd done bar mitzvahs, weddings, graduations, fund-raising galas, assorted benefits, even electoral victory parties. They'd seen it all. The ceremonies of the human race were not things that withstood close scrutiny. They couldn't be reasoned into a state of sensibility. But for them both, Jerome and Tara, occasions and fanfare paid the pills. The moment you let any kind of disparagement into your professional endeavors it had the potential, like a crack in a dam, to reveal the futility of most enterprises, and in this case to embarrass the self-importance of the upper classes. You saw this crack of harsh light increasingly in mainstream media coverage of the Oscars, ever since they were called out for snubbing non-whites—how it's an industry congratulating, fawning over, itself. Anyway, a fete was one thing, and a religious coming of age ceremony like a bar mitzvah or bat mitzvah was another.

"Oh shit, the winner's name is on here!" Tara whispered.

Jerome puckered his mouth, demonstrating tight lips.

"All right," Tara said, squeezing out a dab of polish on the rag draped over her open hand. Starting at the base, she went to work. It reminded her of a job she'd had as a 14-year-old. (She'd lied to the owner of the place, saying she was the required 16.) Suds & Scrubs, a car wash, where the cars were set in neutral and pulled down a conveyor belt. A fleet of kids cleaned it up in three and half minutes, one washing, one wiping, one vacuuming, one Windex-ing. It was pretty miserable, but at least it was kind of indoors, under this canopy-like shed with terra cotta floors, not shitty concrete, open to the elements on either end, where the garage doors went up and down, but the line flanked by electric heaters of glowing orange coils. Tara's fingertips became chapped and her nose ran the entire time in winter. At least it wasn't a greasy griddle or a basket of fries dunked in boiling oil.

By that age she was on her own basically. When she was four, Tara's parents had divorced, and she'd lived with her father after that until age nine, when he was jailed for a felony armed robbery. Her grandmother took her in at that point, out in a depressing suburb called Blaine, but when grandmother died, Tara couch-hopped at the homes of some school friends, back in the city; that dried up after a few months, at which point, rather than get herded through the juvenile system, she hit the streets, working by day, sleeping in shelters, box cars, cardboard digs. She learned the public restrooms she could slip into, like the bus station, the Hennepin County Public Library down on Third Avenue with its pale imitation of the Acropolis. Work was kind of welcome at that point—at least it was warm, on the steamy line—

and it was Suds & Scrubs money that got her into her first rented room, an eight-by-ten number in some creeper's run-down house, that felt like the Taj Mahal not because of spaciousness but because the door actually had a padlock—well, and the room actually had a door, for starters—and so unlike tents and boxes in a Canadian Pacific switchyard and on the grassy median outside the Cedar Avenue tunnel, you didn't wake up to some filthy drunk grabbing your tits, or barfing on you—features that take on the aspect of luxury after you've been out there. The place was at Monroe Street and 10th. Yeah, the super's Marb red smoke penetrated the walls and out one window and into hers, but to privacy and relative safety add a little heat, a shitty single mattress, and there you go—Taj Mahal.

She always figured that her Suds & Scrubs boss, a ratty looking guy named Terry, knew she wasn't in fact 16. There was a certain knowing gleam when he hired her. Never made her fill out a W4, but that was nothing special because he kept timesheets by hand and paid everyone in cash anyway. Okay, helping out the unfortunate. What a champion. He was all right for a while, until he wasn't, when he jumped her in the supply room one time, came up behind her as she reached for a gallon jug of cleaner from a high shelf, put his face in her neck, his hands around her waist, started smearing his lips all over her neck. At first she was like, There's been a mistake, he thinks I'm someone else. Or he forgot he's not at home with his wife. But when she spun around, he grabbed her wrists. You couldn't hear shit back there—the vacuums howling, the compressor motor for the pressure washers ratcheting, the motor that drove the belts grinding. *Don't fight, Tara. Don't fight. I'll break you.*

That was the end of Suds & Scrubs. Lucky for her she was resourceful, gritty, determined. She took all the shit that happened to her and just stuffed it down, down, down, and it was a kind of power pellet, a fuel in her furnace. Yeah, there were times she wanted to jump into a lane of traffic—spotted the places it would work, where drivers didn't stand a chance of anticipating her falling body, whether out of the air or from behind an overpass abutment. There were hundreds of places. But something kept her going. A single cop bought her fast food pretty often, a Wendy's burger and fries in a sack, checked up on her.

Through it all she thought of her uncle. She had an uncle once who had a dog and a motorcycle. She'd stayed with him a few times, back when her father was alive, in some factory town up near Ely. Something like his life was all she'd ever wanted. A couple pillars of freedom she could discern in the otherwise shabbiness of his setup: a place of her own that she could paint and build in whatever fucking renegade configuration pleased her, that she could change every day if she wanted, putting the kitchen on the roof or whatever; a bike, nothing special, just a Kawasaki or Suzuki with saddle bags and a windscreen; and a some dumb mutt to kill the squirrels and shit on the neighbors' yard and just be there at night—to bark like hell if some fucker tried climbing in the window. Like anyone's foolish dream, it seemed enough to stick around for, even if the only apparent point of sticking around was to answer the question that she was the only one in the world who cared about the answer to: whether she was clever or determined enough to *make it* happen, or whether fate had something else in store for her.

One thing Tara understood was that for every new thing she lost and for every person who shit on her good-faith efforts to get it together and make something for herself, when the dream did come, it would be that much sweeter.

She got other jobs. A hard worker. Ethical. Loyal. Honest. Bussing, dishwashing. An Italian place on Stinson Avenue, near ballfields and other Friday Night Lights kind of scenes that were nearly imaginary to her, like she was in a Spielberg movie.

Then came 16, 17, and the surprising new fun facts that penises were way uglier than pussies and chicks far cooler than guys, with their macho bullshit, and anyway, mascara and blush and hairspray and curling irons were expensive and a pain in the ass to tote around when you're living out of our car. Once she brought a gal pal over to her room, and the next day the smoky super of the eight-by-ten suddenly told her to get out, he was renovating, selling, other lies, like she hadn't paid on time or broke some curfew. Jeans could be worn wrinkled and when she looked at herself she saw not pretty but bad-ass, with a hard jawline and cutting eyes and pencil-thin lips. The piercings and ink colored it up, spoke a language to other females like her. She started dying her hair black, shaving the sides with a clipper, the number 1 guard, and gelling the rest upwards spiky like razor wire at the top of fences.

There's a shit ton more to the screaming comet that was her life's trajectory, and it all started with those strokes of a rag against car doors and car hoods and car bumpers, and ended with Tara being where she is now, in the attic of the Winslow's townhome, her lesbian days behind her, not that it was wrong or she miscalculated, it was right at the time, what she needed, and probably brought on by the fucker Terry, her therapist says, but now she's single and dates guys here and there, from time to time. Mostly she just works, though, banking cash. She owns a duplex on Emerson Ave South, rents the lower half out below market value to some young ladies, has concrete countertops poured right now in her kitchen, and after they set she'll shellac them and scorch them with a torch and put some handsome dings in with some 80-grit and a circ sander, and then the trim is bought but not cut for new moldings around every door. Weekends she drives a '64 Mustang to estate sales and flea markets with her English Mastiff Floyd, who is absolutely dumb as a post but loyal to the death, a stalwart beast who makes no complaints. She likes to find old vent grates, lamps, and other ironwork stuff to add to the house, which this year will probably be about twice the value she bought it for. She's 39 now. It's taken almost twenty years, and nearly cost her a kidney at one point, but she wouldn't do much different, given the chance. The whole thing has an ugly beauty about it; it sure as hell wasn't like this hideous trophy, spotless to start with and even more spotless now.

"Brilliant," Jerome said, standing beside Tara, looking on with satisfaction. "I knew I asked the right person."

"Thanks," Tara said, with a smile.

"Not a word about the name on here. Not a word that it's even *up* here. You know there's no cell phones allowed by guests?"

"No shit?"

"Mrs. Winslow seems to think that the name of the winner is a matter of national security. Never mind that more important stuff leaks from the White House every day."

Tara snorted, zipped her lips with a pull of pinched fingers across them.

"Back to work," Jerome said, leading them out the attic door.

For a moment, atop the stairs, Tara looked down on her Grand Soir Gourmand colleagues from above, like a bird in the boughs. She felt like Eva Peron but it was not her nature to sweep her arms wide. She made no proclamation and did not even think of jokingly addressing them as "my people" with the false ardor of the dictator.

—7—

When Lamond P. Jackson walked in, a hush passed over the ensemble, now topping 30 people in size. Jackson, a six foot four black man, toned by the Marine Corps, and wearing field gear fatigues bearing the "digital" camo pattern, dog tags, combat boots, and all, was a physical specimen, no question. But he was also a spiritual specimen. Six tours of duty, Lance Corporal of a troop out of Kentucky, he had served in Afghanistan near the Pakistan border. Specialist in radar and drone surveillance technologies. On an advisory panel to the NSA. Retired. Dozens of times shot, blown up, targeted, discriminated against, tortured, hidden out in desert bunkers, dehydrated and scorched, until roving bands of jihadi nomads passed. PTSD (waning in severity). Testified to a senate committee investigating problems with VA benefits, explaining the lunacy of hoops he and his fellow vets had to jump through, the interminable waits for treatment, psychological services, elevated blood pressure, sleeplessness and other symptoms. Jackson's presence was large—physically, yes, obvious to all instantaneously. But spiritually magnanimous too, a feverishly strong spirit, which everyone recognized but few detected for what it was. They just ascribed it to the impressiveness of his physique, the deserved respect signaled by his uniform, the valor codified in the sculpted medal hanging from his lapel (purple heart). Knuthe saw him and suspected that their awe and wonder was partly their own (reprehensible) subliminal fear of Jackson's skin color, even though his tight haircut and steely demeanor were owed to a kind of serious duty to country, not militancy to extremist views like racial hatred. Recently Knuthe had watched a documentary on Quincy Jones and noticed how in the footage of Jones in the '70s, when his afro was large and his muscles bared, the gifted musician and composer set off some nervous system response in Knuthe about criminality and threat, even though he'd led big bands behind Sinatra and studied orchestration in Paris, for god's sake. There it was, something genetic or cultural overriding all fact and observation to impart a physical response: threating blackness. Totally un-founded in direct experience. Something similar was at play with Jackson upon many others, and they said to themselves that it was his size, his strength, and his fatigues that appeared threatening. They said to themselves that it was war they op-posed.

Jackson moved into the room, and when he did so everyone across the parlor and in the adjacent room where a multi-lane line had formed before the bar momentarily dropped their hopes of winning the award, and all their aspirations figuratively bottomed out, and they said to themselves, "Shit, here's some-one we should truly *honor*. We're all monumentally unworthy." Then, little by little, everyone began to find heartening flaws in the idea of the 2018 FAIR award going to a pawn in an interna-tional death game—a warmonger. Flaws that restored their own chances, which were dear to them, promised them a future re-newed by redemption, making each person unwilling to give them up so easily. Not to mention the chunk of change that for some meant months on the beach in Phuket, for others meant a year off to write that novel, or any other dream no-longer-de-ferred. They would not let that be taken away without a fight. Thank god, looking at Jackson's 46-inch-wide shoulders, it would be an *ideological* fight.

Christine Wong said was standing with Depace and Roselli still. "I support the military," she said. "I do, but I do think there would be a lot of backlash, you know." There was so much con-versation happening now, she did not have to cover her mouth or speak quietly to protect herself from being heard by Jackson. "That would really politicize the whole thing in an ugly way."

"It *would* be a tricky choice," said Joseph Hector Depace. "You know what I say now. I support *service members*. I think that's more correct to say. Or that's how I feel? I don't neces-sarily support the military at large. In fact, in general, I'm against the military. I wish we didn't have to have armies and navies at all. And especially nuclear weapons."

"I know, right?" said the graduate student Merrill Roselli, the third in this trio currently clustered near a lustrous mahogany end table, their clothes bathed in the futuristically clear LED light bleeding anachronistically through a Tiffany lampshade. "Imagine if we could reclaim the entire defense budget and route it to schools. That'd be amazing!"

"I'm glad he's here," Christine said, nodding in the direction of Jackson, easily spotted in the crowd. "It's important that he's here."

"This is about opportunity for everyone," Depace said.

"If there's one thing we understand better than ever, it's that people are good," Roselli said. "It's the systems that need fixing. Right? He's a guy who probably got a GI scholarship. That might have been a good option for him, given his place of origin and family background."

"It's interesting," Wong said. "Does that mean no one's blameless anymore?" She held a glass of white wine at the height of her stomach, which was prominent under her white blouse with three-quarter length sleeves, and its two rows of square cutouts running vertically, showing a spaghetti strap undershirt. It was a lively garment, while Wong herself was not animated in the least. She stood on flats like a pillar, one arm hanging straight down her side, lifelessly, and though she claimed the topic was interesting and posed an interesting question, her eyes revealed no curiosity, and not even her chin turned up as one reverently turns their faces to the stars, pondering the imponderables. It seemed to be a kind of routine or script that Wong was following. Or that she acted pensive out of odious conscription.

"What do you mean?" Depace asked.

"We have these cases now of lawyers arguing defenses on the grounds of psychological conditions. Your honor, my client's brain is wired to respond violently. Your honor, my client's neuropathways made it next to impossible for him to act otherwise."

"Really? I didn't know about this," Roselli said.

"What kind of cases?" Depace asked.

"Oh, I don't know exactly. Like, murders, in some cases, I suppose, and it begs the question of guilt and accountability. Is any one of us really in charge of our decisions? Where do we draw the line? Say someone's addicted, and they steal to feed the addiction."

"Yes, an obvious case."

"But that's not so interesting to me. What interests me is a murder case. Because the same condition that might absolve him of blame—"

"Would actually be a good reason to lock him up!" Depace said.

"Yes, exactly."

"Whaaat?" Roselli asked, fishing the maraschino cherry out of his cocktail.

"Think about it," Wong explained. "It wasn't his bad judgement or lack of morals that made him do it—assuming in this case the killer is a man. It was something out of his control, his brain. The defense argues this to absolve him of guilt, in search of a lighter sentence. But if his brain is really so programmatically interested in murder, what's to stop him doing it again? He's not safe out among society, where his brain arbitrarily drives him to violate the rights of others—the right to live. And that's against the law!"

"I get it. But he can be treated. Just target the area of the brain with drugs. Whatever the murdering part is."

Wong laughed at Roselli's millennial diction. "The Murdering Part," Wong said. "I'm writing a play, and that's the title. It's set in a courtroom, and the lawyer chooses the brain chemistry defense. There will be many allusions to Kafka's *The Trial*."

"Oh my god, amazing," Roselli said. "You're working on your night off. Have you ever read *The 4-hour Work Week*? I love that guy's podcast."

Wong looked at her drink and did not answer. She did not listen to podcasts or read popular self-help books, and she was thinking about death. Death is the only dramatic gesture with currency anymore. Perhaps it always had been, or never was anything but. Television had coopted death from Shakespeare and made it the Only Act of Consequence. Browse your guide. A hypnotized man doesn't know he's a serial killer. Countless villains want to destroy the universe, all of it, all at once, forever, no exceptions, no backs. Jinx, buy you a Coke. Every night on prime time, bodies turn up on beaches, in attics, in the woods, in trunks of cars, in storage units, in freezers. Every network works to maximize its ad revenue, and it's drama that sucks in the viewers, and death is the loudest dramatic sound. The sounds of death manufactured by Foley artists. Bones crunching, blunt impact by baseball bat, tire iron, shovel. Somewhere in Burbank, there must be a computer hard drive that teems with death in audio form, a library of death sounds. Splat dot wave. Scream dot em pee three. Scream oh one through scream three hundred and five dot em pee three. It used to be that only cable networks like HBO and Showtime made gore, showing it past midnight. Then zombies moved into the thirties on your cable box, and they could be shotgunned by the dozen. Then it moved into the major broadcast networks. How could they keep Kellogg's and Kraft on the books offering anything but death? Things got to a point where online retailers saw how easy the formula is. They started making programming. Other electronics makers got into too, wanting a piece of the death pie, a slice of it dripping red and viscous like cherry filling. Visions of death, people screaming in the dark, the lure of death, the suggestion of death, the threat of death. Get it in the can, get it online, and send out the contracts to State Farm, Huggies, the Frozen Yogurt people, Cialis. Get a hard-on and watch death. Watch death and eat waffles in the morning. Binge it, like a bag of chips. Coin the word binge, put it in the papers to normalize it. It's not unhealthy, it's just fun. You deserve some death today—ding! Make subscriptions cheap. Hell, get one parent megacorp to own the ISP and the network, and you fleece the death-buyers coming *and* going. Bundle the services. Death in your ears, death in your eyes, death up your ass!

"If the brain weren't in play, couldn't we treat his morals?" Roselli said. "Target them?"

"That's what gets targeted in prison, theoretically," Wong said. "Prison is a time for people to contemplate their actions and all those whose lives they've impacted."

"You said you're a theater director?" Depace asked, scratching his head.

"Yes, and a playwright," Wong answered, for the first time expressing something with her face—an angle of 15 degrees starboard, taking the line from her chin to her brow point and measuring against a plum line hung from ceiling to floor.

"What I wonder is about the people in plays. Every play I've seen, the people don't talk naturally. Which I understand is necessary. That's how the action gets going. Really, it's the only thing available to the play writer. Their lines. The characters have to talk. With no lines, you have no play. But how do you solve the problem of realism? Because in my experience, people are very reticent and quiet. They keep secrets. They're shy. Take my wife, for example. She comes to this country, her English is poor, she hardly speaks at all."

"Let's scoot over," Roselli said, making a shepherding motion with his arms, as more people stepped from the foyer, under the long archway, and into the parlor, their eyes widely opened in a show of receptivity and proud participation. Or sometimes, fussing with a handbag, eyes down as if moving onto a busy subway car or through a turnstile—nothing more special than that, an onerous period of awaiting them. Or in some cases heads regal and still and drifting slowly forward like an ocean liner gliding into port.

—8—

"Oh, marvelous," Petra Barnhouse said, seeing a woman, Cassandra Mande, in a bright yellow and black *gele*, or head tie, long, flowing *boubou*, the woman's African dress, brocaded at the hems in gold, and a beautiful sky blue *iro* draped down one shoulder.

Everyone standing in Barnhouse's cluster turned to observe the procession.

"These are all foundation people," said Santos Gougoutris, a newcomer—a second-generation Greek, 46, owner of an import-export business, who had connections to Greek government and a few years ago returned to his native country to advise and consult on the financial crisis, but now was back stateside and active in local Greek-American organizations, including acting as president of Opa!, the Madison, WI, annual Greek food festival, street and craft fair; and serving as Facilities Coordinator at Annunciation Greek Orthodox Church in Wauwatosa, Wisconsin. Santos wore a vest with Greek symbols sewn in it.

Moving in unison with Cassandra Mande, a Haitian, in her African garb, were Charlie S., a chief of the Shakopee-Mdewakanton Sioux tribe, wearing a charcoal suit with vest, and a single falcon feather woven into his braided salt-and-pepper hair; Jóhanna Sturludóttir, 53, first-generation Icelander with joint residency in the US and Iceland; Lenore Happybones, trans, nee Mark Johnson, in heels and sumptuous emerald taffeta strapless cocktail dress with oilslick sheen, bowed across the (implanted) cleavage, flesh and build still thicker and heartier than a typical natural female's through the back and shoulders, despite ten years under estrogen's influence, arms covered in long white evening gloves like Audrey Hepburn in *Breakfast at Tiffany*'s reaching to the upper arms, hair bobbed and dyed autumn-leaf red, dangling earrings of many small connected charms, including, if one looked closely, erotic figures, like a porno totem, face enhanced with rouge and a dusting of glitter, and enough trimmings and elegance to fool many of the room's naïfs who never would have presumed this woman carried two Y chromosomes; Juan Ramirez, a scholarly and hip looking Latino, with Buddy Holly specs, medium-length black hair parted down the center, and many incisors the size, shape, and color of Chicklet brand chewing gum bared by a broad smile, face handsomely carpeted in a black beard—the type who might have worshipped Lorca and traced his Mexican motorcycle journey; Darla Emmenberg, 34, in a motorized wheelchair, shrunken and curled with spina bifida, smile beaming under freshly tinted hair, also curled and bouffant, shellacked into place, wearing a black dress with white trim bought during prom season, when dresses for petites are stocked abundantly.

Their titles, as they appeared in the signatures of their foundation email:

Mande — Director, Foundation for the Advancement of Inclusivity and Recognition

Chief Fire Bird Samuelson — Finance Officer, Foundation for the Advancement of Inclusivity and Recognition

Sturludóttir — Outreach Coordinator, Foundation for the Advancement of Inclusivity and Recognition

Happybones — Program Director, Foundation for the Advancement of Inclusivity and Recognition

Ramirez — Program Director, Foundation for the Advancement of Inclusivity and Recognition

Emmenberg — Administrative Officer, Foundation for the Advancement of Inclusivity and Recognition

They moved into the crowd, intimidating some, but pleasing many.

"What a treat," Knuthe said, smiling at the group. "They're all dolled up."

"A good-looking bunch," Hermann Donskoy said.

"Our fearless leaders," Lamond Jackson said.

"A cross-section of America," Depace said.

"A more dignified procession has never been..." Wong mused.

"Oh my god, Oh my god," Evonne Sorenstam-Finch tearfully blubbered.

Gougoutris silently smiled. Thee brutish woman unnerved him.

Tara Voss, passing from the kitchen to the makeshift dining room/bar with her own personal cigarette lighter in hand to light the Sterno cannisters that sit in the tray table openings, said, "Cool."

The Foundation staff mixed into the heavy throng, which included at least 30 people not yet described here, and individual attentions returned to each person's arm's-length neighbor.

Certain parties had parted, as if they were a red sea and the Foundation staff Moses himself, and in the shuffle and hubbub, Donskoy washed onto Knuthe's shores.

"I've noticed one group not represented so strongly at this occasion," Donskoy said, addressing Knuthe. A certain seeking of commiseration or conspiratorial edge flavored this remark. Knuthe could tell he was meant to read into it, that it was about something he and Donskoy had in common. Donskoy, with his somewhat weathered corduroy blazer, faded denim undershirt of the kind whose popularity peaked in the nineties, and his wispy white hair, struck Knuthe as the kind of elderly man who might rabble-rouse, but would go home with food between his teeth, passing gas all the way, having said nothing all evening taken seriously by anyone. Age made all offenses forgivable.

"Would that perhaps be *white men*?" Knuthe loudly said—rebuking Donskoy's intimation that their whiteness was something scandalous that they must whisper about.

Disarmed, Donskoy was speechless.

"That's okay," Knuthe sang. "It's not our time right now. There have been plenty of galas honoring white men down the years. We've had our time in the sun. Since roughly the Roman Empire, after all."

"For some, inclusivity begins to resemble exclusivity," Donskoy mused.

"You and I are here. That's two."

Donskoy turned away, trying on a line about short people to Barnhouse. Nothing so tactless had been tried since Randy

Newman's ill-conceived ditty. Which rode the airwaves back in the time when skins were worn thicker, like the fur-lined coats of the time, and a joke was a joke, something you held in your hand like a cone of cotton candy and approached people happily with.

Taking a microphone attached to a soundboard, wired, in turn, to a loudspeaker atop a tall stand in the far corner of the parlor, Jerome made an announcement that the food was being served, which was obvious, because he did it as the catering staff were simultaneously bursting through the swinging kitchen door and loudly dropping trays into the serving table, one after the other, with their metal tongs and hot pads. He pointed out which was the head of the line, which was obvious, because that's where several tall stacks of clean white plates towered. And he directed everyone to the dining room behind him, which no one had missed because its French doors were being ceremoniously un-latched and opened at that moment by the stunning and unignorable Joyce Winslow; it was a dining room the size of a barrack mess hall, holding several long tables draped with ca-tering-white tablecloths, surrounded by chairs.

"After dinner," Jerome said, "Mrs. Winslow will speak, and of course, we'll have the award ceremony. Bon appétit." He made none of the usual incompetent fudging fidgety moves with the microphone that amateurs make, like creating buffeting sounds with his breath or going unheard because of timidity, holding the thing down near the bellybutton. He snapped the off switch with his thumb and deftly replaced it in the mic stand, a pro.

"I brought a torte," Petra Barnhouse said absent-mindedly, a touch dejected.

"A torte?" said Evonne. Donskoy had shuffled away, towards the food troughs at the start of Jerome's announcement. "That was so generous of you! But it's catered."

"I feel like a bad guest if I don't bring something. I guess it's the Midwesterner in me. Do you think they'll serve it?" Barn-house said.

"You should ask them where it is."

"I couldn't do that."

"I'll ask for you."

"No, no. I don't want to make a scene."

"You went to the trouble. The least they can do is cut it up and set it out."

"Let's just see. They'll probably bring it out later."

Sorenstam-Finch sighed. People were trying. "Shall we get in line?" she asked.

"I'll go towards the end," Barnhouse said, a mild sneer playing upon her upper lip, like when you get a stitch in your side, running.

Sorenstam-Finch looked away, perplexed, disappointed.

"Sorry, my appetite has not been great lately," Barnhouse added.

"Okay, well, I'm going in."

Shared smiles indicated no hard feelings.

As a high schooler, Barnhouse had worked at a secondhand bookshop, a job she adored. She got to handle all those valuable books. Keys to the promised land of knowledge and betterment. The biographies of Benjamin Franklin and Frederick Douglass were two key texts of her youth. And the Narnia series. Escape, uplift, introspection, determination. The integrity of education. The esteem of clear thinking, clear morals, over the muddled lives of slave-owners. The promise of invention (Franklin), the unknown treasures within us all. Seeds watered by imagination, blooming into things like eyeglasses and democracy. If we dared to trust our own God-given resources.

Much of her time at the bookshop time had been spent rifling through customer's boxes of mildewed romance and thriller and mystery paperbacks, of which the shop recycled thousands every week. Barnhouse loved tipping whole bins of them into the recycling dumpster. It was like weeding the world's intellectual garden.

At age 16, Barnhouse reached her current, and tallest height, of five foot three inches, and her current and heaviest weight of one hundred twelve pounds. She played on the lacrosse team and skied cross country. She was fleet, lean, strong, but there wasn't enough of her to produce the muscle needed to outpace girls of five-eight, five-ten and up. On the turf of the lacrosse pitch, her small size let her dash and dart like a fox, but her reach was short and her height a distinct disadvantage when passing. On snow, actually bodies of greater weight seemed to get more slide. Certainly taller girls had longer steps for herring-boning up a 200-yard hill, when she'd fall three-body lengths behind, even when giving it everything she had, laying out until the barf almost came.

"Diminutive," was the word everyone used. Her track coach, her ski coach, her family doctor, even her parents. Once a gynecologist performing a pap smear remarked on the relative size of her vaginal cavity, like it might amuse her too. Her father "diminutive" as well, intending kindness, thinking it was scientific and just factual, free of judgement, without the connotation of unimportance carried by "small." Nevertheless Petra felt lesser-than. Someone always made an issue of it, whether as an ice-breaker or deal-breaker.

Her family was Lutheran. She got A's in geometry, algebra, and pre-calculus. She played clarinet. She'd been to Germany and Italy (her father travelled for business and took his family). But these were not things that people understood about her or that assembled into a conception of her as a person of depth. Always, she was Petra, the short girl. Like a figure from legend or folklore: Petra the Diminutive.

As for benefits. When she first became sexually active, there was novelty, because she could climb atop a boy and not crush him. She was agile, spry, moved energetically. Her boyfriend Craig praised her for it. Car seats—no problem. Hop on. But it wasn't what she wanted praise for. Not above all else, anyway.

And the sexual bounciness, or whatever, had a downside: her breasts didn't even fill an A-cup bra. Her chest looked boyish, and they couldn't be kneaded, they didn't bounce—or whatever else boys liked. Her friends pretended at envy—they'll never sag! They don't get in the way! But she didn't buy it. Small titties were another inadequacy.

This was not the caliber of hardship that earns awards, Barn-house was well aware. She had led a more-than-decent life, with much in it to envy. She was privileged, she understood, in 2018 terms, now that certain events and every one on social media every day did their part to illuminate the relativity of hardship.

Penn State, BA in accounting and finance, had to pay back only half her tuition in student loans herself in the ensuing years—her father paid the rest. Got a job right out of school, actually starting with the college itself, in the Smeal College of Business, okay salary and benefits, married Darrin, who she met not long after, settled in a nice three-bedroom just outside the Black Moshannon State Park, near a township in Pennsylvania called Snow Shoe.

Just on the edge of the Marcellus Shale gas field.

Everything was peachy for 18 years, until Cabot Oil & Gas Corp., of Houston, Texas, came in, in the spring of 2001, and began horizontal slickwater fracturing. Fracking. A term so much like fucking the comedy was obliterated by the uncanny closeness. Fracking up people's life. Totally fracking over the earth. Everyone with a pulse and a conscience knows how the rest goes.

Petra filming Darrin opening the kitchen tap and holding a match to the jet, which ignited—so dense was the methane content. Flowing water, burning blue at the edges. Never seen anything like it. A horrifying sight in the place where you wash your dishes, scrub your hands, and down many glasses of water on the assumption that it's bringing you health.

But then Petra's outrage met so much unconscionable shit that it has both seriously depressed her—not just made her feel bummed, but, like, robbed her of her faith in a prosperous future and cornered her into the only practical view of humanity, American capitalism, environmental prospects, etc., possible, which is one of bleak despair; both done this and fueled her to action. Now she speaks and does an online newsletter and goes door knocking and authors letters to the editors of the Pittsburgh Post-Gazette and the Philadelphia Enquirer and anywhere else that will print them. The unconscionable (also deplorable) shit included the county suing the parent company of the drilling company, after families like hers spent years of buying of bottled water and taking painstaking measures to get clothes washed, etc., with scientific results in hand showing the presence of 2-Butoxyethanol (2BE) in well water, including hers and Darrin's, only to have the scum-sucking soulless demon-spawn lawyers argue that it couldn't be proven that it wasn't there before Cabot's activity or that it came as a result of Cabot's drilling.

2BE is used to make paint and cosmetics. Last Petra looked, there was no one a thousand feet below the water table doing frescoes or touching up their eyeliner.

There were periods of temptation to fight dirty, go ad hominem and slander the quote/unquote energy consultant who testified at the trial—even though her employer was a known advocate of the Independent Petroleum Association of America. Why not go on Facebook and call her a whore? Why not tell the world she'll rot in hell? But Petra resisted, kept her own morals in check, abided her values, even as the years-long ordeal ravaged her looks with tinted bags of sleeplessness under her eyes, and turned the corners of her mouth droopy, like a permanent frown. Even though the injustice had turned Darrin into an angry, bitter, cynical person, something he never was before, something Barnhouse wouldn't have tolerated in a husband ever.

And then the fuckery continued, expanded, closed its grip on her family, shutting the door on the way things were forever. Darrin began waking in the night, itching. Fire on his skin. Pricks, tingles. His skin wasn't dry. There was no rash to see. He hadn't touched poison ivy or poison oak, which some urgent care *specialists* said must be the case—nothing.

Petra remembered one exchange in particular at that awful Allina clinic with the doofus receptionist.

"But there's no rash, no welts, not even discoloration," Darrin argued.

"Oh, well, that can happen," says the doctor, stuffing both hands in his the pocket of his lab coat. Petra half expected him to pull out two closed fists and initiate a game of *Where's the jellybean?*

That can happen. When you live inside a chemical storm cloud, the last thing you want is unverified claims that strongly resemble complete ignorance.

One fucking GPs had the nerve to ask if they'd changed laundry detergent. What stocks did these GPs invest in? And then for Darrin urological problems arose, problems too cruel to discuss and too ironic given that fracking drills *thrust* and *penetrate* so far into Mother Earth. Time off work for tests, days to drive to Philly for advanced tests. Now he's not a team player, not in the running for promotions. Then the shortness of breath. A diagnosis of asthma. Darrin's not exactly leading the pack in the 100-meter dash. Is he carrying some extra poundage? Yeah. Does he like a side of bacon on Sunday morning? Absolutely. But they take walks, and he's active on the job. But he's heaving now, coming up the stairs. Then numbness at the extremities—blood flow problems. Neuropathy. Time off for more tests, and nights in a ward at Mt. Nittany Medical Center, for observation. And days off for fatigue and depression. Next thing you know, boom, he's fired.

And still they can't drink the water, and they can't sell their house. Realtors won't even list it.

The Barnhouses had a neighbor, a guy with a farm up the road, same problem in his wells, some of the same health issues in him. Utter denial. "I still support drilling." Turns and spits his tobacco juice. Maybe he woulda got the same illnesses anyway. We don't know, says the guy.

Research and activism became Barnhouse's spouse. Putting pieces together was like a child's wooden puzzle—one of those with 8 pieces and plastic handles on each piece. That is, *not hard.* Where there's fracking, babies are born small. They're plugging the ground with thousands of gallons of benzene, uranium, radium, methanol, mercury, hydrochloric acid, and ethylene glycol. What do you think could be causing those low gestational weights? The oil companies just shrug, standing beside their three hundred thousand gallons of natural gas a day at sixty bucks a barrel. Anyone who doesn't get the picture needs to have their head examined. Where she had once been deferential, she became outspoken. Where once she had been polite, she became blunt and unapologetic.

In her way she had shed the "diminutive" moniker.

When Flint, Michigan's water crises happened, Petra drove there and stayed two weeks, wrote about it in her newsletter, stood in picket lines, attended the city council meetings, talked to people, let them know she heard their cries. Encouraged them to keep fighting.

She was driving back when Darrin just expired one day. Heart attack. He had worked sales for an Ohio-based concrete company based out of Ohio for 22 years. Concrete and mixing trucks. On-site pours for huge construction projects. It was not a glamorous job, but it was one he was committed to. Darrin showed a lot of loyalty to, it. Some summer nights standing in his back yard, near the fence door, feeling the satisfaction of a good day's work, he thought about how he did well at the job not because he loved it, but because it made their lives stable, safe, and comfortable. He'd look to the house, the shed, the garage...

The garage was the worst. The peg board of hand tools in perfect order. His softball bats. Even the lawnmower, which Darrin had serviced himself—sharpening the blades and cleaning the carburetor and tightening cables. How many hours had he walked behind it, in rows parallel to the house one week, diagonal the next, perpendicular the following week.

Shortly after she began parking in the driveway, coming and going through the front door, a neighbor, Alan, came by, asking if her garage door opener needed repair.

It was the loss of Darrin, combined with the corporate victimization, the sheer topicality of the issue, that made Barnhouse a contender for the FAIR award. That's how she saw it. She didn't need the twenty-five K stipend—that didn't matter. If she won it, she'd find a way to put it towards reparations of the drilling. She'd thought about that a lot as the date of the fete neared. A fund for victims—the people left behind after the sick die? A memorial? Legal fees? Something like that. Any one of those.

But mostly, she thought—she *hoped*—an award like this might restore that innate kindness and hopefulness. It could be a closing chapter to the ordeal, perhaps. Maybe, with the money, she could get out of the house and absorb the loss.

She got in line, inched up towards the plate stack. Bright green asparagus. Slices of pork roast, smelling of rosemary. It looked to be of the highest quality. But all she could force herself to take was some Caesar salad and a dinner roll.

—10—

In the kitchen, Jerome Ardizzone, Joyce Winslow and Candace Winslow conferred, huddling near the door that led from the kitchen to the dining room, where the 60 or so guests were now assembled, seated, happily forking and quaffing—a sight Jerome had seen countless permutations of. There is something about many people gathered and eating that confirms the valor of one's own asceticism. He held the door ajar a single inch, peering through it like a snoop, feeling the full glory of his thinness. Thirty-three-inch waistline—had been since the age of sixteen. Carb-free since 2011.

"So," he said, turning to the Winslow ladies, bearing a confident smile. The I-told-you-so smile. The full-commission smile.

"I still think assigned seating is the way to go," Candace Winslow said.

"It's too late now, mother," Joyce said. Their relationship was not one of the typical mother-daughter harpies. Overbearing, bitterly rebuffing, etc. Joyce was trying to ease her mother's burden.

"Any time you get disparate people together like this, sparks fly. You have to be careful. Everything's political these days, you know."

"Honestly," Jerome said, "I'm not getting that vibe *at all* from this group. You know? I don't think there's anything to worry about."

The three of them stood close in a corner of the busy kitchen, dapper near the sudsy sink toppling with dishware, steam flowing off the dishwasher, steam laced with pork grease. The the sous chef and the prep workers had the sleeves of their white smocks rolled up, and their pants smeared by tomato sauce hand-wipes; some fingers were cut and burned, bleeding and bandaged. The mounds of carrot peels and scraps for compost lay piled around openly on the countertops. It was the Winslow's home, of course, and they could be anywhere they pleased, but the caterers worked tensely, in a state of dangerous self-consciousness, more likely to drop the crystal while the bosses were in the room. Normally they chatted, but all were silent now. Jerome saw their darting attentions, their perked ears. He knew their type, their subverted vengeance and career-making tact. Yet there were always some among the kitchen staff eager to overhear the richies betray their composure.

Joyce wore a pleated black A-line dress by Valentino, with a V neckline and square back, knotted at the waist. Her skin was immaculate. Jerome gazed upon her.

"Are you going to eat something?" Jerome asked. "Out there?"

"I'll go out in a minute."

"You're Director," Candace said. "You have to mingle. Should *want* to mingle."

"I *want* to mingle. It's not easy though. Certain people despise us, you know."

"People despise us," Candace retorted, "but no one in attendance tonight. People on the *other* side."

"There is no other side," Joyce said. "I keep telling you."

"That's an illusion, an indulgent dream."

"No."

"I deal in reality."

Joyce moved to the door, held it open a crack and peered out. She saw Santos Gougoutris, Merrill Roselli, and Chief S. happily chatting and chowing.

"I'll just let them enjoy themselves. When I join a group, the dynamic changes, people get uncomfortable."

"Nonsense. They're grateful. Is there any other group doing what we do?"

Jerome was keeping out of this. "Is there anything I can do?" he interjected.

"Just stand by, Jerome," Candace said, not looking at him, but touching the back of her wrist to his chest.

"Money changes everything," Joyce answered without pause. "You're only kidding yourself, pretending not to notice."

"Like hell if I'm going to apologize that my husband was a successful in business."

"What you fail to understand, mother, is that this isn't 1955 anymore. 'Successful in business' doesn't mean thumbing the stock ticker and reading your gut. Dad's company impacted a lot of people." Joyce lowered her voice. "They were ruthless with unions, let's not forget."

"He was ethical, if that's what you're getting at. And more compassionate than your Exxons and your Shells. Lord, this is no time for family therapy. We run the Foundation for the Advancement of Iniquities and Reparations. If we—"

"Inclusivity and Recognition!" Joyce yelled. "Jesus, mother!"

"Oh, all this drama. If you think I'm going to waddle off in search of a martini now, and that all I really care about is myself, you're wrong! We've done a hell of lot of work to put this event on, we have a room teeming with marvelous people, and I'm going to celebrate their diversity, their—their—their.... Everything! Their humanity—"

"There it is," Joyce said wearily.

"Now you've made me look doddering. I'm not doddering, am I, Jerome?"

Timed impeccably and full-throated, Jerome said, "Of course not."

Candace huffed, arranged her pearls. Freshly dignified: "I'm going to celebrate their humanity with them." Even more reverently now: "They're beautiful, they're deserving, and they've been through hell. I want to make it up to them. That's just how I feel about it, and you can't stop me."

Joyce put her hand on her mother's shoulder. "I know, mother. I know."

"Don't patronize."

"I wouldn't dream of it. For whatever reason, you've shown your devotion to the have-nots down the years. And tonight's incarnation of your largesse is probably your best-intentioned, the eagle's feather in your cap. It would take the New York Giants' defensive line to keep you from assuaging your guilt tonight."

"I don't need your armchair analysis, either."

"I'm getting uncomfortable," Jerome said, with a curl of the lip.

"This is complex relationship, Jerome," Joyce said. "What did you think? This was a Toys-4-Tots fun-drive?"

"Yeah. Well." He started texting Gabe, *The Winslow women...* he typed. Just in case it blew up into something, he'd be prepared.... *are having words*. Send.

"Jerome, you don't need to alert Gabe. I get the picture. I know how he is," Joyce said, stepping close to him. "You're very capable, I've noticed." Her eyes were steeled into powerful earnestness, and her pelvis grew somewhat outthrust. Jerome flushed, feeling the preamble to a loin-swell: blood swirl about the inner thighs, a tingling of the testicles. A kind of primitive clarity in the front lobe. Generally oversexed, Jerome often had an innuendo at the ready; this one came without heed: *I rise to many occasions.* In the movies you would always add the lady's name, as a direct address, providing an ironic contrast between the vulgarity and the formality. *I rise to many occasions, Ms. Winslow.* It's more tantalizing that way. But he held his tongue, literally bit it between his teeth, letting Joyce see his tortured restraint.

"Darling," Candace said, "I want you to plate up and get out there, sit down with whoever and let them get to know what a wonderful person you are. Okay?"

"Okay, mother. I will."

Joyce turned and headed out the other door to the serving trays. Jerome saw, through the swinging door, Joseph Hector Depace, pocketing a dinner roll.

"All that stuff about money," Candace said, taking Jerome by the elbow—her signature gesture at this point. She was being very direct, and Jerome appreciated that. Better than some crock of shit served on a platter of tight smiles. "Of course she's right. But what can you do about it? It all boils down to the illusion that anchors so many American lives, that wealth, vis-à-vis happiness, has no point of diminishing returns. Which isn't true, you understand. Enough money, and it does become burdensome. *A problem I'd like to have,* people say. In other words, no one really believes it. They continue to truly expect that *they'd* be the exception to the rule, if they hit the jackpot. I don't know what it will take to disabuse people of that prevarication. And so they look at you different. They think you're a savior. They think you have everything they want and that you have become better than them. That you are anointed. But that's not so. The wealthy are still people, you see, Jerome. Money changes nothing about human nature. Absolutely nothing. We still feel. We still ache. You understand?"

"I see, Mrs. Winslow. And I want to say, I really appreciate your candor."

"Thank you, Jerome. Now I want to ask you..."

They moved away. Tara Voss, holding a Wilton piping bag, star-tipped, filled with fresh whipped cream, raised her eyes to Michael Dulka, her coworker, who was pouring heavy cream into a mixing bowl in which a machine cranked three beaters around in a cataclysmic whorl or near misses. Tara's eyes imparted intrigue, and actually rather than contempt or scorn, a bit of respect. Michael just pinned his eyebrows up. Neither of them was foolish enough to repeat a word that Mrs. Winslow had said. And really, what was there to mock?

Tara resumed squirting four stars of white, fluffy whipped cream onto each pumpkin-pepita mini-pie. The pies were loaded onto a round serving tray, which she rotated 4 inches at a time to bring the next pie close directly under her nozzle.

Joyce reached the dinner table, bearing her dinner plate. One doesn't achieve the level of physical fitness Joyce had attained by eating heaping plates of meat and starches. Her plate bore very small portions. Every chair was taken, however, and the parlor was full of several dozen people eating on their feet or sitting in the sofas and chairs, plates on their laps.

Andrew Knuthe leapt up from his chair, with rejoicing exuberance.

Mr. Ramirez stood too. "Ms. Winslow, please, sit here," he said.

"Oh, no. That's okay, that's okay."

"I'm finished," he said, showing his clean plate. "*Por favor*. I insist."

"Bless you," Joyce said, taking Ramirez's seat.

The thing she feared most was an inquiry into the ways and means that the award recipient had been selected. Wasn't breaking bread together just the kind of intimate ceremony that invited this line of questioning? Wouldn't the gala's resemblance to a lavish American holiday meal just invite boundary pushing and provocative, loose-lipped inquiries? In Jericho, the disciples ask Christ, So tell us about your dad? What's he like? No, no, no. But speaking of unchristian sentiments: she also feared a scandal around the surrendering of mobiles. That's the term Joyce had come up with: "surrendering." It was used in the invite and other promotional materials. We will ask you to surrender your mobile. This was a deliberate replacement of anything like confiscate, take, abduct, or sequester. Shit going down at America's southern border had made any suggestion of forced separation stomach-turning.

To Joyce's left sat a Korean-American man in his thirties, a man she knew as Jeong-Hwa Pak, a doctor and political dissident in exile. He went by the initial J., amounting to "Jay." To her left sat Evonne Sorenstam-Finch. Turning left and right to indicate she was asking them both, she said, "Do you think everyone's okay without their phones?"

"I'm enjoying it," J. said. "For once, I'm free of the compulsion to check it every few minutes."

"Mmm," Joyce nodded, chewing. "What about you, Evonne?"

"What's that?" Evonne said.

"Are you coping without your mobile? Or are you going through withdrawal?"

"I'm totally in withdrawal!" she cried. Her lips few taut and seemed to quiver slightly. "I'm quite attached, I admit."

Joyce and J. delivered her uncertain smiles. Was she really suffering and aggrieved? Or did she have one of those theatrical manners of wit?

"I want to Insta everything. The food. Everyone's dressed up. It's torture."

"Torture? A bad choice of words," J. said. Ug. Yes. Everyone winced.

"I know." Joyce's show of false commiseration. "It's just a few hours though."

"I'm curious," J. said. He spoke very slowly. He wore a gray blazer over a peach-colored t-shirt. He was 38 years old. Black hair shaved to millimeters. Widow' peak pattern. Sage face, placid, disguising outrage. Clearly learned. A man of much sub-dued force. For four years in the early aughts, Pak had supplied the South Korean newspaper Daily NK with insider reports from Pyongyang—all the news that the Kim dynasty sought to keep within its borders, primarily about dissent among the populace, vandalism to monuments, statues and murals, for example; but also dissent within the government; as well as gaffes Dear Leader may have committed; the most illustrious of his illustri-ous deeds; the details of famine and shortages, and the facts, when possible, on the tremendous costs of Kim's missile pro-grams, which he pursued while his countrymen and country-women starved. When Pak became a research scientist in med-icine at PUST (a university funded by Chinese and US Christian sources), and spoke out about nuclear missile tests, he was jailed. After serving three years, he left the country, and granted interviews and published anti-regime articles, exposing the fal-libility and fallacies of the dynasty.

"Did you decide on the policy because you didn't want to have the event publicized?" J. asked, arranging his napkin in his lap, after dabbing his mouth.

"A few reasons," Joyce answered. "Really, number one, be-cause of Prince?" Because this was unexpected, it seemed to warrant a question mark.

"Prince, the musician?" asked Lamond P. Jackson, from across the table.

Joyce explained. "Yes, Johanna learned from her son..." She scanned up and down the table until spotting the blond head of Johanna Sturludóttir. "Johanna's our Outreach Coordinator."

Everyone glanced in Johanna's direction.

"Johanna's son is a big Prince fan. He collects recordings of his concerts, you know. He was playing one in his room, and Jo-hanna overheard. Prince was saying to the audience, Put your phone away. Put your phones away. This was in Europe."

"Oh, I heard about this actually," Evonne said. "I'm also a huge Prince fan."

"Who isn't, right?" J. quipped.

"May he rest in peace," Jackson added.

"Apparently," Joyce said, "on this entire tour with his band Third-Eye Girl—I love that name, by the way—before every show, one of the band members would come out and talk to the audience, asking them to not take pictures, not take video. Turn your phone off. You're going to be more present if you do. You're going to engage with us more fully. You're going to hear and feel the music. And that really, for them, to be on stage playing music and look up and see everyone paying attention to their phones was really hard."

"I saw a clip on YouTube," J. said. "Prince stopped the music in the middle of song. People were using their phones. He said. 'Photographs are for teenagers. They've never been anywhere, so they gotta take a photo to prove it!' "

"Oh, interesting," Joyce said. "He was a man who was not afraid to speak his mind."

"No doubt," Jackson said.

"Johanna proposed do something similar for the fete, that we also invite people to be present. This is a chance to be with each other and be fully present. Let's not water that down. It may be uncomfortable at first, but if we all commit to it, then we share that challenge."

"That's nice," Evonne said, her pitch dropping desolately.

Sturludóttir had by this time caught wind of the topic or overheard her name and was listening in on Joyce's heartwarming summation. This origin story, this creation myth. She kept her eyes on Winslow until she looked her way again. Then they shared a knowing glance. The fact was, the prime concern was that of attack. Several hundred diverse persons gathered in one place. Multicultural persons. Immigrants. Dissidents. Activists like Barnhouse. Military personnel like Jackson, who had been discharged for a tweet in support of Edward Snowden. Gays present. Trans people present. A party celebrating inclusivity! It had the potential to be another Charlottesville, or Pulse, or San Bernardino. An attack was possible from either side (though there were no sides). Someone who hates acceptance. Or possibly someone snubbed by the Foundation in some way they'd overlooked. It was not likely that anyone at all had been left un-invited, but the possibility nonetheless remained that someone out there felt betrayed, ignored, overlooked.

At an all-staff meeting, the Foundation staff agreed on ways in which social media could work to aide someone wishing to inflict harm on the event. Say you have people posting from the event using the dedicated hashtag that the foundation had already published: #FAIRaward2018. The post includes name of the location, as populated by the app, using location detection. Even something close by could be dangerously incriminating. Or even, say, a posted photo from the gala shows a view out a window, and out the window is a some telltale feature of Washington Avenue—for example, the neon BLG restaurant sign (Bar La Grasse). A deviant mind could locate the exact room in the exact building in which all these people they loathe stand helpless and contained, like sardines in a tin waiting to be crushed.

With most everyone at the dinner tables finished eating, the banter about mobiles tapered off. Catering staff intercepted plates from the many guest-candidates who had left their seats and were walking about, eagerly looking for a bin in which to bus their own dishes. Joyce took a last bite, and set her plate down. She turned around to observe the noise. When voices are new, they reach our ears with surprise. Candace had been greeting guests at the door, guests who had continued to arrive throughout dinner. Joyce felt badly for them—the food was gone, every tray emptied. Excusing herself, she left the table and wove through the crowded parlor. Yes, the trays were empty, and a staff-person removing them. The bar was open again. Coffee urns were put out.

Locating her mother, who was holding someone's hand, in a long, enduring shake/clasp, she said, "I'm sorry to interrupt. The new guests—they understand they've missed dinner?"

"Yes, I've explained, and they know. In some cases, they've come from dinner out."

"Okay, I just didn't want—"

"They understand, dear."

Just then a woman's terrified shriek: "Oh!"

Everyone drew their eyes to the floor.

"Man down!" someone yelled. "Man down!" As if this were the deck of a ship.

Joyce and Candace rushed over. There on the carpet, a man lay on his side in the haphazard loose-limbedness of the unconscious.

—11—

It had started on Saturday morning, the previous weekend, for Monti Taylor, 31, an Australian living in the states some 6 years, after studying on exchange at the University of Champagne-Urbana, Illinois. He just couldn't manage to get out of bed. Which give him a scare, because it wasn't the first time, just the first time in a while, and it had been about eleven days since his meds had ran out, even though he'd broken some in half and skipped days to extend their life as his prescription dwindled down, keeping some of those precious SSRI molecules in his noodle. Monti's medical coverage had come through Gail's plan. No more Gail, no more coverage, no more meds. The dried-up supply represented four months' worth. Monti's doctor had done all he could, writing up a double-size batch at once, but that was some time ago, when the separation first began. Now the papers had been served, about a week prior, and Monti had gone to the office of the Hanwell family lawyer—a busy guy!—and signed.

From the warmth of unusually clean bedclothes, Monti reassured himself. Listen, mate, you've moved everything you own, you've just got a right to be shit-kicked. He was staying in the guest bedroom of his pal Ked and Ked's wife, Olivia. They had a huge craftsman bungalow on 32nd Street, near Colfax Avenue, entirely redone. All Monti's shit was in their garage now, stacked like so much bric-a-brac. Little end tables he'd been dragging around since college, in Illinois. A bin full of crap trainers, green from grass mowing, melted rubber from dripping solder. Why did he keep them? They seemed so replete with personal history. A painted tea tray that he'd used to de-seed bags, roll joints, cut coke, count Oxy tablets by moving them aside with a table knife two at time. The tray was the dearest thing to him. The colorful swamp reeds, the blue water of the pond, the ducks alighting. Taking off, into the sky. Just like they're getting high. *Let's get out of here. We're gonna be shot at in a minute.*

Yes, let's. Let's flee from danger, even if it is our natural habitat.

What the hell does that mean? Monti wondered.

Ked and Olivia weren't home—that was the fucking strange part. But to be in their home without them felt damn good. Solid people. They were somewhere in Los Angeles, where Olivia was having a show of her sculptures. Or they were planning the show, viewing the gallery space for the first time, and being selecting and arranging pieces of Olivia's to put in the show. Something like that—Monti had had a hard time remembering.

They were always up to so much, those two. Ked had business there as well. He shopped for instruments, vintage guitars, to get a particular sound for a record or take on tour. It was all an incomprehensible muddle. Their lives weren't like regular folks'. They floated above the laborious fray, making art. Must be rough. Writing off travel as research, necessary inspiration. Monti tried to pretend he related. Yeah, mate, I'm hanging on a girder welding rivets in a bridge for sixty-five an hour. You're writing a check for 6K for a Les Paul once owned by Ace Frehley.

But despite all these differences, there was loyalty. Ked texted him the garage code, which led to the house. Texted him where the spare key was, in the kitchen drawer. Told him to move the car out, put his things in there. Sleep in the spare room. They'd be back in ten days or so.

Being in their house just made Monti feel like a bigger shit, when he finally roused himself from bed. Letting Dingo out in the back yard, he stood on the back deck and smoked a cigarette, watching his skittish, tan-and-white beast, with its stump ass and smashed face, its ping-pong-ball eyes and dysplastic hips. The neighborhood posh qualities gleamed in Monti's eyes. Nice trees, full with summer green. Blue sky, no wind. A beautifully soundless neighborhood, and the pristine assurances of security system signs nailed to light poles and outbuildings.

Then—fuck—Monti pinches the butt out, calls Dingo, and the door handle's either jammed or—no, no, he locked it behind him on himself! You fucking idiot!

Thankfully phones are on people every day, every *moment* of every day, and he found the garage code in it, and got back in the house. But no Dingo! He wouldn't come no matter how much

Monti called. Had to hunt him down, somewhere down the alleyway. Which was like the nicest alleyway he'd ever seen. No weeds, no junk, no broken glass, no graffiti, the back ends of Lexuses, Audis, Range Rovers. The American signifier: the car.

Sitting on a crazy snazzy wood stool at the kitchen counter with a sigh, Monti texted his boss. *I gotta take the day off. Family emergency.* Total bullshit. He just couldn't face it.

The silence of Dingo's collar is loud. He's being conspicuously still. "Dingo, get off the couch!" Monti turns and confirms. Dingo's big beady white eyes look back with attempted innocence. "You know you're not supposed to be up on there." A jangle and a thump bring him down. "Dumbass."

Monti spent the morning shuffling around the place, reading texts from Gail, his ex-wife, about shit that was undone at the house, some stuff he'd left there, which wasn't his problem. I don't want those fucking gadgets. Juicer. Rice steamer. You bought them. You never used them. Obviously, I left them behind on purpose.

Moving from room to room, he looked at Ked and Olivia's stuff, seeing it in fresh contrast to the shabby belongings of his own that he'd just hurried into a rental truck, having to do it all in the 8 hours that Thania was away. (Thania was another story— a 3-month-long mistake.) The bookshelves loaded with art books, photographic tomes of musicians. Who was Piet Mondrian? Who was Patti Smith? Monti's life was just shit. The sight of these things just cast him into the broad perspective that he hadn't amounted to shit. He was a fucking lowlife petty criminal and scammer. Mixed race—we don't say mulatto anymore—aboriginal mum, white dad. Never fit in. Did okay at school but nothing special. Started causing trouble in high school, and they forced a tutor on him, and gave him the college scholarship out of pity, and the advisor in the study abroad office had recruited him for the new exchange program, Monti believed, to get him off campus, where he was doing nothing that impressive and probably just making everyone else nervous.

He was a fake. Unloved. Something just wrong with him that made it impossible. His own dad he texted and called and emailed with problems, and the man was just, like, unmoved.

Couldn't be bothered. Never offered any sympathy. Even to say something basic like, *Sounds hard-going*, was beyond him. Never a word of encouragement. Just Farmer's Almanac kind of stuff. Gotta keep in the scrum. Whinging won't do you any good. What was he, an Okie in the Dust Bowl? I fucking moved to another country, Dad, with no more social or academic skills than I ever got from you, a road-paver with a permanent can of Foster's in your hand.

That was at the heart of it, no question. That Foster's can. Stateside, Monti'd outdone his old man. Didn't stoop to lager. Vodka tonics, bourbon cocktails. Tall, in a pint glass.

He had the old man jealous for a time. There was satisfaction in that. Coming into Gail's family money. Four years, not that Monti didn't work, but it was a different kind of work, not sweating it out under the sun, steaming tar in your lungs. Way better than that.

Hanwell Mercantile. That was the Gail Hanwell family business. A lot like Crate and Barrel, Restoration Hardware, even Pier 1, but not a national chain. Just a few shops: Chicago; Hartford, CT; and the one Monti and Gail ran, in suburban Minneapolis. They take some vintage armoire, and Duke Hanwell, using a designer/draftsman, specs it out—the measurements, the cuts, the drill holes. Then they have it manufactured in places like Lichtenstein and Vietnam. They batter it up so it looks ancient. Burnished patinas, they call it. In business, you have to have the language. Wines are no longer nice, it has to be notes of blackberry and clove. All these things Monti learned, his palate developing way beyond lager and hot tar.

Hanwell did wicker patio chairs. Crockery. Stemware. Throw pillows in Moroccan patterns. Even oil paintings. Monti was on the lookout—there was at least one *objet d'art* in Ked and Olivia's place that was a Hanwell. He had all this under his belt now, but it was unravelling, and tottering around Ked's, looking out their windows on a city that seemed to be bucking him off like a bronc rider, he worked backwards in search of the miscalculation. He was very much a "no regrets" kind of guy. But then Australians tend to be overly aphoristic. Laid-back sometimes meant so passive and inflexible that you were doomed to repeat mistakes.

Monti had dropped out of C-U and was working welding jobs—something he knew how to do quite well, from home, back on their ranch outside Adelaide, where his dad fixed smashed-up cars on the side. When the frames were cracked and no-longer insurable, his dad put these cars back on the road. Illegal but lucrative. Monti's grades had dropped. Living in a frat house, skipping class, selling weed, and having more fun at all of that than writing papers. He was looking for a way out of studies, and it was crazy how it happened. Early summer, took a road trip to Minneapolis with a fellow "teek" (Theta Kappa Epsilon), Jimmy, to see a band at the famed club where Prince had filmed Purple Rain, and to score a big brick of pot that Monti and Jimmy would take back to campus, split up, and resell at a profit to freshmen. It wasn't even supposed to be Monti going; another guy had been booked to make the trip, but something came up, and Monti took his place.

Drinking at this little dive bar near Cedar-Riverside, and he starts chatting with this wild-but-fine looking girl. Gail Hanwell, celebrating the end of final exams. Monti had forgotten all about them, that it was finals week, that were exams at all.

She could put it away. Whiskey sours. They talked and laughed at the bar. Monti's father would have called her "brassy," a compliment. Monti liked her eyes, her straight sand-colored hair. What's to like about sand-colored hair? He didn't know, but it was sexy somehow. None of the easy sex appeal of bleach blond. They lost each other for a while, while Monti and his friend threw darts, and she roamed around clinking glasses with girlfriends. But at bar close, they spotted each other and locked arms like old friends, heading out into the night. When she suggested they cab it to her place, Monti bailed on Jimmy. It was one of the hotter hookups of his life, with Gail purring over his accent and his muscles. She carded the taxi fare, saying it was a write-off, and took them up into this high-rise condo downtown, across the river, by the lock and dam, far from any campus.

"Pretty swish dorm," he said.

This wasn't a dorm, and she wasn't a student, she confessed. Yeah, it was finals week—her only for her gal-pals. She worked for her family's company. Her place was ridiculous. Fourteenth floor. Smelled of sandalwood. Three-bedroom. No roomies. All kitted out with stone statuary, exotic lamps, African masks, wool rugs. The sofas in the TKE house were torn and stained and probably should have been confiscated by people in hazmat suits. Gail's were white leather that still creaked when you sat on them. At TKE, they had drank keg beer, naturally enough. Gail poured Japanese scotch, and they smoked hash oil and made out on the balcony, before moving to the bedroom, where they passed out half-dressed.

Her voice. It hit him in the morning. Sober, he was powerless to ignore it. There was a thing in it. This twang. Thrown back in the throat. Like she had a golf ball sized tumor on her larynx. Anachronistic. Years ago, Frank Zappa had put out this "Valley Girl" song. It played in Monti's head.

An outsider, Monti didn't know enough about America's regions to pin it. Later, she'd explain it, because it did embarrass her too—boarding school had done it. That's how these obscenely wealthy east coast girls talked. Okay. He'd met east coast people, but never heard anything like Gail's twang. But he believed her, because what else could he do? At this point, three weeks from the day they'd met, she'd asked, and he's said Okay to moving to Minneapolis to be with her.

Probably the other thing he would come to understand about the Hanwell's American type was that her father was a good old boy. A Northerner, yes, a Michigander. And a democrat. But suspicious of the browns. And Monti was coffee with cream, that tired old image so near at hand to everyone. To put it in Mr. Hanwell's terms, Monti, with his aboriginal blood, that reddish tint of Indian, was like rosewood. He was a square Ming end table. Pair this coloring with the rebellion and dissent, the resentments that Gail always had towards her domineering, truly crazed parents, and Monti came to look like a middle finger incarnate. None of which occurred to him till around wedding planning time. This is my guy. Don't like him? Too bad. Think this family is holier than God? Think the Hanwell English bloodline is so pure? I sully it and dare you to speak against it.

Monti stayed in that Monday night, taking it easy, doing what

he considered self-care: smoking weed in Ked and Olivia's opulent living room, watching movies on their massive HDTV, having only a bloody Mary, then a cold beer or two. Craft IPAs from
Ked's fridge, that were 9% ABV or so, and came in a 700-ml bottle. But it's all relative. What would crush a lightweight was a
chill night for Monti. Before bed, he texted work again—the
emergency continued, had grown in fact. He needed another
day off, so put his father on a deathbed for this one. Savored
that. But the excuse had to be strong, because there was a dead-
line for these custom railings going in the lobby of some high-
end residential place being built down on Washington Avenue.
Monti was doing all the welds, starting with the lobby, then the
elevator shaft.

All week, the unravelling of the life he'd had, what he'd gained
and lost, were with him like a head cold. Like a flu bug physically
in his body, giving him chills and sweats, making him weak but
not hungry, taking the refreshment out of water, even the re-
storative power out of Gatorade, which was Monti's morning-
after go-to. Tuesday afternoon, when the pristine white walls of
Ked's place started to close in, and Dingo's dumb stare made him
want to smack the mutt, he took the light rail to Electric Fetus,
a record shop on the south side, flipping for an hour through the
CDs and vinyl, looking for the album that would make it all co-
here. Monti was old enough to still think of an album's second
half as "Side B." He thought there might be something out there
whose side b would, lyrically, clue him in to what lay in store.
Tom Waits? Some underground hip-hop dude? An obscure Blue
Note reissue?

The thing that jumped out at him was a Prince disc, to his
surprise. Monti loved the guy—who didn't? But he was a fan of
the hits, like most, and knew little of what the Purple One had
put out since the last single he could remember, "Cream" in,
what?, roughly the early '90s? But he spotted this disc called
"The Truth" on the staff picks shelf, liked the look of it, and come
to find out it was an acoustic record. Not 100 percent stripped-
down folk, not like the funky little glyph man had turned into
Neil Young. But the guitar was acoustic only, and added to it
were lush vocal dubs, synth and strings, and acoustic bass,

bongos or congas for drums. Very spare, and channeling some dark, dark shit. "Don't play me / I already got played." All the spiritually uplifting stuff Prince was known for, not to mention the sexy pop grind stuff, the high-energy stuff dripping with anticipatory juices—not present. There was bitterness about being overlooked in favor of more frivolous artists of the day. "I'm the wrong color / and I play guitar / I'm over thirty / And I don't smoke weed." There were obscure metaphors about uniformity. And the title track. "What if half of everything I told you / turned out to be a lie?" No swagger, but questioning. No seduction, but isolation. Monti didn't know the dude had it in him, but it was chilling, struck a nerve.

Monti went away from the store, not thinking he'd found what he needed but thinking he'd found a curious artifact, a local novelty, considering that Prince himself had been known to shop at the Fetus. The disc ended up in Ked's player all week, getting spun daily. It made Monti feel righteous. Half the shit Gail had said did turn out to be a lie, he felt. And slowly he realized that he had in fact found the soundtrack to the present moment, exactly as he'd wanted. That gave him hope that the he was on the right, if fucked up, path.

—12—

They had married and moved into Gail's high rise place and started running the shop together. Pulling out of that heated underground garage in winter, enveloped in heated leather, protected from the bitter cold, while suckers scraped their frosted windows in the howling wind. No better feeling. Pulling into the back of the shop, parking askew across the back door, because who could call them on it? Hanwell Mercantile, Monti and Gail proprietors. It was a dream. Here he was, gone from a dropout drug dealing in fucking nowhere Illinois, to one half of this multi-million-dollar business. Through Gail's force of will, he was declared and introduced as the expert on furniture design. Shop displays were his jam too. In time, Gail said (and so Roger and Frances agreed, wholeheartedly—she had them wrapped around her delicate finger) Monti would make custom furniture, in a workshop studio. They would find a building. He could do ironwork stands, ironwork tables, shelves. Whatever. Plus wood—he felt he could move into wood pretty easily.

Gail did everything else. A master bullshitter, Monti came to understand very soon. Talking things up. Wonderful to *see* you. How *are* you? That was the line every time the bell rang on the shop door. Hit that emphasis hard with the throaty twang. She cared, it said. They were her customers. *Aren't they great?* she'd say of some wood dalmatians, paint faded, wood rain-split. *Oh my gawd, and a steal at two hundred a piece.* She had mixed in antiques now, brought to her by a hired picker who drove to flea markets down in Iowa, Nebraska, buying only what Gail approved by texted photo. What Monti came to understand, and what Gail preyed upon, was that HM (as they called it) customers wanted to be known for their disposable income. They loved mingling among the shop owners themselves—parking their Audi A8 and waltzing in dressed in actual corduroy pants and loafers on a Saturday, actual Ralph Lauren sweaters. It was a class game. You confirm me, I'll validate you. One up, two up, three up. How much did you blow on that? *Fantastic.* I blew five hundred on a lamp.

People loved to say that they were "summering" places. Monti learned to smile and let his accent out. He didn't think of his homeland as cultured, but it was different, and a signifier of culture here. Sheep, Shiraz, gold, opals. Monti was the handsome accessory, the interesting multi-cultural twist. It was he who had hung the vintage gas station sign from the beams so high (climbing like a monkey), it was he who was in the back now unloading these *great* new bed sets that had just come in. Was he the brains or the brawn behind the operation? It had to be something—let them guess. Though Monti was guessing too.

What Mr. and Mrs. Hanwell Sr., Roger and Frances, did, was fly to China, haggle with the manufacturers, look over the prototypes. It was they who bought the shipping containers and did the measurements of dimension and weight and calculated the retail prices based on their target margins. It was they who shifted the money around, bought and sold warehouses where hordes of items were kept. Later, Monti learned, it wasn't a business they'd grown from scratch. Roger had been a partner in it, when the company had another name, in another city, and *his father*, Gail's grandfather, now deceased, had lent (or gifted) the money to buy it out. A play right out of the Trump playbook! Roger had changed the name to his own family name, Hanwell Mercantile, making it his own, and moving it from some town near Duke University, to the family's home turf, Minneapolis. Not that Roger was talentless or underserving of credit. He had worked. He had learned a hell of a lot about ins and outs. But now gramps had been paid back (or not), and the company was netting millions a year. The Hanwell seniors had three houses. They had horses. They had pools.

They had competitors. Which meant they had enemies.

Enemies, Monti gathered, they had made by burning people along the way. People cut out of deals. People bought out and disclaimered and NDA'd into impotence. Former partners they'd fought off legally. Designers they'd hard-balled and fucked over. Monti didn't know the details. There were intimations, allusions said with a brittle laugh, over lobster dinners. Monti didn't need to know. As long as he stayed on the inside.

Monti thought of as Roger as "Duke." Yes, Duke University was his alma mater. But also, with his flaring temper and phlegmatic ways and store-bought distinction, he resembled a character in a novel that Monti enjoyed. Duke Fitzgerald, a Michigan-lawyer-turned-Montana-rancher. Frances then necessarily became "La," the French feminine article, after the fictional Duke's wife. Hanwell Mercantile was Frances' wig bank.

The fucky thing, dawning on Monti only very gradually, in the face of much denial, was that Duke and La were shafting him. Monti had no salary. He got no paycheck, no direct deposit. Yet he was within HM's walls 35 hours a week, and laboring outside it another ten to fifteen. His recompense was that they'd bought Gail's townhouse. It was paid. Monti also never touched a gas bill, electric bill, mobile bill, either at home or at the shop. He put his own meals, gasoline, everything on a company credit card. Which, he knew, meant that they treated his expenses as business expenses and wrote them off on their taxes. Okay, fine. Yet, sometime into year two of running the store, Monti came to assess, he was giving his life over, and what did he have to show for it? If Hanwell vanished in a day, he'd have no cash, nothing in his name, not the Jeep Grand Cherokee that only he drove, not the bed he slept on. Only his clothes. Whereas, if *he* vanished in a day, Hanwell would have all the assets, all the fruits of his labor, and what would they miss? How would they measure the loss? Any monkey could climb the rafters and hang signs.

Yeah, it was cool that if he needed a tool or any material for a display, he just bought it. But they always asked how much it cost, and balked absurdly, as if it would break them. In the end, they'd concede, wearily. They had to make it seem like he was a draw on them, a threat to their solvency. Compressors, rivet guns, table saws—Monti loved having the latest, right out of the box. He bought all DeWalt tools, the top of the line. His father would have said it a waste, and that was the best part. Sometimes Monti routed a single piece of edging, and the thousand-dollar router went in a cupboard forever after.

Meanwhile, Gail began travelling extensively. Driving to the flea markets where her picker had identified items fitting the

Hanwell brand. Because, she said, it was too hard to judge by a photo. She'd OK'd some stuff that looked good, but when it arrived, it was horrid, had to be trashed. Couldn't sell it. This was a waste. And she flew to places like New Orleans because, she argued, the store needed items that had a different flavor, that looked exotic to northerners. Not the same old Red Wing crockery.

She got home exhausted, complaining of the physical toll of travel. But while she was away her Insta account always showed neon martinis and snifters of amber and orange peel.

She and Monti smoked weed together at home. That was almost exclusively—that is, it became about the only thing they did together. Gail had a guy who delivered to their place, half ounces of insanely sticky stuff with white crystals on the buds. When it was in the house, Monti could smell it in a drawer in the next room. Standing around the kitchen island, passing a pipe back and forth, eating take-out, doing texts about business, finances, everything. Duke and La never came to their place. The Hanwell family did not do family dinners in which they cooked for themselves. They did not do holiday gatherings with aunts and uncles and cousins. The first Christmas of Monti's life in this family, they all went to Tunisia, stayed at a resort in separate rooms, never spoke of the holiday, of relatives, of gifts, of good cheer or glad tidings or peace on earth. They met on the beach, and dinner, and at the bar.

In-store events. Postcard invites to the customer list—must be hand-written, insists La. The Thompsons of Shady Oak Road. The guy's actual name was Chip. Chip, like Mitt Romney and Biff from *Death of a Salesman*. It was lost on them.

Monti did graphic design and the print orders, including for the cards. He was in the website's back end now too, putting inventory online. The Hanwells said just take photos of things in the shop. They looked like shit. Monti went to National Camera and walked out with a couple grand in lights, screens, backdrops, special product-propping stands, lenses, filters. Saturday afternoons saying, "Twenty percent off" four hundred times. Drinking enough Riesling in the shop until the edge came off. Sleeping in an Eames chair when it was slow.

How *are* you?

The penetration of her fakeness. Wanting to be in the back storeroom where he'd set up the photo studio. The perfect clarity of white light. Gail had acquired some jewelry at an estate sale. The hard edge of a turquoise stone against the backdrop. Infrangible.

Saturday night, home smoking weed, ordering Thai delivery, texting Duke and La the day's totals. By midnight, faceplanting in front of the TV. Sundays weren't even a day off. If Monti said that they wanted to take the day, get out of the shop, go on a hike, or go to the beach, Frances would harangue them both with all the things that needed to be done.

Gail bought the dog without discussion or planning. You can name it, she said. He picked Dingo. A six-pound Pekinese. She carried it around like the women she watched on TV carry their rat-dogs around Beverly Hills. She started calling it her therapy dog, and expected that to be taken as a legitimate effort toward mental health.

Monti started putting pressure on Gail to put pressure on Duke and La to get him his workshop they'd promised him. He flashed around the Insta and Etsy accounts of other custom furniture designers, saying this is what he'd build. Iron coffee tables and shelves with wood tops, shellacked. He knew a wood supplier who had fine walnut, cherry, Hawaiian Koa, everything. The HM base would love this stuff. It would be one of a kind. Reclaimed Japanese shuo-sugi-ban—cedar boards burnt to keep termites out. Taken from rafters and beams of monasteries at the top of Mount Fuji itself! Okay, maybe not. But you could tell Chip Thompson that. Factually, it *will* last forever. Gail got nowhere on the workshop issue, they fought about it, and Monti went directly to them, made ultimatums—ugly but necessary. They bent. He had to ride them, but within a couple weeks, they secured a little brick building over in near North East, on Central Ave., and gave him the key. He set up all the tools, built workbenches, had a ventilation system installed for the sawdust. Hanging out in there, he worked his ass off, and it felt great to escape the four walls of HM where Gail was beside him every moment, talking, talking, talking all day, either to customers or on the phone with her picker or on the phone with suppliers and creditors or on the phone with her parents or talking directly to him in the same way about the same fucking shit and never of love, companionship, dreams, fears, tenderness...

He put on music, smoked up, set up a Mac and monitor, and started designing pieces. He felt creative, worth something. Like he had an identity. A future. Was Gail even capable of being impressed? He'd have to find out. Were the Hanwell's capable of valuing, or recognizing the value of, something they hadn't conceived themselves? He knew he had to produce something fast. He kicked out a basic square coffee table with a burl top, irregularly shaped. He bent the legs different than everything he saw online, used rods and blow-torched them hot enough to curl letters into them, twisting with plumber's wrench. Letters of the alphabet. M, t, h, m. Monti Taylor. Hanwell Mercantile. That individualized it. But he thought they'd appreciate the show of solidarity. It sold for $650.

"Yeah, but how many hours did you put into it?" Roger said. "I just wonder if custom is really sustainable?"

"You pay me nothing, Roger. There's no labor associated with your production costs. Just materials."

"The lease on the building. Utilities. Tools!"

"Well, what you do want? You want me to work in outer space, with quantum mechanics, just forming custom pieces out of nothing?! For fuck's sake!"

He'd started expressing frustration with them at times. The impossibility of their logic.

The workshop gave Monti's marriage a chance to breathe. But it was a chance for the fire to spread as well. He kept weed and a veritable cocktail bar there. Tito's in a cabinet. To keep costs down, he hired an assistant, an apprentice, someone to make the cuts to his designs, to do the hand sanding, staining, charring, chain-beating, painting, drilling. Ross was his name—a friend of Gail's weed dealer. Ross needed a place to stay as well, so Ross slept in the back room on a mattress for a time. Don't tell Duke and La, he said. DO NOT tell Duke and La.

Monti getting home late to Gail, considerably buzzed. Red-eyed. Pointless fights. She'd fucked up something with an antiques dealer, someone who'd shipped all these furnishings from France that she'd ordered. The guy had gone around her, up to La and Duke, complaining of non-payment of $30K. Her stories didn't add up. A check she wrote, a check she cancelled. A refund. Flawed goods. A dispute. Which was it? Nothing added up. Monti wouldn't put himself in between her and her parents to solve it—no way. Yet he got it in the ear from both sides for a week running.

Sort it out, Gail. I'm sick of hearing it!

Nights on the couch. The leather couch that still creaked. Or maybe it didn't anymore—maybe he just wished it did.

Gail's go-to thing now was to fly to the Hartford, CT, store, on the premise of helping them cull "dead" product, to get their monthly numbers up. Optimize their storage. Refresh their inventory. When she went, she stayed with friends in NYC, not far, she claimed, "right there." Google maps showed Monti a bloody three-hour train journey.

Insta shots of club lights, people awash in dance floor foam.

What the fuck? Monti texted. No reply. He called. No answer.

Did he care? He's at home on the couch in front of a 60-inch widescreen, all the weed he can smoke, champagne in the fridge. Order anything he wants for dinner on the company dime. Escargot, if he damn well pleases. If his old man could see him now, probably had his thick fist around a Foster's at that very moment—except for the fact of Adelaide being 16 hours ahead.

He could have gone out, hooked up, gone to a strip club, nightclub. Anything. But he didn't. A cheap kind of superiority. Cheap and sad. But integrity seemed to be worth something, some price that he would reap in the end. Hell, it wasn't even personal integrity. It was loyalty to Hanwell Mercantile.

All told, they stayed together four years, more and more separate. More and more superficial. No real feelings. Just the image of their youth and interesting backgrounds and their wealth and the idea of family business, like it was love and devotion and sacrifice that brought them so much prosperity and joy. What a crock. To her credit, Gail did go to a shrink, trying to get out from under the spell of her domineering parents. Trying to learn boundaries and limits, communication. Monti went along some sessions, to support her. The unflappable equanimity of psychiatrists. What would it mean if Gail did insist on a set schedule, with some weekends on, some off, with holidays? The guy had a hilarious euphemism: "I'm just curious." Whatever he was just curious about was basically what Gail should change, tout de suite. It was easy to see. What would it mean if they had a store manager or assistant manager, who could take some of the duties? Gail pulling tissue after tissue from the box, insisting on the impossibility of these changes, the cruel things they'll do. They'll cut off some expense of hers that they pay. And would that be so bad, to be just a little more independent?

Sane questions with no sane answers.

And then, ludicrously, when Gail asked her parents to attend a therapy session, they said it was too costly. "Two hundred dollars an hour, Gail?!" Roger said. Literally holding a forkful of prime rib at his lips, a 1995 Chateaux Latour at his elbow. "For god's sake!"

About six months prior to the fete, Monti insisted on a salary for himself. If that meant paying his own expenses, fine. But he needed autonomy. They flipped. They raged. They mocked. He held the line. It drove them to a kind of lunacy to have people question their motives. To be asked to accommodate others was a heinous afront, a kind of sacrilege. They gave reasons they couldn't—plenty of reasons. They'd have to pay employee taxes. So pay them, Monti said, like thousands of businesses do. It was the beginning of the end. His pushback was forceful now, not just frustrated quips, but actual resistance—felt by them as insolence, as from an ignorant schoolboy.

Behind it all was the fact of his coffee and cream skin. His red cherry patina.

Weekend sales. Weekend shipment. No, he's busy. Can't make it.

They didn't deal directly. It wasn't their way. He got a call from their lawyer, Larry Blackwell, making vague insinuations, threats. If he was out, he'd be out. There'd be no coming back.

What does that mean, Larry? Hmm? Gail is my wife! How am I out?

Gail felt pressed to pick a side. She nearly cracked. They were working at her privately. Monti isn't committed. Monti doesn't understand business. He's a threat to the company. As if he'd bring it all down, the whole operation, Hartford, Minneapolis, *and* Chicago. She stayed at their home for a weekend, citing some reason they needed her there, some chimney cleaning ritual or god knows what. The annual chestnut harvest. It was utter bullshit. He didn't say, Them or me. He didn't have to. He just let it hang there unspoken.

Then, that Saturday, he was in the store, and there was a notification on the iPad they used as a cash register—a reminder about a departure out of JFK Sunday night. JFK to Minneapolis. In the name of Gail Hanwell.

When she got back, in the coming days, he stalked in feigned ignorance, in wait of an opportunity. Then, when she fell asleep in front of the TV, he snatched her phone, went in the other room, and swiped through her photos. There. A series of herself topless amid a swirl of bedsheets. At the edge of the photo, in the dim lamplight, a foot.

A foot with fucking nail polish on it!

Flirty text messages from Karen, a 914 number.

Jesus. Not another man. Another woman!

The blowup. The blowout. Door slamming. Gail unleashed her beside-the-point anger at him for snooping in her phone, as if this was a court of law where evidence gets dismissed if improperly introduced.

"You lied, Gail. You lied. Admit it."

Denials. Insisting there's nothing happening in the photo. "I flashed her my tits. We were just mucking about."

"Why so sedate, so sultry? Why a series of ten? There's nothing in your posture here suggesting surprise or embarrassment. These are intimate shots."

She laughed. "Give me a break."

"And the texts?"

"That's how girls talk."

"Yeah, no, I don't think so. You said you were at your parents, for fuck's sake."

"They made me go to Hartford!"

"You can't blame them for everything, Gail. At some point, you have to take responsibility."

Hypocritical words, maybe. Monti just wanted to abdicate his responsibilities, or prove (to whom?) that he'd already proven himself capable, that he deserved a *new* set of responsibilities. Clear ones. Fair ones.

Ross, the living burnt fuse. Monti found him at the shop, doing this armoire. Monti bent his ear. Ross pulled out a twisted baggie of little white pills. OxyContin.

The tipping point. A night of forgetting. But it's only a night.

Gail left their place, started staying elsewhere. Didn't even take Dingo. Angry texts about that. You left your dog, Gail! He needs to be fed, you know.

From there it was just a fast descent down the mountain. He kept up his responsibilities to HM. Opening the store, closing the store. When he and Gail were there together, they worked, and he kept his distance, smoking cigarettes out back, organizing the back room, changing displays, repairing things. What had ever happened with the French guy? He was crazy, Gail claimed, which meant she'd fucked it up somehow. It occurred to him while gluing some joinery on a table that she had tried to do what her parents had done successfully to others down the years—rip the guy off.

Gail said the word first. Divorce. He snatched at it. You got it. He didn't need this. Life was too short.

It was four months until papers materialized. Four months living by himself at their place. She took away her clothes at some point, one day when he was out. She didn't care about anything else. She'd retreated. Deeper into her untenable Hanwell enslavement. He knew she'd lay low, out of his reach until everything was settled and their lives divided again. Then she'd resurface, an unblemished facet in the family crown jewels again. With a smile, she'd tell the Chip Thompsons of the world that Monti and she had split up, amicably. You know, one of those things that just didn't work out. How *are* you? Have you seen these chairs we got in? Aren't they graaaaaaayte? Her tongue halfway down her throat.

Monti wrote up an assessment of the salary they owned him,

turning what amounted to an invoice, totaling $220,000. There was petty haggling, all administered through Larry, this human-slug hybrid. Monti got seventy-two thou in the form of a paper check just like those written to the Chinese distributors and everyone else. The price of business. What were Monti's dimensions and weight? Were they satisfied? Please rate your satisfaction with Monti.

He tried to move into furniture making, or display design, or antiques dealing for other outfits. But of course they all operated just as HM operated: slim margins, banking on their own expertise and optimized resources, set connections, always trying to keep labor and costs down. Always trying to consolidate gains, maximize their foothold in the market. He got work through the contractors he'd hired to do the workshop ventilation. What a comedown. Installing prefab cabinets, insulation, tile, trim, etc. Residential and commercial. At least he was site supervisor, managing the tweakers who showed up late or not at all, the lunatic meth-heads who brought a shotgun to a rural home to hunt deer foraging near the site. The guy seriously was going to shoot. Monti came out of the house at 8 in the morning, looking to see if he'd arrived, to find him with the gun laid across the roof of his truck, sighting down at a buck at the edge of the woods.

After work Monti started going straight from work sites to the downtown bars he'd resisted before. Nothing at stake. Duke and La knew he'd been faithful to Gail in matrimonial terms. But he didn't need to be now. He bought rounds of drinks, plates of appetizers, to people he'd just met. Two hundred bucks a night, easy. Of course you make friends fast that way. Of course some desperate young thing turned up.

Her name was Tania. A skinny, skinny thing who dressed in tight pants that showed off her ... everything. She was tasteless, unapologetic. Her father was a builder. Owned a big commercial outfit—Monti knew the name from signs on cranes parked in open pits. She was a hostess at a hibachi place when Monti first hooked up with her. A couple weeks later she was fired—calling in sick too much, sleeping off late nights at Monti's. It was a drunken flesh-fest of the most blatant kind. There seemed to be something sophisticated about her bald statements. "When you're done with me...." she'd say. "You don't care." "You're not listening." And he wasn't. And he didn't. But at least they were honest. They got high and drunk, then they got naked. They did it again as much as their schedule allowed. He paid for everything. That was the deal.

When he had to leave the townhouse, Tania didn't help lift so much as a pair of socks. He's packing, and she won't even go to the U-haul store and bring him some damn cardboard boxes. But she let him move into to her place, the top floor and attic of a house in an obscure little neighborhood of St. Paul, by Como Park. There, the depth of her dysfunction was revealed. She lived on the couch, watching My 600-Pound Life and other shows about the world's dispossessed and degenerated, laughing cruelly the entire time. In the attic was the monument to her damage: a disturbing corner set up with an easel and paints, surrounded by an array of empty beer bottles, like those tiered arrangement of votive candles in churches. Here she put on moody music and jammed the broken glass of Corona bottles rights right into the canvas and oils. Here she stood until dawn, drinking and painting. She couldn't mix for shit, had no eye for depth, shadow, light, nothing. Everything was figurative. Shapes smeared right out of the tube. Faceless homages to pure dead hope. Silent cries for help that she hung only on her own walls, never inviting anyone in.

She expressed a similar terrifying ferocity in bed, and this became the thing worth seeking out to Monti, for its obliterating power.

But when his money dried up, and he began talking about what jobs they should get, how to join forces financially, Tania kicked him out, calling him a loser.

Which is when he called Ked, a distant friend made through Aussie connections. He and Olivia had met Gail once—they'd had dinner years ago, early on. Ked was ten years old than Monti, and been around the world. He seemed to understand Monti was caught up in a tense family drama that would one day likely shatter him.

Monti had turned over the key to the workshop to the family, via Larry. He knew Ross had been fired and no one was using the shop. He went there and climbed in a back window, totally unsecured, unguarded, and out of sight. There was a security sensor on the back door. The code still worked to disarm it. Letting himself out, he took away a bandsaw, a six-thousand dollar table router, lots of expensive jigs. He had it all sold, for a song, on Craigslist in a day. With the money, he bought several dozen Oxy from Ross, and a sack of weed from Gail's guy, who he met in Gold Medal Park, a park with no jungle gyms, no ponds, no tennis courts, just public art for the condo owners—theater directors and the like—walking their dogs.

"What's up? I coulda came to your house," the guy said.

"Not my house anymore," Monti muttered. He was becoming adept at imbuing everything he said with self-pity. Well, who else would offer pity? His parents hadn't supported him when things were good; they sure didn't want to hear from him now that his life had hit the skids.

Rather than drain Ked and Olivia's cabinet, he picked up some Laphroaig and ice, bottles of Ked's craft beer to replace those he'd drank. There was this party happening at a residential place that Monti knew about. The people were Hanwell Merc regulars. The Winslows. Mrs. Winslow, and the hot daughter Joyce, ran a foundation. The elder harassed Roger and Frances constantly to donate, getting them to part with maybe a thousand bucks a year. The party was a fundraiser for the needy or something. The Hanwells were invited because of their donor status. Monti dug out a flier about it that he'd tossed in his Jeep. He thought he might like to go—good chance to meet someone new. Someone with some class.

At Ked's, he began showering and imbibing. Music loud, the Prince disc. Shaving. Dressing. The experience of buttoning a shirt in the mirror began to resemble watching a film. He jumped when his father reached around his shoulders and to tie his tie. Then he succumbed to the embrace.

"What that a Windsor knot, pa?"

"Never mind, you little shit."

"Aw, pa."

He got onto Washington Avenue about 9 pm and parked the

Jeep on the curb, feeling a touch puckish. Two meat-heads who looked like they were from New Jersey took his cell phone. Monti threw a minor fit, until realizing that the meatheads were serious. "Ok, fine," he slurred. Then, brandishing the ticket with the digits to reclaim the phone: "Are these the winning numbers? What time is the draw?"

The men were unshaken.

"Lighten up," he said, and walking away, "What are you guys, sponsored by Brylcreem or something?"

The most adorable woman let him in. He introduced himself as Monti Taylor-Hanwell, trusting that Joyce hadn't been in the shop recently, catching news of his and Gail's divorce. Candace's smile said, No, he'd cleared the hurdle. "Pleasure to make your acquaintance," Monti said with a solemn nod. It's possible he had said "quake your amaintance." Her arm swept in an inviting gesture—a narrow sweep, but the place was packed, people behind her. Duke and La and Gail would hear about Monti's appearance eventually, but fuck 'em.

—13—

"Roll him over," said Evonne Sorenstam-Finch.

Joyce Winslow crouched down and did the honors, pulling at Monti's shoulder, twisting his spine. The man was loose as a goose, an utter rag doll.

"Is he all right?" Merrill Roselli asked.

A tight circle closed in around the sloppy, lifeless figure.

"Give her room, give her room," said Hermann Donskoy. "Stand back."

"Is there a pulse? Check for a pulse," said Lenore Happybones, peering over people's heads, aided by her stilettos.

The man was on his back now, his jaw slack, eyes closed. To all, the broadness of his nose, the way his forehead bulged, the singularity of his eyebrows, the way they met at the center, the thickness of his lips, and the roundness of his cheeks, and the brownness of his skin, was revealed. Backdropped by the bamboo flooring of the Winslow's townhome parlor, the primate resemblance was amplified. This was a Kubrickian moment—a creature from the past and future, dropped into our realm in a helpless state, ominously foretelling our death. A second of silence whipped through the room.

With a little whir of its motor, Darla Emmenberg's wheelchair drove up, parting the figures forming the gawking circle. "Is he drunk? He looks drunk."

Joyce mushed her fingers into the man's neck, in search of a pulsing jugular. Dropping her ear close to the man's mouth, her face drew clenched into a revulsive pucker. "Oh dear." She looked to the people around her. "Certainly *smells* of booze."

"And ganja!" Cassandra Mande said. "I can smell the ganja from here!"

"Somebody call an ambulance," Evonne Sorenstam-Finch said.

"We can't! We don't have phones!" said Charlie S., the Indian Chief.

Joseph Hector Depace mused, "This was an oversight. A medical emergency and no phones."

"I said from the start," barked Donskoy, "if my wife drops, she can't reach me. Now this man has perished on our shores..."

"Sir, is this triggering for you?" Sorenstam-Finch said to Donskoy.

"What?"

"Everyone, calm down. He's breathing, he's breathing. And I have a pulse. We have our phones in back."

But people were talking over one another and not everyone heard Joyce's plea.

"This is a scandal! There'll be a wrongful death lawsuit! The foundation will be cleaned out."

"The event coordinator has a phone," Joyce said, more loudly. "I have my phone."

"We need an alibi!" cried Santos Gougoutris. "Everyone, let's get our stories straight!"

"Santos! I'm surprised at you. A good Christian," said Lenore Happybones.

"Who is he anyway? Search his pockets, Joyce!" said Johanna Sturludóttir, stepping forward.

"I don't know if that's a good idea. Does anyone know this man?" Joyce called.

"Never seen him," said Lamond Jackson, unfazed by this. It's not like an IUD went off.

"No idea," said Andrew Knuthe.

"He's a drunk! An interloper!" said Christine Wong.

"Yeah, what kind of wastoid crashes *this* party?" said Roselli. "We're trying to recognize good deeds and deservingness..."

"He sure looks like a junkie," said Santos Gougoutris. "Get him out of here!"

"Hey, come now," said Jeong-Hwa. "We should treat this man with dignity."

"He may be an addict," added Petra Barnhouse factually, standing beside Jeong-Hwa and touching his arm.

Joyce pulled the man's eyelids up, looking for signs of life, or perhaps an indication of intent. All she saw was two unresponsive globules of something like bloodshot gelatin.

"These guys are all junkies, a drain on the system, and I'm sick of all this coddling," said Gougoutris.

"Please, Mr. Gougoutris," said Joyce. "Let's keep a civil tone."

"Civility died along with chivalry," said Darla Emmenberg. "I'm with Santos. Why should we taxpayers pick up the tab for rejuvenating these degenerates who can't control themselves?"

"Okay," said Joyce, standing up. "I'm going for my phone. Excuse me. Excuse me." She wove through the crowd.

"Search his pockets! Let's find out who he is!" shouted a man.

"Don't touch him!" Joyce called over her shoulder. "Please! Nobody touch him!"

"If we find out who he is, we can help him," Evonne Sorenstam-Finch warbled tearfully.

"How can we help him?" Wong asked. "We can't reach anyone."

"If we had our phones, we could do facial recognition," someone else said. The conversation quickly burbled to an indistinguishable froth, nothing that any one person could absorb, no single voice leading it, no direct through-line, lacking any trajectory towards resolve.

"Honestly, I bet that would work," said Roselli cheerfully, turning to find and address the person who had suggested facial recognition. "Technology will save us!"

"I think the Foundation will regret taking them away—our phones," said Ramirez. "It's a major liability. If this man croaks, I mean."

"*He* doesn't need his phone. Who's he going to call? He's toast."

"If he starts puking, roll him over." This was Hermann Donskoy.

"Yeah, remember Jimi Hendrix?"

"I've seen it happen."

"Jimi Hendrix choked on his own vomit?"

"Of course. You didn't know that?"

"That's an urban legend."

"An urban legend? What's that?"

"Let's toss him out the window. That'd be hilarious."

"The scandal here is not the phones. It's our own inhumanity.

You hear me?" Petra Barnhouse. "Our own hypocrisy!"

This caught some attention. Barnhouse stepped forward, her feet between the splayed legs of the drunken man.

"Who's a hypocrite?" Depace asked, not catching the gist.

Barnhouse spoke up, rotating to address the crowd at large, a skill she'd learn at the Centre County council meetings and the town halls and the Flint, MI, coffee klatches and the press conferences and other speechifying events surrounding the incident of her poisoned well water. "Odds are, this man came here for the same reasons we did," Barnhouse mused. "To be awarded the trophy. Did you ever think of that?"

Just then the front door opened and closed. No one could see over the throng, who had entered, but the slowness of the door's movement seemed to suggest apprehension, like that of people encroaching mid-scene. "See, they're still coming in. All in search of the same thing. A chance at the trophy. Just like you." Turning. "Just like you." Turning. "Just like you." Turning again.

"This is getting saccharine!" said the voice of an elderly woman from deep within the crowd.

"I don't want to be preached to," said another voice.

"Shh!"

"Let her talk!" said Happybones, wielding her feminine power through her masculine windpipes.

Barnhouse continued. "And just like me. But why do we presume he's so different than us? So he's had too much to drink. Haven't we all at one time?"

"I *don't* drink," Mande said, defiantly.

"And if he's smoked marijuana?" Barnhouse speculated. "Is he a criminal? Or did he only wish to ease the pain—the pain that we all—"

"Mom! Jerome!" Joyce said, bursting into the kitchen.

Candace and Ardizzone both twisted a startled 180 from within their conspiratorial huddle over the sous chef's work on the carved radishes.

"What is it?" Candace said.

"Somebody passed out."

"Who?"

"I don't know. You better come see. You too, Jerome."

"Keep carving, and neater!" Candace yelled, storming across the kitchen with Jerome in her tailwind. Candace's heels clapped against the hardwood. When she reached the people-thick center of the parlor, she cleared a path. "Step aside, please!" Candace called, reaching. "Step aside! Coming through. Excuse me." She stopped before the morbid, splayed figure as a plumber stands before a malfunctioning toilet tank emitting that annoying hiss of constant refilling. Monti Taylor, unconscious on the floor, was like that useful but unpleasant apparatus whose every part must be assessed when it goes buggy.

"Oh," Candace said, with evident relief.

"You know him?" Santos Gougoutris asked.

Using the discretion of someone of her class, whose family has been in the public eye, she made no reply. Chatter erupted.

Candace addressed the group like an adept tour guide, quickly squelching any suspicious gossip. "Listen up, everyone."

The hum quieted.

"Your attention please."

Silence.

"Thank you."

"We need you all to clear some space here. We're going to be calling a doctor. The doctor will come at once and attend to the patient." Diplomacy in action. She knew Roger and Frances Hanwell would prefer that their son-in-law not be taken to a public hospital. She didn't need it getting out either, bringing scandal to her event. A private doctor is a privilege of the well-to-do. Privacy around blunders and mishaps. The precautions against scandal.

"Who are you calling?" Andrew Knuthe asked in full voice.

Candace described the doctor as highly qualified, an associate of hers for 25 years. The fallen man would get the utmost care with less delay than if he were herded through the ER, that's for sure.

Some murmuring as the guests deduced that Mrs. Winslow

was choosing not turn him over to medical authorities. Why would that be? Was a cover-up in play? Candace asked that everyone now please enjoy dessert—a pumpkin tart—and coffee, being served in the next room.

"Please, let's resume our celebration," she said with a charming smile. "Mingle. I see such diverse faces here, it's wonderful, and I'm sure many of you have not had a chance to be introduced to and visit with everyone just yet."

Seeing the front door open, she pointed towards the foyer, drawing her guests' attention away from the besotted Taylor-Hanwell. "See, and newcomers are still arriving, so I know there are more friends you can make yet tonight. Ha ha. Thank you. Have some cake. It's over there. Thank you, everyone."

Smiling, smiling. The throng shuffled uncertainly towards the enlivening promise of stimulants.

Candace grabbed Lamond P. Jackson by the arm. "Mr. Jackson, stay nearby, would you? I'd like to have someone of your caliber—that is, experienced in emergencies, you know?"

"Yes, ma'am," Lamond said. He took one stride back towards the body and snapped into the familiar pose of standing at attention. He was capless tonight, but he could all but see the brim of his camo "cover" just above his narrowed gaze, shading his eyes from the sun bouncing off Kirkuk dunes.

"If he gets on his feet," Candace said, leaning against Lamond's broad chest and inadvertently feeling its impressive breadth and strength, "put him down again."

She placed the call to Dr. Rajani, while Ardizzone and Joyce stood by awaiting instruction.

Dr. Arjun Rajani, the Winslow family GP who was compensated handsomely for his services in the manner that functioned like a retainer, though, in taxation terms, as far as the feds were concerns, that certainly wasn't the nature of the payment: such payments were not allowed due Mr. Rajani's status as an advisor to the Foundation and shareholder in a private equity firm that invested in medical technologies that Rajani's colleagues developed, some of whom (the colleagues) had submitted nominating applications for the FAIR award on behalf of their patients, relatives, or friends. For example, Joseph Hector Depace, who was presently involved in double-blind clinical trial of a new anti-depressant, which if successful and marketed correctly stood to become quite lucrative. These connections weren't entirely immoral or nepotistic, but they did have a tendency, in Candace's experience, to unravel when an otherwise innocent circumstance (a man drinks too much) leads to politically motivated probes and inquiry.

Candace, her iPhone to her ear, listening to the ambient sounds of Dr. Rajani's household (TV, a barking dog), as his wife fetched him from another part of the house. "Friend of the family, I don't mind telling you," she said to Lamond, again conspiratorially, this time pointing her toe at the motionless Taylor-Hanwell.

Lamond nodded sternly. He had derived that much.

Rajani got on the line saying, "Candace, what are you doing? It's the fete right now, no?"

She gave him the scoop. "I need you to come to the house, Raj. We've got a got a guy on the floor. Drunk as an Irishman. Roger Hanwell's son-in-law."

Networks of wealth and connection, woven through the average community riff-raff. Access. Expedience. Efficiency.

Rajani asked a few basics about his condition—pulse? breathing?—said he was out the door in two minutes.

Candace hung up with a satisfied sigh. But before she could revive herself, a guest, the Asian theater director, was at her elbow, accusing: "You know, I think it's only fair that if you can have your phone, we should be able to too."

Candace had to diplomatize her way through that one. Not gonna happen. "Thank you for sharing your thoughts on it. I understand completely. However...the sanctity of the award, scavenging news outlets..." Wong began to open her mouth again, and Candace cut her off: "Excuse me, we have to attend to the gentleman."

Ms. Wong stalked away.

Seeing her mother had finished the call, Joyce moved in to confer. Jerome shadowed, walking—he was an expert in this—with his eyes on his phone and thumbs hammering. He'd already told Gabe *We got a drunk guy on the floor.* Gabe had replied to go fetch Abbas and Kendal, the two security guys. He'd recently starting contracting security for dinners and galas himself, directly, rather than through a third party. It was all licensed and insured, and done under another DOB beneath the Premier umbrella: that way, Gabe could still hire out muscle if even the meal calendar dried up.

"This looks bad," Joyce said, ignoring the question. "Let's move him."

They decided on the kitchen. Jerome lifted Taylor by the boots, Jackson by the armpits. Joyce and Candace cleared the trail through the densely packed room. They made the kitchen, and the door swung shut behind them.

"Block that door, will you?" Candace said to Tara Voss, the first hired staff she saw. "There's a stopper at the bottom, a latch at the top. Over here, gentlemen." She crossed the room, around the kitchen island, stopped to supervise the handling of the cargo. "Easy now."

The other caterers, including Michael Dulka, watched the processional steering through their workspace, as one watches a motorcade coming through town. It looked like they were toting a rolled up carpet in a suit. Dulka envied the peaceful rest of the obliterated.

Voss kicked down, at the bottom of the door, the hinged steel arm capped by a rubber stopper, and threw the gate-style barrel bolt at the top of the door.

"Here?" Jerome said, reaching the opposite side of the room.

Taylor issued incoherent vocalizations.

"Oh, god, he's waking up," Joyce said.

"The pantry?" Candace said, looking around in a panic. A lifetime of covering up dirty family secrets, covert abortions, wire transfers in false names, properties sold for a dollar, children transferred from schools. Jerome re-gripped and huffily inhaled. Even though Jackson had the heavy end, he was as easeful as if carrying a picnic basket. They all filed into the store room, into the aisle down its center, between the two rows of storage racks. They dropped Taylor against the wall and propped him up.

"This is a new one for you, eh," Candace said to Jerome, who brushed his hands and took a knee, breathing deep.

He straightened, buttoned his suit coat. "Phew," was all he could say.

"Lamond, maybe you could go watch the door for Dr. Rajani," Candace said. "Indian man. Escort him back."

"A military escort," Joyce joked. "He'll appreciate that."

"Yes, ma'am," Lamond said. "Happy to help." He went out.

The idea lingered in the minds of some in the room that the African-American Lamond, though a decorated soldier, someone who had sat in meetings inside the Pentagon, and ridden in C-130s over the Sinai Peninsula, an expert in drone surveillance … well, there were uncomfortable—anyone under 30 would say "awkward"—overtones of the servile black man leaving the pantry of the wealthy white matriarch. Oh, god, would the nation's antebellum past never cease its haunting?

"What a pickle," Candace sighed, leaning on a stack of 50-lb bags of basmati rice in the steel shelving.

—14—

George Opfell, 54, of Houston, Texas, stood in the parlor, talking to Lenore Happybones and Jeong-Hwa Pak, holding a little plastic cup of plain seltzer. It didn't even have lemon in it, that's how sensitive George's organs were. Because George had a non-functioning kidney, he did not drink alcohol. Six foot one, 260, a rotund midsection shaped by much barbequed pork, brisket, and ribs. A cheerful, resilient face muddled by the ugliness of pocked skin (teenage acne, chicken pox) and a nose like those fungal growths you see on dead but still-standing birch trees. He wore a pink polo shirt under a powder blue polyester blazer, black Dockers brand pants, which in total did not match, but were the best-condition of his duds not destroyed by the rising waters. The sole of George's left shoe was thicker than the right—a custom orthotic to accommodate the shortness of his left leg. George was in very good spirits. He'd taken some pain pills on the flight, and they continued to provide relief to his many aches. And he had one of his favorite things—a captive audience for his stories of Hurricane Harvey's wrath and power.

"I live in the Mason Park area. We were hit hard. The flooding was 12 feet. Here, before I forget, take my card." His fished in a pocket, producing a rubber-banded packet of business cards. He asked Lenore to hold his drink, and she did. He unbound the rubber band, and somewhat unnecessarily wetted his thumb on his tongue to separate the cards. Doling them out, he said, "So I'm a photographer as well."

"Oh, wonderful," Lenore said.

J. looked on with interest.

"At my website, I've got a bunch of Harvey pictures. The aftermath. Streets like brown rivers. People stranded on rooftops. The wreckage. You know, when the waters receded, it left just *untold* volumes of debris. People's lives scattered everywhere. Furniture. Photographs. Their prized possessions. Everything. I shot as much as I could. But I had to get dialysis still, even during the flooding, which was a big problem. So I went to my sister's pace in El Paso. They got a good hospital there. Mt. Kettering, I think it is."

"I can only imagine," said Lenore, recognizing in George the features of a certain garrulous type. There is a fine line between the admirably open-hearted and the life-sucker who must saddle you with his every woe. Lenore was interested in hearing about George's artistic side. She asked what George's specialty was, whether portraits or nature stuff, or...

"I do lot of landscapes. When I was more able-bodied and could travel, I'd drive out to west Texas, shoot the ranchland and the expanses. But not only that. Galveston and the islands. Wildlife. Whatever grabs my interest, really."

"And do you show your work?" asked J.

"I do, I have a gallery space that I own back in Houston, in the downtown area. A lot of time, I go around to the cafes and talk to the owners about hanging some photos."

George stopped to let some passersby sidle through.

"After you, after you. Lively party now," George remarked. "Anyway, really I do it for the love of it. I just love the visual medium. I love finding that surprising image, the one hidden in plain sight. I love the ritual around a day's shoot. The gear, the anticipation. The post-production stuff, not so much. But actually, I'm pretty into the techie side of it now. I'll probably go back to my hotel room tonight—you know, the great thing about it is, wherever you can carry a laptop and get online, you've got your travelling studio. I've got a series from Nashville, where I went recently. So maybe I'll get those up tonight, so y'all can see them when you go to the website."

How charming, Lenore thought. George Opfell, Houston amateur photographer, and nice guy, yes. But FAIR award recipient, 2018? Alas, no. "Well, thank you for being here, George," Happybones said. "Wonderful that you could make it. It sure has been a pleasure to meet you."

"Yes, thank you, you know my wife—"

"Bye bye, now," Happybones said with a smile, turning, and coming immediately upon Darla Emmenberg, who seemed to be struggling to move, chair and all, through the thick crowd.

"Everything good, babe?" Happybones said, looking down at Darla. They'd been coworkers at the foundation offices for three years now, keeping cubes nearby each other. The problem at the moment was, you'd normally stand back a piece from Darla's chair, so the poor girl didn't have to break her neck craning up at you to talk. But now elbow room was at a minimum. Adding the height of her heels, Happybones veritably towered above, making a sightline nearly impossible.

"Peachy keen," Emmenberg said, with characteristic sarcasm, head lifted as if beseeching the Lord above. The buoyancy of Darla's spirit was a true treasure. Candace and Joyce (they ultimately made hiring decisions) recognized it in her. Darla's position was a sad one—not to say a sinecure, but Administrative Officer, the title says it all, she's pushing pencils and sending emails. In the office, Happybones could count on her, however, to perform her duties with vigor and cheer. But then sometimes, just every so occasionally, her ebullience became affected, and Happybones saw that the child—how terrible that she thought of Darla as a child, because of the smallness of her body!—did labor under the strain of her affliction in ways that none of us could imagine. Think of being permanently seated. Sure, at night, she left her seat and slept in a bed, and other times floated in a tub to clean her stubby limbs and ill-sunned flesh. But her life was spent on her tush. She did not know the pleasure of a sassy strut, a sexy sashay. She had never leapt over so much as a toadstool and never would. Never mind cartwheels, somersaults and—don't even think of a life sans horizonal hula.

"Oh, darling," Happybones said. "Shall we get you some wine?"

"Blaze a trail," Emmenberg said, meaning through the bodies, seen by Emmenberg as a forest of legs and rumps. Legs in creased slacks, legs in hemmed skirts, trunks adorned in cocktail dresses, little belly rolls muffin-topping above visible panty lines, rumps draped under the coattails of blazers, hands in pockets, the brass buttons dangling. Emmenberg had thought many times that she should take up pickpocketing.

"Pardonez-moi!" Happybones called loudly into the pervasive vocative thrum.

Emmenberg pressed her joystick in the forward, or thrust, position, driving past many preoccupied guests, many champagne flutes clutched, under the many chins held up in the attentive position, her eye caught by a red woman's blazer decorated in dime- and quarter-sized sloganeering buttons and pins, saying

ENOUGH.

and

~~Thoughts & Prayers~~
Policy & Action

The red blazer had practically jumped off the hanger when Gabrielle Rauch dressed for the fete. The red of her anger. The red of her audacity, her willingness to call attention to herself and all she believed in, all she stood for. The red of alarm, because it is time to take action. The red of danger, because our children are in danger, our country is in danger. The red of blushing—for she was ashamed of her country's leaders, the senators and congresspeople who kowtowed to special interests, who broke campaign promises, who failed to protect those in most need of protection. The red of the blood spilled on the floor of room 4A, Edison Middle School, in Rauch's town of Brenton, 50 miles southwest of Albany, out amid the rolling farmland of the Catskill Mountains.

"Do you believe it, Mrs. Rauch?" Hermann Donskoy asked. "Do you believe it was staged?"

She felt it was her night. She had prepared an acceptance speech. The fates were on her side. No issue was more important. It's not that she had suffered more, but that her suffering was emblematic. Innocents. *Children.* She had that feeling of all eyes being on her, just as she had felt riding on the float through Brenton's Main Street, on a hay cart, a sash across her bosom, a tiara on her head, back in '71, waving to the adoring townspeople, Neil Denning seated on a hay bale beside her. King and Queen, Otsego county 4H Club.

"I *do* believe it, I'm sad to say," said Mrs. Rauch. "How else can we explain it? It serves their purposes perfectly. It has the ominous characteristics of an event that is, I feel, beyond fortuitous."

"The deep state," said Merrill Roselli.

"Let's not go there," said Mande.

Petra Barnhouse was silent. Donskoy, Roselli, Mande, and she comprised the four persons forming an audience around Rauch—something of a celebrity, the most heinous kind of celebrity, as the coverage of Brenton accelerated and expanded. The peculiar twist to this latest addition to America's most shameful list, the list that had begun with Columbine, included Newton, Orlando, San Bernardino, Vegas, and countless others.

What Rauch believed to be staged was the entire massacre itself, and its chief feature: the surprising and inexplicable fact that the assailant had used not an AR-15, not a sawed-off shotgun, not a Glock 9, but a blowgun and poison darts. WTF?, an entire nation (and beyond) had asked of the breaking headlines, when the anchors took up their customary positions outside the site of the massacre. And since then, in the following months, came the expected investigative reporting, the interviews with the CEO of Cabela's, the sporting goods store, which stocks the Terminator, a 36-inch blowgun that fires a dart at up to 350 feet per second, and stocks another weapon called the Cold Steel (is it the steel that's cold, or the users' heart?), which can deliver lethal poison into a body 20 yards away, and is "powerful enough to penetrate plywood," as boasted on the packaging. The noiselessness of these weapons is touted as an advantage in the merchandising. A pack of 50 "mega spikes" costs $19.99, and none of this weaponry and ammo requires any ID to purchase.

All for hunting, of course, say the CEOs and the manufacturers. All for hunting. These products have been around for centuries. An ancient technology. Because they're silent, they won't scare away prey.

But a typical classroom is under 20 yards deep—how convenient.

"I remember watching the Eye Witness special on Channel 4," Rauch said. "Those scenes in the woods. How they fired those darts into that buck. That poor animal didn't know what hit it. The stunned look in his eyes. The terrible slowness with which he staggered away. That's what they did to my baby. My Ryan took one in the neck. He didn't know what hit him."

"What kind of chemical do they use in the dart?" Donskoy asked, uncomfortable with sentiment, much preferring to discuss technical details.

Petra Barnhouse jumped in. "I don't think that's something Mrs. Rauch wants to discuss."

"It's fine, honey. I can handle it."

Roselli short-circuited the issue, coming out of a seeming reverie. "I saw online—Mrs. Rauch, you probably know this—Walmart sells a Nerf—," air quotes, "Fully Loaded" end air quotes, "kids' tactical vest. It has a bandolier, ammo clips. Part of the Guns-N-Strike Elite series. I'm not making this up. Some friends of mine have been picketing at their local Walmart."

"Disgusting," said Mande.

"You can picket all you want," Barnhouse said. "Do you think they'll pull them from the shelves?"

"They might," Roselli said.

"The kid who did this was a hunter?" Donskoy asked, peering with concern at Mrs. Rauch.

"He was not," Rauch provided, a little fatigued. This stuff was all out there. Did people not read the news? She considered it the duty of every citizen to debrief themselves on the latest assault operation on the most vulnerable population in the world—children. As it had done with the siege on Bin Laden's compound, the New York Times had created elaborate info graphics showing cross-sections of the two-story Edison school building, tracing the path of assailant Craig Hartigan's route from the entry point at the south doors, to the gymnasium, where he took his first victims during their game of air hockey, and where he dropped the first empty steel quiver for .625 caliber darts; out the opposite gym door to the west hallway and up the stairwell, with callout inset boxes captioning the simultaneous events, such as the principal's call to 911, providing sidebar factsheets such as the elapsed time of Hartigan's murderous pass through the gymnasium (one minute, ten seconds); and his route to room 4B, Ryan's Civics classroom, led by Ward Prinz, a veteran Edison teacher of 18 years. This cartographic almanac of horror was Rauch's blue book in her recovery from grief. It's factuality assuaged her feelings of raggle-taggle outcomes and causes—her feeling of being absent from this essential event. She printed the page and studied it under lamplight past midnight with cups of black coffee. She read it aloud to her sister Joan. To retell Hartigan's actions was to recreate it under her control. The illustrator of the infographic had even captured the billowing of Hartigan's trench coat, and this sight seemed bring Rauch herself into the building, making her the witness she wished to be, *ex post facto*. Feeling present and connected to the reality of the occurrence was, Rauch realized, required in order to promulgate her great terror and remorse, and to sharpen the rage she felt towards this ignorant, ignorant beast who had ruthlessly robbed her of her son.

That Hartigan had taken his own life, via a self-inflected dose of the same ricin compound used to coat the tips of the darts he'd shot into Ryan and 15 others (12 child students, two adult teachers, one adult custodian), was no consolation to Rauch. And as for the fact that many, many otherwise engaged citizens and news-reading people knew nothing of the massacre's specific timeline, or where Brenton was located exactly, and who these children were—that is, lacked the compassionate will to realize the totality of the injustice, the sheer vileness of the crime, the idiocy of our federal government having no restrictive laws around obtaining blow darts and blow dart guns... that was just unfathomable.

What Rauch never entertained was the possibility that the otherwise news-reading and concerned public also struggled to keep their lives on an even keel, to keep their own daily feelings free of the clinging spider's webs of despair and ennui that threated to snag them at every incident of engagement with media—which, in 2018 was a near-perpetual occurrence.

"Ricin, Mr. Donskoy," Rauch said. "To answer your question. It's made from the castor-oil plant. Highly toxic."

"Interesting. In my time, it was mustard gas."

"I read that blowguns are illegal in a couple states, but everywhere else it's fine?" Roselli said.

"California, Massachusetts, and DC.," Rauch answered bluntly. "Illegal there. Blowguns are banned in the UK, Ireland, and Australia as well."

"They should be banned here. Every state," Mande said defiantly.

"If I should find myself with a platform," Rauch said, gesturing vaguely to the room...

The trophy, thought the canny Petra Barnhouse.

"...then I'll be sure to work towards getting federal legislation passed."

Merrill Roselli said something about a hashtag campaign.

"It's a very small-minded person who thinks that social media activity is the same as reality," Rauch said.

Barnhouse felt a jolt of glee. The frontrunner stumbles! Indecorous remarks! Demerits!

Roselli stuttered. "Well, I—that's not—if you—" His blue eyes blinked and blinked.

"When a body is bleeding, we don't *protest* the wound," Rauch said. "We suture it."

—15—

"I can't believe it's her," said Yvonne Sorenstam-Finch.

"Believe it," said Juan Ramirez.

"I'm looking at this red blazer, and it's—"

"Oh!" Ramirez, startled, spun around. Someone, in passing, had bumped the elbow of the arm to which his Pinot Grigio-holding hand was attached. His quick reflexes averted a spill of more than a few drops. He shook his hand free of the spillage, and turned to spy the offender slink through the throng unaware.

"Getting crowded in here," Evonne said.

"Yeah," Ramirez said, running fanned fingers through his medium-length hair, resituating himself in the configuration of encroaching bodies that, he was glad, pressed him closer to Sorenstam-Finch, whom he was entertaining designs upon. He liked the tight bun her hair was tied in. It was like how a person would do their hair upon waking up in a tent. He liked tents, and he liked camping. Plus the tautness was suggestive to Ramirez—maybe she liked to have her hair pulled. Her green eyes were big and mysterious, ringed by black mascara lines. Underscoring their intensity. Thick eyelashes, the bridge of her nose flat in a non-Anglo way. What was she, exactly? The beige tones of a Caucasian, but the contours of an Occidental. Clear, smooth skin with imperceptible pores. She almost seemed photoshopped. Her mouth sat low on her face, a long gap under her nose, above the upper lip. But it wasn't ugly, though it was slightly amphibian. And her lips rested in a slightly protruding pout, like she had chewing tobacco in, which made Juan think of things in her mouth in general. When she spoke, her bright white teeth shone through, and the hugeness of her mouth, like Julia Roberts', was revealed. Was she a singer? She seemed to have the sharp beauty and political positioning of an Ani DiFranco or Joni Mitchell.

"Gabrielle Rauch," said Evonne, reverently. "She's been very outspoken since the Brenton massacre. Very inspiring."

"Absolutely," Ramirez said. "She should run for office."

"That'd be amazing," Evonne said.

"Has she come out with a position in response to Greeley's statement?"

"Not yet, I don't think. Greeley's was just yesterday."

Djink Greeley, founder and CEO of Ntrepid, a space exploration firm—rocket building, civilian space-tourism, etc.—had tweeted a video accusing the National Rifle Association and the White House of orchestrating the Brenton blowgun attack, which had successfully taken the vitriolic focus off guns and gun legislation. Every cable news channel was now replete with pundits and spokespeople saying, *This just proves, guns don't kill people—people kill people. Guns aren't the problem* and so on. The proverbial heat was off the NRA, the narrative successfully reshaped. And the fact that Hartigan was a Muslim-American—forget about it. How did they get him to do it? That was the question. It was eerily convenient. Greeley called for an FBI investigation and a raid on NRA offices and servers, said they should be looking into Hartigan's background for connections to the NRA and contact by any government agent, who Greely believed recruited Hartigan and trained and guided, armed, coerced, and motivated to carry out the attack.

"My favorite part is how they say that Greeley is 'politicizing' the Brenton tragedy," said Ramirez. Ramirez's salty tone made it clear that by "they," he meant the opposing party.

"Oh, I know," Evonne said.

"They're all politicians. They'll all do it. They all speak out against what the others think and believe and do. And then rather than address the nature of what *they* think and believe and do, they say it's shameless how the other party is politicizing the issue."

"I've been working on a design that shows a body. When it comes to limbs, for example, right and left cannot survive without the other. You see? If we split a body the center..." Evonne provocatively drew a line from her throat, down her exposed chest between the lapels of her eggshell blazer, and over the black blouse underneath, through the channel between her breasts, all the way to her belly button. "...the body cannot survive. Both sides will die."

Ramirez swallowed hard and tugged at his shirt collar. "Like the Judgement of Solomon," he said.

Sorenstam-Finch smiled.

"So you're an artist?"

"I work in advertising. This idea—I want to make it poster—there's no client. Unfortunately, the campaigns I work on are more for things like money market funds and cloud-based computing solutions. But if a client comes along wanting a message of nationwide political unity, I'm going to be ready."

"Fantastic. I'd love to see it sometime—your body. That you're designing."

"I'd love to show it to you."

Ramirez and Sorenstam-Finch's eyes locked, as they each sipped their beverages. She took a deep, deep inhale of breath and closed her eyes, directing it towards the tremendous fear burbling up in her solar plexus, a breathing technique learned from her therapist Dr. Lukas Martin, who worked in nontraditional modalities such as, primarily with Evonne, somatic cognition. That is, becoming aware of and working with the responses within the body. Not working with feelings *as ideas* but as real events happening in the flesh, organs, nervous system, and glands. It was the only modality yet to help Evonne deal with the trauma she'd endured of being kidnapped at age nine and held hostage in the basement of the psychopath Warren Dudzic, in her hometown of Grand Rapids, Michigan. Actually, to get away from the black and white thinking that was characteristic of her coping mechanisms, it would be more correct to say that somatic work was not the *only* modality to benefit her, but rather the latest and very healing step in her journey, which began with powerful anti-psychotic drugs and other traditional therapeutic practices practiced incorrectly by quacks who failed to comprehend the magnitude of her experience and who made all kinds of stupid antiquated Freudian assumptions. Anyway, what she was doing now—momentarily ignoring Ramirez—was sending breath towards the quivering parts of her body, around the sternum, including the heart above and the belly below, to calm herself, as she felt sexual excitement surface, in response to the handsome and alluring Mr. Ramirez, and as the prospect dawned of potential romantic contact. All her work under the guidance of Dr. Martin was directed towards the reclamation of not only her basic sanity, which meant restoring her belief that the world was, or could be, a safe place; that men were not all predators wishing to constrain, harm and abuse her, and so on; but repairing and rewiring her body's response to those healthy attachments and healthy sexual interactions which we all crave and require to be happy human beings.

Evonne was released from captivity at the age of 15, after which she spent strange years back in the fold of her bewildered, mortified, and ultimately incredibly grateful family (mother Stephanie, father Thomas, brother Brian), reentering school (the upset to her educational trajectory was another saga entirely; the psychopath Dudzic had let her read extensively, and discussed world events and history, and so on with her—part of the nurturing behaviors that allowed Evonne to attach and even love her captor). By the time she graduated high school, the media flap about her abduction had died down, and people forgot her name a little bit, and then she actually went away to college on time with the rest of her class, studying communications at the University of Michigan at Ann Arbor. There (as Evonne Sorenstam), she met Michael Kenneth (M.K.) Finch, a record-holding swimmer and debate team captain, magna cum laude, a big-hearted Christian with a possible Christ complex, in his outsized wish to heal and redeem Evonne and her life. Finch had a devotion to chastity which fit her fears around sex just great—a devotion which Evonne thought would lift once they married, but did not exactly lift, rather turned into a domineering thing where MK insisted on sex at certain times, ordered her to shower and wear certain things, became paranoid about her involvement with other men, even innocent men like her physical trainer and her boss at Janklow & Janklow—and furthermore became accusatory, delusional, verbally abusive, and controlling—trying to keep her in the house, keep her out of civic involvements, even limit her use of the telephone. This was all revealed to be caused by Finch's maniacal guilt and fear of discovery around the sex he'd been having with the young men of the swim team at Carlow University, Pittsburgh, PA, where they'd moved, and where he was head coach (Go, Celts!).

Evonne had been 25 years old when they married, and for seven years they'd remained married, having no kids (thankfully, Evonne felt), and divorcing eleven months prior to the fete. Evonne planned to change her name back to Sorenstam, but was meeting some kind of subconscious resistance to it, her current working theory being that it was Evonne Sorenstam who had been kidnapped, and Evonne Sorenstam-Finch who had overcome The Atrocity to triumph in love. But that love had turned evil in a scary way that was crazily reminiscent of her captivity, and so had she chosen to re-captivated herself? This was an open question, among many, being addressed under Dr. Martin's care, and what that meant was that in Dr. Martin's office, in the Shearing Professional Building, in Pittsburgh's Troy Hill neighborhood, Evonne sat once a week, at first discussing the events of the week, however mundane they might be, and when striking on a triggering event, Dr. Martin would say, "Let's work with that for a moment. So go ahead and put your feet flat on the floor. Close your eyes, good, and just relaaaaax. Take a few deep, centering breaths, and I want you to focus on that feeling. You're back there in the office, and you're on the phone... Okay, are you back there? You're in the office? Mm-hmm? Good. Okay, your coworker is being demanding and rude, he's barking those orders at you like you said. What do you feel in your body? What's coming up for you?"

It might be vanished limbs or a thick throbbing in the frontal lobe. It might be painful tingling in the joints or any number of physical sensations. Most often it was a tension and electrical-type sensation in her chest and stomach—fear. Fright. Her body telling her, freeze, fight or flight. FFF. That was a key to so much. So, so much. Dr. Martin was an angel, and somatic work helped her stay with her feelings, *have* them, and not do crazy things in response to them without even knowing it.

Paired with Dr. Martin's therapies—his keen counsel, his deep empathy—was Evonne's adoption of other alternative wellness modalities. She was a convert to holistic homeopathic practices. Every Saturday morning she received acupuncture by a real Chinese person named Yi. Frequently she arrived home to the Troy Hill condo she'd moved into (fifth floor, no basement; Evonne didn't do basements anymore, and she didn't do macaroni and cheese, which Dudzic considered his specialty) after the divorce to find packages on her doorstep—packages from NaturalRemedies.com that excited her with the promise of growth and healing, a new life created in her own mold. She was experiencing individuation and knew that when she was ready for a new relationship, it could only be with a man who respected this process in her and was pursuing or had attained a similar kind self-discovery, who had wholesome self-care practices. Evonne's entire kitchen cabinet was stacked with fish oil, ashwagandha root powder, bladderwrack, rosehips, kava kava, St. John's wort, and much, much more. That didn't even cover the teas and essential oils.

Tuesday nights was yoga at a neighborhood studio—hatha, other traditions. It was astounding how, broadly speaking, Americans believed yoga was about flexibility and contortions and knew nothing of the spiritual component of meeting yourself where you are, acceptance of your limitations, while patiently *stretching* your potential and being present with yourself. Most weekday mornings at home Evonne did a 15-minute meditation on a zafu at home. She read books by Pia Melody and Pema Chodron. She listened to several self-help podcasts, but not the idiotic ones by bros trying to optimize their outputs, maximize their efficiencies. Her whole conception of what went in her body and mind and how things affected her had been overhauled one hundred percent from the understanding that her upbringing and education had given her on that front—which was next to nothing, a rudimentary idea, at best, of nutrition helping her body grow and the facts of history and diagrams of food webs contributing to intelligence. And basically, the more she practiced these things and the more people she met at the coop and in the aisles of bookstores, the more she meditated and did somatic work—she even did somatic practices on her own now, during stressful moments, during relationally-challenging encounters of any kind—the more holistic wellness as a field and homeopathy as a field interested her and became her passion—all she wanted to think about and read about and talk about, to the point that her daily work, in advertising and marketing for Janklow & Janklow, came to seem hollow, false, meaningless, unfulfilling, superficial, even degrading, insulting, and asinine. Which was an inner conflict that itself required treatment with somatic work.

She was rightfully very proud of her progress and grateful for the support of people like Dr. Martin, Yi, her yoga teacher, and Pema Chodron, who taught that no matter what horrors we'd experienced we could still return to our basic place of goodness, our innate openness and joy. And because Evonne knew empirically that she had advanced spiritually and had overcome so very much pain, and had grown a fair amount of wisdom—namely that she couldn't change the past but could shape her future—and had developed such a powerful sense of empathy and compassion for all suffering beings, she did wonder if the FAIR award wasn't destined to be hers, the culmination of a long process of moving out of victimhood. She wondered if the stipend—the cash prize of $25,000—would be hers to help fulfill her dream of opening an holistic wellness center of her own, buying or leasing a space in Troy Hill and having a library of books for people and after-school services for kids, a safe place where they could come and not be on the streets getting abducted, and where people could get herbal teas and go to private rooms to do breathing techniques, and a thousand other resources that Evonne wished to provide to Pittsburgh's fine citizens.

And yet the damaged part of Evonne was not one hundred percent healed. There was a deep, deep part of her, unavailable to examination and control by her conscious mind, which believed that in order to get what she wanted she would have to perform sexually—just as she had had to please her captor Dudzic, for so many years, in order to get what she wanted (to live; have decent clothes; drink water). And so even as she observed the handsomeness of Juan Ramirez and felt a genuine desire to get to know him and enjoyed his views on the Brenton massacre and Djink Greeley's accusation, ideas formulated that if she could take him to a back room and felate this foundation staff member (or committee member or delegate or representative or whatever they were), then she stood a better chance— perhaps the only chance—of walking out of the Winslow townhome on this night, arms aloft in victory, the recognition of her suffering crowned, her soul whole at last.

"Let's get another drink, and, I don't know, look around," Evonne said.

"Yeah, great," said Ramirez, his head making an involuntary twist of delighted surprise.

Evonne took him by the hand and led him through the crowd. "Hi, Mrs. Barnhouse!" she called, passing Petra, the delightful and deserving woman she'd met earlier.

—16—

Petra was on the move, looking for a new clique to join, when she crossed the path of Evonne Sorenstam-Finch and Juan Ramirez, and simultaneously spotted Andrew Knuthe, the handsome, kindly Biology teacher.

"Hi, Evonne," she said, continuing to approach Knuthe, smilingly warmly.

"Hello," said Knuthe. Neutral, open to interpretation.

"I owe you an apology," Petra said.

"What?"

Face to face. His red beard and ruddy forehead, pink ears, purple nose.

"What, you're going to make me say it again!"

"No, I just—I can't hear you, that's all."

She spoke up. "I'm sorry, I was kind of judgmental earlier about your hunting. I'm sure you sensed it."

"Ah, don't worry about it. It's a tough one, animal rights. Not the first time I've met a vegetarian."

"Yeah, well, we could *discuss* it. That's what I wish I had done. I'm capable of civil discourse." She smiled, a quick, slapped-on smile to charm him.

"Of course you are. I can tell that."

"I'm actually something of an environmental activist," Barnhouse said.

"Is that right?"

"Where I live, our well was poisoned by fracking."

"No shit. Cabot?"

"Yes indeed—Cabot."

"Which county are you in? Huntington? Blair?"

"Centre."

"Oh, yeah, Centre County. I know it. You guys got shafted in that verdict."

"That's one way of putting it!" Barnhouse clasped Knuthe's forearm.

They laughed, locked eyes, drew a few inches closer to one another, compelled by the bustle around them, their desire to continue hearing and being heard and avoid the congestion of strangers.

—17—

The parlor's several chairs and sofas were now lost from view to the majority of guest-candidates, who stood about the room, from wall to wall, in one dense group resembling some parame-cium or bacteria under a microscope—abundant, loose group-ings, all aquiver with small movements, some worming through the sea as if questing to distinguish themselves, or pair up. Most of the sofas had been given up to elderly or infirm or overweight or otherwise distinguished people. On the main sofa sat Balooja Inamdar, a Bangladeshi-American woman, 49, her head covered in an orange hajib. She wore a modest dress with long sleeves and high neck line, that fell to her shoes. Only her face and hands expressed the brownness of her skin, the color of fertile soil. She had organized a media campaign and raised funds for activism and made a presentation to congress about some proposed leg-islation that would require labels on clothing to disclose whether the goods were made in safe conditions in inspected facilities. Inamdar's sister had died in the 2013 collapse of the Savar building, in Dhaka, Bangladesh, which housed, among other things, a clothing factory where her sister had worked as a seamstress.

"Do you go to many parties?" Inamdar said to the man next to her—they'd made introductions already: Avi Sobol, 60, gray-bearded, sidelocks (*payot*) dangling in spiraling curls down from temples to jaw. He wore a knit kippah and a black suit.

"There are many celebrations in my community," said Sobol. He voice was raspy. He had a cold. "This time of year, not so much."

Inamdar asked about the community referenced—where it was. Cincinnati, Sobol said. Inamdar herself was from California. Neither of them were living in expectation of an award. They did not particularly crave an award, either, or feel it was necessary. For them anyway. They recognized that in each other. Yes, they supported the foundation in its mission, had never spoken against it. But they had lives to lead, other matters concerning them.

Sobol was hard of hearing and for whatever reason had delayed and delayed being tested and fitted for a hearing aid, despite the pleas of his family. The din of the party made it difficult for him to make out what Inamdar was saying. He leaned her way, squinting. His resistance to the challenge of conversation was weakening as the years went on. The remainder of the evening held a shape in his conception of time as a dutiful but not strenuous couple more hours, sitting through the ceremony, hearing a speech or two, and then concluding.

"When are they doing the honors?" Sobol asked.

"They are setting up the next room, I heard."

Sobol nodded. He didn't know what she meant exactly—what room, setting up what exactly?—but it didn't concern him. He would find out soon enough. To him, the award was a cultural signifier, not a ceremony of any spiritual validity. Only g-d in *shamayim* would bring the end of suffering. The award was noble, though, in that it made a statement about which persons in present-day America we wish to no longer hold at the fringes, like modern-day lepers. Unfortunately, Sobol felt, it was likely to go to a transgender person, because this was very popular now, this switching teams, which was an abomination. Sobol was not one of these Zellman, Reform types—or worse a Reconstructionist like that Pennsylvanian, Wenig. He was Hassidic. True.

—18—

"Are we having fun yet?" Michael Dulka said, taking hold of one end of a folded up folding table in the dining room, whose doors were closed to guests while it was being reorganized.

"Tons of fun," said Tara Voss, taking hold of the table's opposite end.

They carried the table through to the kitchen, and into the service elevator, which was being held open by a big bag of rice dropped in the path of the auto-closing door. Voss stepped aside, giving room for Dulka to upend the table and stack it with the others. They went back for additional tables, passing Jerome and Joyce, who were overseeing the conversion of the room from cafeteria into a consecration hall. They were pointing and making slashing gestures at the emptying room, as of imagined ideal arrangements.

When the elevator could fit no more tables, Dulka conferred with Voss, expressing his interest in their being the ones to take them down to the van. Voss went to her handbag, at the kitchen island, the prep station, and on the way back, got Jerome's attention with a smokey-smokey gesture at her lips, which Jerome OK'd with a nod, engaged with his phone now.

Dulka sighed heavily as the elevator doors closed.

"Hard part's over," Voss said.

"True, true," he said, watching the floor number lights change, five to four to three...

"Do the chairs, clean up."

"I don't' know about this crowd," Dulka said. The elevator dinged, and the lurch to a halt momentarily sloshed Dulka's inner-ear fluid, making him queasy. He'd always been extremely sensitive that way. As a child he had many inner ear infections, and couldn't ride even the Tilt-a-Whirl without getting sick, much less those monstrous contraptions at amusements parks that toss you around like a pizza dough. Something psychic played a hand today: the whole meaning of the fete unbalanced him. The world, he felt, was shifting further and further under his feet—the cultural and political tectonic plates had broken up from the ground he grew up on. "There's something ominous about it, don't you think? Something ... not right?"

Dulka stepped out, back-first, held out his hands to receive a table. "Just tip one down, I guess." Voss let one tip into Dulka's hands, then picked up the bottom end. That worked. Only a few yards to the van, parked with hazards blinking. The garage was cool, as if air conditioned, and Dulka's sneakers squeaked on the glossy concrete as he back-pedaled, and the squeaks echoed.

"Seems like a bunch of good-intentioned folks," Voss said, speculatively. "I try to stay out of clients' business, just do my job."

"Yeah, yeah, of course." They slid the table into the back of the van, went for another, Dulka hustling to catch the closing elevator door.

He said that something felt forced about the occasion. Like the foundation was idealistic. "The wrong side of history" was a phrase you heard a lot these days. Everyone scrambling to get on the right side. But are there really only two sides? "You know, I was on the debate team in college. You learn about rhetorical devices. There's a logical fallacy called Either/Or. That's making things out to seem black and white, like there's only two options. We'll either adopt affordable health care, or everyone will die. Well, no. There's always a continuum to real-world outcomes. There are gradations to everything."

Sliding in the second table, Voss swore and yanked her hand away—her finger got pinched in the leg's hinge brace. She stuck the finger in her mouth and sucked. Pulled it out with a pop. "Fuck."

"All right?"

"Pinched." She shook the hand.

"Anyway, these guys seem to be trying to usher in a future like *Avatar* or something, where technology and tribal primitivism are one. Or that scene of the Imperial Council in *Last Jedi*—all these lizard people in robes and crazy hats, like it's the intergalactic United Nations, every species working in harmony. That'd be great and all, but we can't force it."

"Dangerous ground, Michael," Voss said, picking up the last table, her injured finger folded into her palm.

"I know, right? You can't say any of this shit. And it's not that I'm a bigot or don't want world peace—I fucking *do*! Of course I do. But aren't there practical limits on this shit? I remember when the term 'global community' came around. I'm sorry, what? That's an oxymoron. A community is by definition small. Or smallish. The entire globe cannot be a community. That's too much. I'll make Rice Krispy bars and bring them to the fourth of July picnic in *my community*. Okay? I get to know my neighbors in *my community*. But I can't make Rice Krispy for the global fucking community, and I sure as hell cannot get to know the entire global community. I guess that's what feels odious to me. Don't ask me to do the impossible. Can I leave just a little brain space to watch the Yanks? Or does that make me a second-class citizen?"

"You're hilarious."

"I'm serious."

"You should do standup. You're like Louis CK or something."

"Oh, thanks. A pariah."

They got the last table in the van, slammed the door, and drove the van through the garage until they found a space. Locked it up and left it.

"Heater?" Tara said.

"Yeah."

They walked to the exit ramp, deliberately under the sensor that triggered the garage door to open. The chain motor leapt to life, roaring and rattling. Fresh, warm air rolled under the raised door. They stepped out into the night, relieved to see the ordinary sky, with its pink and purple hues cast on the clouds by the lights atop the IDS Building, and the white ring from the Norwest Building. They lit up two cigarettes with savor. A perfect little breeze blew. Washington Avenue was desolate.

"I want that feeling back that it's okay to just live your life, do your thing, without having to take on other's people shit every day and, like, feel guilty for your prosperity," Dulka said, not really done with his rant.

"Now you're talking about white guilt. I get you. The thing is, their hearts are in the right place."

"Yeah, yeah, no question. I mean, I guess so."

"We're all the same. We gotta stop with the exclusionary stuff."

"What if that's just human nature?"

"It probably is. But there's not going to *be* human nature if we keep it up."

"The thing that gets me is, it doesn't make me a fascist. It doesn't make me a social conservative either. I believe in equal rights for all. I hope Virginia ratifies that constitutional amendment, giving women fair treatment. That's not radical to me. Should the border be wide open? Eh, not sure. But I'm not saying, Allow discrimination. I'm just saying, there are limits on the capacity of even the human spirit and especially the human brain and probably our social resources too. I can't hold all this information in my head. Oh, you're this religion, so I have to be sensitive to this. You're that religion, so I can't say that. Maybe I worship peanuts in the shell. Stop eating peanuts in the shell! You're killing my god!"

"Now you're talking crazy."

Dulka laughed, a laugh betraying much chest congestion and lung fluid. When apparently healthy people cough with an unexpected death-rattle you must view them differently. Some level of self-sabotage has been exposed. It's like you've seen their report card, and their intelligence has gone down. They are miscreants, misbehaviors. You regard them with circumspection. You become stand-offish. "I know. Ultimately, though, the one thing that I can't deal with anymore is this—I call it emotional flopping. You've seen these soccer players, the defender puts a toe near them, they hit the deck. Oh, my leg! It's broken! They're rolling on the pitch. There's this basketball player, Vlade Divac, he used to do it. 7 foot 1, a little elbow and he'd send himself to the deck, sliding back, arms flailing. The Vlade Flop. Now you get it with everyday events. My favorite black actor didn't win the Emmy—pen an Op-Ed that it's racism, and everyone on the committee should resign. A Senator uses some turn of phrase that has a vaguely race-oriented derivation a century ago—he should hang himself and kill his children and burn his house down. This is politics now. Politics is no longer seeking office to effect legislation and represent a populace. It's Flopping and counter-Flopping."

Both their cig butts were done and flicked around midway through Dulka's rant.

"Back to the grind," Dulka said now.

Upstairs, Jerome said the chair and podium guy was pulling in *right now*.

"You have a chair and podium guy?" Voss joked.

"I do. He's the best chair and podium guy in town."

They headed back down in the elevator, Jerome with them. "What a nice night," he said, out on the street. They found the truck in the residential U-shaped drive at the front entrance. The driver brought the truck over, they opened the garage door, but the clearance was too low. The garage had eleven, and they needed fourteen-five. That was fine. The folding chairs were on a wheeled racked, and the podium could go on a hand truck. The driver brought the rack to the ground on a motorized lift, and they wheeled it to the service elevator, and that's how they got it done.

Joyce described the arrangement that'd been decided on. Voss and Dulka unracked chairs and arranged them in rows. They got going a little ways when they realized they were boxing in the empty rack—leaving an aisle too narrow to wheel it out. When the podium was brought in, Jerome clipped in the mic cable and ran it to the mixing board, and Joyce went to the back of the room to eyeball the positioning. She signaled left, and Jerome nudged it over a foot or two.

There was a banner as well. Jerome and Joyce hung it, and then everything was shipshape, and they surveyed the room with satisfaction. The room was ready to receive everyone. There would probably have to be SRO, Joyce pointed out, but that was fine, people could stand at the back for a while. It wouldn't kill them.

"Awesome."

"We better check on my mom and Dr. Rajani," Joyce said.

"You go ahead..." Jerome said, a contemplative look on his face too deep for an Event Coordinator. Spinal surgeon—yes.

But Event Coordinator—no. "I've got some other things to take care of," he added.

Stunned silence from Joyce. "There's a medical emergency, Jerome. We need your help."

"What can I do? Except carry the guy somewhere else?" He shrugged the shrug of the helpless. Joyce gaped, all her hurt feelings right there darkening those sensuous green eyes. "I mean, Mr. Taylor is kind of guest issue, don't you think? I'm Event Coordinator, and he's a problem guest. You know what I mean?"

"Great," Joyce muttered. "You're leaving us in the lurch."

You're maybe watching too many seasons of The Bachelor *or something,* Jerome wanted to say. Instead: "Premier is not insured for medical emergencies. I shouldn't even have carried him. You know what I mean?" Jerome proffered his phone like Exhibit A. "Gabe is coming down hard on me on this one."

"Okay. Fine. I get that," Joyce said. Eyes tossed to the heavens, an inch-wide head-shake, once, twice. End of that. "All right, well..." She stalked away, heels clopping, dress fanning in the breeze.

—19—

In the corner of the parlor farthest from the entrance and farthest from the room where the food had been served and the bar was now set up—a hotspot of activity—was a loveseat backed up against some built-in bookshelves holding many items of international origin such as wooden figurines, native finger cymbals, a giant gleaming shellacked conch shell. These items were artfully arranged amongst hardback art books with such names as Kahlo and Rubens on their spines, books held erect by decorative marble bookends. Warm lamplight, the handsome whorls of the mahogany wainscoting. (No elegant townhome is complete without handsome mahogany wainscoting.) Here in this picturesque corner sat Johan Damgaard, Dane, 38. Hair the color of silkworm silk: nearly translucent; shaved close above each ear, to the crown, showing the fairness of his scalp; long where not shaved, providing a dramatic contrast in lengths; and the long parts, swooping in a curve away from the forehead but stiffened and made heavy by thick, goopy pomade, and so immovable, and always creating the precise desired effect no matter the movement of Johan's head. Worn, in other words, in the fashion of the day. Narrow face, long pointy nose with nostrils barely slits. Eyes like two licorice gumballs. Cheeks like an excavated hill for tears to run swiftly down.

"I remember I used to sit with my Sisi," Damgaard said. "on the hillsides *aaaall* afternoon. Sisi means cousin in my language. For hours and hours we would laze in the grass on the hills outside my town, soaking in the summer sun, with no greater care than dreaming up creatures we saw in the ever-shifting shapes of the clouds. My cousin—Liva was her name—was one year older than me. Just enough older so that I was filled with fascination of her. Oh, how I admired her. She always seemed to know something about the waarld which I had not yet learned. She always said things that I could never have imagined on my own. My brain was too feeble. Observations of things I had failed to notice. Conclusions I lacked the wit to draw myself. I envied her so strongly. But I also loved her madly. When she took my hand to lead me across Jyllandsgade—that is the main road in central Aalborg, where I come from—the world seemed to stand still, the earth to stop spinning entirely. I was captive to the sight of her flowing brown hair, her long limbs, and especially her electric hazel eyes, which were as big as my own swelling heart."

"When we grew tired of staring at the clouds or grew too warm lazing in the sun, we would walk down the hill and into the grove where the *gerlaap* trees grew. Do you have *gerlaap* trees here?"

"No, I don't think so," said the young woman beside Damgaard.

"I did not think so either. I think the gerlaap tree only grows in my country." He sipped his scotch on the rocks, which was melting fast due to the number of bodies in the place and their close proximity.

"There in the shade of the *gerlaap* groves, I would hoist Liva up into the branches. Then she would pull me up after her, and together we would climb among the limbs, high in the shaded boughs, moving from limb to limb as easily as if among the rooms of our own home. In fact, this was our home—or something just like, for it offered safety, a type of above-ground privacy, and held us at a remove from the outside world. It was heaven to me. Our goal, of course, was to reach the ripest and biggest of the *gerlaap* fruits and eat them. Which we did, in abundance. Have you ever eaten a *gerlaap* fruit?"

"No, I'm sure I haven't," answered the young woman beside Damgaard.

"I didn't think so, since the *gerlaap* trees, as I said, only grow—to my knowledge—in my country." He sipped his scotch—a very good scotch, Glen Livet. "The fruit has a husk which must be peeled off. The husk is hard and bitter. But inside is the tender, greenish flesh, full with seeds. One eats the seeds, like with a pomegranate. They are crunchy. The flesh is moist and sweet, kind of like a kiwi or passionfruit."

The young woman smiled appreciatively.

"At the end of an afternoon, there would be so many empty

gerlaap shells on the ground beneath our tree, that we were not required to climb down the trunk to reach the ground. We could simply roll off the limbs, and it was only a short fall before we landed safely in the pile of empty husks. By now, our bellies were as big as bowling balls. Then we would walk to the riverbank, where we would wash our sticky hands and faces, and drink the clear, cool, sparkling water. Amazing, no?"

"Johan, you tell such beautiful stories. I can see them like a film in my mind's eye! Why haven't they made a film of your stories? People would love them! You'd be a millionaire."

"Many people have told me this," Johan said drily. With a tremble of his hand, he rattled the ice cubes in his drink, shaking the Scotch off them, then tipped the cup to his lips. "And yet what would I do with millions of dollars? The only thing I need to live is my stories. And stories cannot be bought. Not for all the money in the world." This Damgaard said with an air of calculated disinterest.

"What happened to Liva?" the young woman asked. "Are you still in touch with her?"

"Ah, no, unfortunately, fate was not so kind to Liva. The joys we shared on that hillside and in the *gerlaap* groves would be among the last she would know. Liva was away at boarding school when she caught ill and died. It came on very suddenly. I was on my way to see her when she expired. By the time I arrived, it was too late."

The young woman closed her eyes. Tears, one at each eye, emerged from under her eyelids like sleepy animals from their burrows. Trailing down her cheeks, they washed away her foundation makeup, drawing lines like those children draw on construction paper, the color of sorrow.

Damgaard took the woman's hand in his. "Would you stay with me tonight?" he said. "The life of a travelling storyteller is a lonely one. I'm so far from home, and it is not only trains that sadden me, but planes and taxis, shuttles and busses as well. I always feel that with every journey I make, I am travelling to the Herlufsholm School for Girls. Always I am too late to save Liva."

The young woman's throat flexed as suppressed tears travelled down her sinus passages and into her throat. Her cheeks and neck flushed the color of a Queen Elizabeth rose petal, onto which fell the shadow of Charles Knott, founder, CEO and lead architect at Knott Architectural Design.

"Pardon us, folks," Knott said, shuffling in side-steps into a position not unlike a dentist would assume if he wanted to straddle either Damgaard, the young woman, or both, in the interest of gaining leverage to manually extract a rotting molar.

Knott, 48, wore cobalt blue wide-weft corduroy pants, belted, and a black turtleneck. His eyeglasses bore a tortoise shell pattern. There are many variations of middle-aged baldness, and Knott's was the type wherein the remaining hair is still dark and full, and the hairless pate totally bare, no stragglers, and its skin a healthy and tan tone, unblemished by age spots. It is a rather attractive baldness, of which Knott was justly proud.

Beside him another figure inched in: Boris Czecknik, Serbian, also an architect.

"Good evening," Czecknik said, with an academic air. He sensed he was interrupting some kind of canoodle.

"So you see here," Knott explained, "it's actually a yellow poplar that they used for the built-ins. I like it."

"Is it a rare wood?" Czecknik asked.

"You can get it easily enough."

"Pricey?"

"Fair, I'd say. And that's a modern touch, and what I really love is, look up here, the egg and dart molding." Knott pointed up, and both men gazed skyward. "Typically in an application like this you'd see probably dentil or cove molding. Nothing wrong with that. But this was, I think, a daring choice, showing some cleverness even."

"This is unique," Czecknik confirmed.

The men squeezed onward in an apparent counterclockwise tour of the entire townhome. "Down here you can see, nothing special, typical five-inch baseboards, topped with quarter-round trim."

"Mm-hmm. Question."

"Yes."

"Approaching the building, we see neo-Gothic features on the exterior. Gables topped with finials. Windows with decorative crowns. Arches, parapets, towers."

"Yes, yes."

"It's unusual to see this in new construction. How do you account for—"

"There is no accounting for genius," Knott said with a laugh. "It just happens..."

The men's voices were buried by speculative chatter as they moved further along the crowded room to examine its other features.

Damgaard and his female friend had gotten up to fetch fresh drinks by this time, and when they left, their places on the love seat were immediately snatched up by Chief S. and Hermann Donskoy.

Donskoy, holding a small plate of the pumpkin torte topped by four handsome dollops of whipped cream, said, "My dogs are barking."

"Dogs will bark," Chief S. said, nodding solemnly.

"It's an expression," Donskoy clarified.

"I know." Chief S. turned away. On the bookshelf, he saw a magazine with a sophisticated looking cover and picked it up. He needed a little reprieve from socializing. He thumbed to the table of contents. The review of the new Ty Whitely biography looked interesting. Chief S., like everyone, had read *The Whole of England* as a schoolboy on the reservation, and liked it OK. When the movie came out, he saw it. It, too, was OK. He turned to the review.

You•re History

by Brock Hollington

In 1955, when the writer Ty Whitely was just a boy playing whist with his mum on the veranda of his family's disgustingly opulent home, a sturdy breeze blew in, toppling the rose trellises which Whitely and his mother so admired. Their gardener, who earned only pennies a day, rushed to the rescue, and in the process of wrestling the contraption, sprained his ankle. The gardener's shriek rang out "like a caged lion with a thorn in its paw." An entirely similar scene happens in Whitley's massively best-selling novel "The Whole of England" (later a wildly popular BBC television series and feature film, read and studied in high school classrooms and universities until, mmm, only somewhat recently, when it has fallen out of favor). Chaz Thornburry, the novel's naive and privileged protagonist, rushes to the aide of the lawn-servant Grundy O'Connell, who falls while trying to right a toppled windmill on the expansive lawn of the Thornburry estate. "No, Chaz!" yells Lady Thornburry. "Leave him be. Grundy is poor, and therefore not deserving of our help. He can fetch an ice pack from town but only if he takes the horse cart and pays for his own horse-oats." This theme of economic disparity would pervade Whitely's entire body of work---all seven novels, two novellas, three volumes of journals, poetry, and correspondence, and the plays that comprise the Somerset Quartet. It is a theme which haunted Whitely and was worthy of many readers at the time but which now we, as arbiters of intellectual tastes, are obliged to discredit.

A Whole Lot of Bluster: The Life and Shameful Times of Ty Whitely, the new biography of Ty Whitely (Revisionist History Press, $28), by Kell Darlinberg comes out this month, and, boy, did Darlinberg get it right. Whitely has come under increasing scrutiny since his death, in 1998, of cirrhosis of the liver, for both his political views and his questionable position as a man of letters and native of an Anglocentric country populated with Anglocentric institutions, many of which had ties to the British imperial government, who were a bunch of colonizing pricks. I'm here to pen this ostensible book review in hopes of securing my position on that ever-narrowing ledge called "the right side of history."

Let's rush things along and get to the disparaging, disowning part, shall we? Whitely was born in some town and went to a school that was expensive, and this we must regard as despicable now, because wealth, we know, invariably makes moral clarity impossible. He was an early reader of several philosophers, themselves suspect: with most of them, a hop, skip and a jump through their little black books, or old-timey Rolodexes, and you land right in the lap of someone like Der Fuehrer himself. So fuck this guy and his upbringing. This is not the kind of person we want representing the literary arts, that much is clear, and Darlinberg adroitly recounts the many mistakes Whitely made in his thinking and actions throughout his ill-conceived life. For example, choosing to record, in his journals, his early love for Penelope Rosewater (also a Caucasian and so not very sympathetic figure by today's criteria). What a joke.

I basically want to endorse erasing Whitely entirely from whatever annals he's in. I'm for pulling extant copies of his novels. I'm for commissioning a rewrite of "The Whole of England" from Grundy's point of view. Whatever it takes. There were some awards he was given in the sixties. There's no reason we can't just do a new ceremony for those years. It wouldn't take that long or cost that much.

At age 25 Whitely had so much opportunity compared to what others had, it's sickening, and he probably didn't even appreciate it. His father got him a job as a records keeper for the London woolen mill called Thackleson's. There, by day, he worked in pretty considerable comfort, it has to be said, and at night wrote his novels. Like Herman Hesse and Anthony Powell, Whitely was devoted to his craft,

and could churn out a decent sentence, and that was once seen as admirable, and people were willing to him a shot, but Darlinberg is correct and valiant to name Whitely's style of storytelling "narrow and self-important." Indeed, when other writers from more recent time periods do the same from *their* point of view, the fact that these works are contemporary ensures their correctness, as far as I, a paid academic who has never tried to write a novel, can discern. The current attitudes of out-sized humility and paralyzing anxiety over race issues, gender norms, and so on, clearly constitutes a need for a new canon, one that will be everlasting and never subject to reconsideration. Let me be the first to applaud the wiping of the proverbial slate. Craft and form can suck it. Whoever suffers the most injustices wins. Their story is best and the most important, forever, no backs.

And so, in conclusion, Ty Whitely equals an embarrassing period in our cultural history, and please just let me keep my job, please. I'll do anything. I'll mop the floors. It's all I have now. It is my *Whole of England.* Wait---no! I didn't say that!

I didn't say that!

Chief S. looked up from the page. "Journalism," he said, "is not what it used to be."

"Nothing is what it used to be," answered Donskoy, raising his voice but not his affect. He was weary. "When are they going give out the damn award so we can all go home?" He sat stock still, his left armed draped down the arm of the love seat, holding an empty paper plate and plastic fork. He did not even turn his head to address Chief S., and did not care that his view was of a bunch of legs and butts, odd to be looking so closely at for so long. It couldn't be helped. And neither, Donskoy felt, could America. He let his senses go slack, let his muscles relax, closed his eyes and took a deep breath. His hearing aid did its job and isolated sounds in the frequency range that most human speech occupies and amplified them, creating a dimensional soundscape in his consciousness, the appearance of a darkened space, such as that behind his eyeballs and between his ears, the same relative dimensions of the room, in which hundreds of disembodied voices spoke, in spatial terms relative to the arrangement of bodies in the parlor. It was just like when Donskoy had listened to Morse code broadcast by the Chinese—the monotonous dots and dashes taking on depth within his consciousness, morphing out of their flat binary sound, his perception providing the z-axis, as when you look at one of those hologram posters and a previously chaotic, meaningless image turns into a sharp and angular figure. The patterns describe contours; and panning back, the contours become edges of objects and figures, nations and populations shaped by ideologies...A frightening moment of clarity like those had by epileptics. The airlessness of the room and its growing heat amplified Donskoy's keen catatonia.

"...do consider them separate tracks," said Christine Wong. "The arts and the sciences. Each has its place. But—and of course I'm biased—I think it's obvious that the arts are rightly taking the ascendency, even as federal funding is pulled. Science won't save us. Why are so many cosmologists staring at Mars, Jupiter, Saturn. Oh, there's signs of water. Life may have come from there. This planet may have supported life at one time. So what? There's life dying right here, right now. This star-gazing is a type of tragic denial masquerading as discovery. Mapping the genome. Where did our ancestors come from? How can that information possibly help us, as California burns and the Maldives will be gone soon, and what are they doing about it? Now, the great works of art might not be saving our lives in the biological sense, but they are saving our lives in the present sense, in terms of what our daily experience is, and how we interpret our present reality and cope with the awful truths that science refuses to face.... Yes, precisely. That's my prediction. The award *has to* go to an artist. It's the only choice that makes sense."

"...don't do that? You should try it. I bet you'll want to try it after tonight," said Merrill Roselli. "No, I don't want to bet. Not real money... Because of everything she's done around the BBM since it happened.... Yeah, no, that's the sad part...I would place a side bet that she accepts it on behalf of all the loved ones of BBM victims... Probably not. The lobbies are too strong.... Of course there is... If you don't think there's a blowgun lobby, you're naïve.... I don't know. Soon. It's gotta be soon..."

"...Regina Pampagno. Nice to meet you...I'm sorry we're so late.... OK, great. Thank you."

The creaking of a door hinge. Laughter. Coughing.

"...wildlife too, down in the islands, on the coast near Galveston." The voice of George Opfell. "I used to drive into West Texas and shoot the oil rigs, sunsets, but my foot is not so good anymore, and it's my right, so even working the pedal...What I would I do with it?... Oh, probably new equipment... So who do *you* think? ... Really? Okay.... I don't know.... All I know is, Harvey was a once-a-century storm... But we've now had three once-a-century storms in eight years, so..."

"...Taliban are taking back control in Afghanistan," said Lamond P. Jackson. "Roughly half the territories now. You're starting to hear it in the news, which doesn't mean it's just started happening. That just means the Pentagon is *ready* for you to know... I think so. I'm speculating, as a civilian. This is not official intelligence or official anything, but yes. That's usually what it means... Might be air strikes, might be drones..."

—20—

In the pantry, Candace Winslow conferred with Dr. Rajani, both of them leaning over the still-blotto Monti Taylor, slumped against the wall, mouth agape, mouth-breathing in deep draws and hair-curdling gusts of his booze-soaked breath.

Rajani had advised to let Taylor sleep it off. The patient's pulse was a steady and strong 58 BPM, his breathing regular. Waking him could yield an unpredictable outcome. Rajani was dressed in some linen pants and a t-shirt under a linen sport coat—a man at leisure interrupted. At his feet, the obligatory leather kit bag. He had not used the Narcan, only the stethoscope for breathing and heart-beat, and the flashlight for checking pupil dilation.

"Can I lock him in here?" Candace asked.

"No medical reason you can't. It's not like he'll run out of oxygen. I don't think he's dangerously dehydrated or anything."

"But?"

"But he might come to and be a little unhappy to find himself in this situation. Or frightened."

"Maybe he uses the place as a toilet."

"Yeah, perhaps." Rajani stood up, and Candace afterward. "Or harms himself in a rage."

They had discussed Monti's status as a friend of the foundation, vis-à-vis Roger Hanwell, a donor. Rajani understood.

Candace paced the entire three paces that were possible in the small room, checked her wristwatch, and spun around. "Okay, well," she said conclusively. "Nap time continues then for our young friend. Thanks, Raj. You know what to do..." She trailed off, eliding the unnecessary description of billing protocols established long ago, when Joyce was a young girl needing treatment for the usual colds and fevers, chicken pox, what-have-you; and when Mr. Winslow had found frequent need of medical attention for withdrawal from benzodiazepines, or stress-related shortness of breath when his company faced SEC meddling, and any number of other recurrent bodily and cognitive torments such as hallucinations and paranoia.

"Yes, of course," Rajani said. A man in the confidences of the wealthy is a confident man. He tossed his instruments back in the case, snapped it shut. Kissing Candace on the cheek, he said, cheerfully, "I'll see myself out. Good luck with the event."

Candace kept her arms resolutely crossed and continued to scowl at Taylor. After hearing the sound of the door latch, she muttered, "Lord, have mercy."

You may now select an Outcome Branch™.

If you think Candace should head to the podium in the banquet room and announce the commencement of the awards ceremony, turn to page - 122 -.

If you think Candace should delay the start of the ceremony, turn to page - 176 -.

You have chosen to start the awards ceremony

—21—

In the kitchen, Candace found her purse in the cupboard where she'd stashed it. She checked her keyring, found the key she believed went to the pantry, and tested it in the lock. It worked. She locked the room. The catering staff saw her, so she met their suspicion head-on. "Yes," she said from the center of the room. "I've locked the door on him. It's for his own safety. He's out cold. If any of you hear a disturbance, don't let him out. Alert Jerome or me or Joyce. Understood?"

The caterers assented, variously. *Okay. Sure. Yes, Mrs. Winslow.*

"Thank you for your discretion. Where's Jerome? Jerome!" She kicked out the brace stopper and reached up and threw open the barrel bolt on the swinging door, and pulled it open to meet a wall of bodies—partygoers, oh-so-hopeful hopefuls. The conversational roar that poured into the kitchen was thunderous. She squeezed out into the sensory tempest, and the door swung shut behind her. She wove through the room wielding a polite smile as a machete. "Hello! Hello! You made it! Welcome." Everyone tried to arrest her, bend her ear. Would the ceremony start soon, they all wanted to know. "Mrs. Winslow," they said. "Mrs. Winslow." "Excuse me," she pleaded. "I'm sorry. Urgent business… Patience, please. Thank you. Pardon."

She found Jerome in a tense-looking conference with Joyce, his arm draped on the fireplace mantel. They looked like a couple of 17-year-olds at the drive-thru after a sock-hop. Pulling up on them was like getting tossed by a wave onto a small beach. The shelter of two confidantes in a sea of… what we're they, exactly? Less like barnacles than the rest. As much as Candace loved the foundation and believed in its purpose and mission, one did come to feel like a constant sow with all the squealing piglets hustling for a teat.

"There you are!" Candace said.

"Where you have been?" Joyce said, stepping back from Jerome. "We were looking for you."

"Looking for me? You're standing here in a huddle."

"The room is set up—" Jerome said.

"I should hope so." Candace gave his countenance an up-and-down perusal. He was dapper as ever, but there was some element of slovenliness now. Moral duplicity, a betrayal somehow. "Well, I don't have time to argue."

"How's Monti?" Joyce said.

"Still dreaming," Candace said.

"You left him in there?"

"He's in lockdown."

"I thought Dr. Rajani would revive him."

"There aren't enough smelling salts in the county for that."

"That's fine," Jerome said, trying for encouragement, congeniality. "No harm, no foul."

"No harm, no foul," Joyce speculated.

"I mean, in there, he'll do no harm. Like the Hippocratic oath."

Joyce brought her wristwatch up to face-level, giving everyone at it a look, really, in these tight quarters. "What about the ceremony? Everyone's restless."

"Absolutely," Candace said, resolutely, without moving an inch. She seemed to gather herself—rubbing her hands, muttering *Okay, right, mm-hmm,* and so on, savoring the moment as one does at such a juncture that one knows it may not be possible to revisit ever again if one carries out one's wishes, as one is resolved to do, however ill-received one knows they will be.

"Mother!"

"Here we go. Attic first."

Weaving in reverse. Parting parties with a wedge-like hand proffered like the splitting head of a maul, like a travelling karate chop. Pardon, pardon. Thank you. The anticipatory eyes, so multi-hued, expectant, and some ob-sequious even at this late moment—too late to sway the decision, surely. But worth a grin. What isn't worth a grin, when a grin costs so little?

Jerome went to the attic; the two women guarded the stairs. He emerged like an obstetrician from the delivery room, bearing the infant fresh from the womb. Gold, precious, and tri-columned. So many of life's wonders occurred naturally in triplets, triads. The trio was nature's coded miracle. Rock, paper, scissors. Small, medium, large. Solid, liquid, gas. Larry, Moe, Curly.

They went to the banquet room, where Candace stood before the podium, and Jerome and Joyce went to the French doors leading to the parlor. Curtains over the doors kept the candidates from reacting too excitedly. Jerome paused with his hands on the doorknobs, turned back to Mrs. Winslow, who issued the confirming nod.

Waters flow over dikes and into rocky crevices and along dry streambeds in search of low ground, settling in a plain. A thin stream of tap water flows into an ice cube tray and overflows to neighboring cells, as described in Nicholson Baker's *Mezzanine*. So the guest-candidates for the 2018 FAIR award flowed into rows of chairs arranged in Mrs. Winslow's opulent townhome, dropping their asses into seats they hoped not to remain in long, that they hoped to rise from triumphantly, hands to their disbelieving mouths.

Lenore Happybones, Cassandra Mande, Evonne Sorenstam-Finch, Juan Ramirez, and several others sat in the front row. Santos Gougoutris, Petra Barnhouse, Andrew Knuthe, and several others sat in the second row. Johanna Sturludóttir, Johan Damgaard, Damgaard's young female companion, and several others sat in the third row. Avi Sobol, George Opfell, and several others sat in the fourth row. Gabrielle Rauch, J. Pak, and Charlie S. sat in the fourth row. Lamond P. Jackson, Merrill Roselli, Christine Wong, and Hermann Donskoy sat in the fifth row. Joseph Hector Depace, Balooja Inamdar, and several others sat in the sixth row, with Darla Emmenberg parked at the row's end. Joyce

Winslow sat in a chair beside and just behind the podium. Dozens of others filled in the gaps and other chairs, and their plights, injustices, and iniquities, the transgressions they had endured, included the following:

+ receiving a wireless modem attachment from the manufacturer of their blood-sugar measuring gadget, and being told they were receiving the gadget so that the device can check for firmware updates, only to discover that in fact data about the frequency of their machine use was being tracked and sent to the insurance company; the insurance company subsequently deeming their use of the machine insufficiently descriptive of a severe diabetic condition, and/or kind of negligent, in self-care terms, and therefore indicative of medical fraud, basically, and the insurance company revoking coverage for the device and for all diabetes-related treatments, leaving the patient to fall into a diabetic coma, and for a foot ulcer to advance, resulting in loss of limb (her right leg): Rosalind Duffy, of Sioux Falls, SD, third row.

+ being discriminated against for decades by the ballet and dance industry, despite being a talented and highly trained dancer, because of breast size (too large); being denied lead roles in touring troupes, in performances of, among others, Tchaikovsky's "Nutcracker Suite," leading to depression, diminished income, abuse of and addiction to appetite suppressants, related side-effects including insomnia, high blood pressure, and "rabbit-like" heart rate: Denise Underhill, St. Louis, MO.

+ being discriminated against by Harvard University admissions department: Cheng Lui, 20, Nashville, TN.

Candace stood at the podium. In her yellow cardigan, she looked matronly and scholarly, like a librarian. Cardigan sweaters imbue their wearers with apparent sagacity and restraint that cannot be achieved by any other knitted garment. "Thank you, everyone. Thank you," she said. "Thank you for your patience." A reverential hush inflated the room, pressing outwards on its walls, depressurizing its center. "Twenty-eighteen has been a *hell* of year." Agreeable chuckling—a dispersal of anticipatory tension. "With MeToo, we've seen a hashtag grow into a powerful social and political movement. This fall, the midterm elections brought historic reform to the houses of congress. The first Muslim woman congressional leader. The first black woman mayor. The first transgender mayor. The patriarchy may not be toppled, but some significant bricks in its edifice have been knocked out. It's being disassembled peacefully, through electoral and legislative means, which is even better than violence. At the same time, the horrible lineage in the family of mass-killings has born, all too soon, its next offspring. Adding to Columbine, Virginia Tech, Fort Hood, Tucson, Aurora, Sandy Hook, Charleston, Orlando, San Bernardino, Las Vegas, Pittsburgh—we now have Brenton, New York."

An awkward smattering of sparse applause and the hushed sound of somber grief, swelling anger, confusion.

"May the victims rest in peace and their loved ones have solace."

Murmured assents.

"Meanwhile, our president foments hatred, models ignorance, denies responsibility, praises dictators and dictatorships, pathologically lies, denounces a free press and covers up for a governments that murder outspoken journalists..." Candace shook her head in sad disbelief. "The list of atrocities and offense grows and grows. Asked what he's grateful for at Thanksgiving, our pompadour in chief said, Himself. He's done tremendous things."

Affronted sniffing, morbid groans.

"Indeed he has done tremendous things. Notorious things. Incredible things."

The audience stirs in aggravation.

"Children detained at the border, torn from the loving embraces of their parents and caregivers. The innocent incarcerated. The gender-fluid humiliated by obscene bathroom laws. The working man and working woman neglected and abused. In this climate—and there's so much more, people, as we know—the task of choosing a recipient of the 2018 FAIR award grew even more challenging than usual."

Burbling excitement. The sound of folding chair pad

foam expanding and contracting, as buttocks lift—people sitting up, repositioning themselves in elevated postures as their bodies respond to the promise of recognition, that sweet, sweet salve. Apply it here, nurse. Succor my ailing spirit. Dab my worried brow with the cool, moist washcloth of validation. Cauterize my wound with the healing laser beams of your attention.

The sanctimonious parts over with, Candace's voice relaxed into a quick conversational tone. "It's not an easy process. It never is. We, the foundation staff, work with the advisory board, from a pool of 300-plus candidates and applicants. And I want you all to know, the so-called 'process of elimination' doesn't apply here. No one is eliminated. The foundation is not in the business of eliminating anyone. In fact, we can't do that. We cannot eliminate you. All of you will go on, continuing to be strong and valiant and determined and worthy, as you all are. The award recognizes one; but we are all one. At this time, on this point, I'd like to quote his holiness, the Dalai Lama, who said, "Whether one is rich or poor, educated or illiterate, religious or nonbelieving, man or woman, black, white, or brown, we are all the same. Physically, emotionally, and mentally, we are all equal. ...We all aspire to happiness and we all shun suffering. Each of us has hopes, worries, fears, and dreams. Each of us wants the best for our family and loved ones. We all experience pain when we suffer loss and joy when we achieve what we seek. On this fundamental level, religion, ethnicity, culture, and language make no difference.' And to that I would add that we all want our suffering, pain, transgressions, hardships, and the injustices inflicted on us recognized."

Sturdy applause.

"Yeah!" Candace was loose and relaxed now, even moved by that power of the quote. "So, before I announce this year's winner, I want to say, Thank you all for complying with the no-cell-phones policy. The withdrawal symptoms will abate once you have your phone back, I assure you."

Laughter.

"The anxiety. The twitching thumbs. The ranging eyes, in

search of a screen." She smiled at the laughing audience. "No, seriously. There are a number of serious reasons that we instituted the policy, and we understand it's an inconvenience and a hardship, and we thank you for your sacrifice."

Mixed-tone applause.

Candace signaled to Joyce, who rose from her chair and lifted the tablecloth draped over the trophy sitting atop the table.

Applause and cheers. Wolf-whistles.

Candace, loudly: "Here to present the trophy to this year's winner..." Candace gestured to the front row, and made a waving motion. "the 2017 FAIR award recipient, Hollis Fillmore."

Hollis Fillmore stepped up beside Candace and, smiling, faced the audience, his hands clasped before him. A dazed-looking Caucasian in his fifties, with a puffy head and a gray beard, he wore a tan tweed suit jacket and maroon tie. He nodded gratefully a few times. No one could remember what Hollis had experienced exactly, no one remembered why he'd been recognized only a year ago, but they clapped anyway.

Joyce brought the trophy to Fillmore, who took it in his hands.

"And now..." Candace produced a sealed envelope from beneath the podium. Wedging a finger under the glued flap, she vamped at the audience with a cheeks-drawn-in, wide eyed look, shoulders shimmying as if overcome with anticipatory glee.

"The winner of the 2018 Foundation for the Appreciation of Inclusivity—"

Joyce lashed at her mother, grabbing her arm as one grabs a badly misbehaving child. "*Advancement!*" she hissed in her mother's ear.

"God dammit."

Laughter. When a genteel socialite issues a vulgarity, it's a real knee-slapper.

"For the *Advancement* of Inclusivity and Recognition,

is..." She drew back the flap, and removed the card.

If you think the winner should be Petra Barnhouse, turn to page - 130 -.

If you think the winner should be Andrew Knuthe, turn to page - 134 -.

If you think the winner should be Hermann Donskoy, turn to page - 139 -.

If you think the winner should be Christine Wong, turn to page - 144 -.

If you think the winner should be Merrill Roselli, turn to page - 148 -.

If you think the winner should be Joseph Hector Depace , turn to page - 152 -.

If you think the winner should be Evonne Sorenstam-Finch, turn to page - 156 -.

If you think the winner should be Jeong-Hwa Pak, turn to page - 162 -.

If you think the winner should be Gabrielle Rauch, turn to page - 166 -.

If you think the winner should be Johan Damgaard, turn to page - 172 -.

You have chosen Petra Barnhouse as the winner of the 2018 FAIR award.

—22—

"...Petra Barnhouse!"

Delighted applause.

Barnhouse rose from her seat. As she sidled out of the row, Candace spoke on: "Petra lost her husband to ailments brought on by poisoned well-water, poisoned at the hands of the hydrofracking industry. Since then she has become an activist, journalist, and organizer, leading her own community in legal battles against Cobalt Drilling, and joining the fight in Flint, Michigan, where water safety is a big-time issue."

Fillmore handed Barnhouse the trophy and stepped backwards—there was no limelight, but out of the proverbial limelight. Barnhouse endearingly studied the trophy's features, read its engraving, regarded the triumphant, vaguely seraphic figure atop it holding the wreath, and smiled in wonderment. Throughout, the audience applauded.

"Ladies and gentlemen, our 2018 FAIR award winner, Petra Barnhouse!"

The applause strengthened as Candace stepped back from the podium and gestured for Petra to take it. She did.

"Wow. Thank you." Diminishing applause. "Thank you." The obligatory fussing with the microphone's height. Silence. "Wow, I'm really gob-smacked. I wasn't expecting this. I want to thank the foundation, Mrs. Winslow, Joyce, and all the staff, who I've enjoyed meeting tonight and getting to know."

Light applause. Barnhouse smiled at Happybones, Emmenberg, Mande, Chief S., and others in audience. She turned to Joyce behind her and smiled.

She set the trophy atop the podium and grasped its sides, the default pose of the authoritative lecturer. "You know, we only have one Earth. Our Earth mother. The one who nourishes and sustains us. If a child stabbed its mother, wouldn't we punish that child? If a child drained a mother's blood, wouldn't we stop that child from doing so again? If a child injected a mother with uranium, radium, methanol, mercury, hydrochloric acid, wouldn't we take away that child's implement? We would. Of course we would."

"Yet only two states with considerable fossil fuel reserves have banned hydraulic fracking: New York and Maryland. Yes, hundreds of towns, counties, and tribal territories have banned it. But over 21 viable fracking states allow it. And the industry, the drillers, are fighting back. In Texas, Oklahoma, and North Carolina, laws have been passed limiting the abilities of communities to ban fracking and related activities. In Broadview Heights and Munroe Falls, Ohio, the industry fought in the courtroom to strike down bans. There's a war going on, and if we don't win it, it's not only Earth that will suffer, but all of us. It's a public health crisis, and as is far too common, our federal legislators are in the pocket of the lobbyists, and our president is just generally blind to good sense and uncaring about the health and safety of the American people, beholden to corporations and the wealthy."

Applause.

"We need to do a lot more. This war isn't over. I appreciate this award. I think it clearly demonstrates that the health of our planet is the premier issue of the day. If the planet isn't healthy, *we* aren't healthy. If the planet doesn't survive, *we* don't survive. So thank you to the foundation for this award. I dedicate this to my deceased husband, Darrin. I plan to use the stipend to help victims of well-water poisoning. Thank you."

Resounding applause.

Candace appeared at Barnhouse's side, taking her elbow and turning her to face a lone chair placed at center stage.

Using that perfected gesture of hers, the open-palmed directive like that of dog handlers on the plastic turf of the Westminster Kennel club during exhibitions, Candace led Barnhouse to understand that this was her special seat, and she was to take it. It was a plain padded folding chair like all the rest, nothing throne-like about it, but there was that ennobling gulf around it saying None are close; saying, She stands apart; saying, Today we recognize. There Barnhouse sat with the trophy on her lap, a smile fixed to her face. While Candace made closing remarks at the podium, Barnhouse's mind drifted off. She thought of Darrin, pictured his handsome oval face, with his thoughtful green eyes. She seem to see him working a platter of ribs at Famous Dave's BBQ, a favorite place of his, red sauce all around his mouth. But then she managed to place him elsewhere: in their kitchen, igniting the methane coming from their kitchen tap with a match, bonded in their horror, outrage, and confusion. *You did it, honey*, Barnhouse heard Darrin say. *Congratulations. I love you.*

She wiped away a tear, but it was not a heavy sorrow. She felt light, so very light. The trials (literally), the battles, the persistent anger, the years of rallying a fighting spirit, of garnering animosity, gathering evidence of misdeeds, of regarding the world in an oppositional stance, facing one's country and leadership and laws every morning with the intention of combat—much of this accrued psychic burden was leaving her. It was going away. Barnhouse noticed that she couldn't even really feel herself in her seat. She was near weightless. And tall! Incredibly tall! A giddy grin dashed through her lips, which she was quick to squelch—it would appear rude with Candace was saying inspiring but serious things about the Foundation's mission. But it was funny how earthbound everything looked. She seemed to see the room and its occupants, the stage, and even her own lap, as if from the boughs of a tree or a first-floor balcony. Accepting this phenomenon, owning her new stature, she turned her head thoughtfully to attend, in thought and in consciousness, to the final words from Mrs. Winslow.

The End

You have chosen Andrew Knuthe as the winner of the 2018 FAIR Award.

—23—

"...Andrew Knuthe!"

Delighted applause.

As Knuthe sidled down the row, Candace spoke: "Andrew Knuthe is a Middle-School Biology teacher in Tulsa, Oklahoma. He was fired for refusing to teach using classroom materials rewritten by oil-industry groups, curriculum that spread falsehoods about fossil fuels versus green energy. His beloved wife Shari died of breast cancer. He started an anti-bullying awareness group at his school. He's a much-loved teacher, devoted community leader, and self-described positive-thinker. His foundation Meanwhile, In Reality raises money for youth STEM education. Visit meanwhileinreality.com."

Fillmore handed Knuthe the trophy and stepped backwards—there was no limelight, but out of the proverbial limelight. Knuthe whimsically glanced at the trophy's features, read its engraving, and regarded the triumphant, vaguely seraphic figure atop it holding the wreath. He smiled with uncertain pride. Throughout, the audience applauded.

"Ladies and gentlemen, our 2018 FAIR award winner, Andrew Knuthe!"

The applause strengthened as Candace stepped back from the podium and gestured for Knuthe to take it.

"Wow. Thank you," Knuthe said, pulling up to the lectern. Diminishing applause. "Thank you." Knuthe adjusted the microphone, flinching at the amplified creak of the gooseneck arm. "Oops. Hello. Wow, I'm really shocked. I wasn't expecting this. I want to thank the foundation, Mrs. Winslow, Joyce, and all the staff. This is a real honor."

Running his hand through his beard, Knuthe listening to the light applause while looking out over the assembly, a group so motley it tickled him. In his youth, he and his brother had spent Saturday mornings watching WWF wrestlers like Baron "The Claw" Von Raschke, "The Incredible" Hulk Hogan, and the like. Sometimes, during a title belt ceremony, for example, fights broke out: A Battle Royale, this was called, a chaotic spectacle that brought 8-year-old Knuthe out of his seat, cheering, with men in capes flying from the ring to the stands, sliding under ropes, folding chairs wielded as weapons. In a Battle Royale, everyone was an enemy, and blows were delivered in every direction. Complete pillory. Now for this group before him to bully each other for their differences would be to stage a Battle Royale to end all Battle Royales. Knuthe's breathy chuckle created a wind-buffeting sound in the mic.

He set the trophy atop the podium, grasped its sides, and struck the pose of the contemplative lecturer. "You know," Knuthe said, "not 18 months ago, I was a happily married man—13 years married. I enjoy my job quite a lot, as challenging as it is, but I had been at that some fifteen years as well, and may have been a little stagnant. Like we all do at times like those, I prayed to God. 'God,' I said, 'if there's something more for me, bring it on.' Well, it wasn't long after that prayer, about a year, that I lost my wife Shari to cancer."

Uncertain dim exhalations as of very mild laughter.

"The moral is, be careful what you wish for. And not long after that, I was handed a pink slip by my employer, the Osage County School District. Of course, that decision was reversed, when the board was advised that they'd likely lose in court. Nevertheless, my life was sufficiently shaken up, and that point I amended my prayer to say, 'God, if you have anything regular and boring in store for me, bring it on.'"

Straight-up unmistakable, grateful laughter.

"Well." Knuthe tipped the trophy back to regards its face again. "Nothing boring about winning the 2018 FAIR award. Actually, in my estimation, I think the turns of fate that I endured and the saga that my story provided to Joe Q. Public is not so much about Biology standards or Biology curricula. It is not about the rightness of evolution or the wrongness of Creationism. I think my story is about the way we treat each other when we don't see eye to eye."

Many thoughtful utterances of "mmm."

"Yessss," said Cassandra Mande.

"And here's the beauty of it: both Biology and Christianity have advice for us. Evolution might rely on 'survival of the fittest' and winner takes all and so on, but it actually also incorporates the best of *cooperation*. Saying nothing of species that rely on each other, such as the Egyptian plover removing insects from a buffalo's back—that's called protocooperation, or mutualism—there is also the fact that on the genetic level, species learn from their mistakes and adopt better practices or traits. I'm talking about in the evolutionary sense, across millennia. This is something that humans might do as well. It'd be great if we all did it—maybe a little faster. On the *qui vive*. One trait I think we could all stand to adopt is... or drop, rather. Well, what if, for example, xenophobia could be pegged to a gene and that gene cut out of the genome? If it could drop off, because it simply isn't useful to us, in an evolutionary sense? That would be amazing, I think. When we fear others who aren't like us, where does it get us? Either fleeing to our separate corners or fighting for territory—whether physical territory or intellectual territory—these days, vying for rhetorical dominance on social media, and controlling the narrative in the news. That's the message we teach in my after-school group **Meanwhile in Reality**. We got the name from one of my students' favorite catchphrases, which basically means, movies may tell you otherwise, the media may tell you otherwise, but Meanwhile in Reality, bullying hurts, discrimination hurts a whole lot, and racism just hurts us all, hurts the whole country. Hurts our dignity. Hurts the human race."

Spontaneous, feel-good applause.

"Thank you. Well, I appreciate this award. I think it clearly demonstrates that humane treatment of each other, despite our differences, is the premier issue of the day. If we don't treat others with kindness, we feel mean. If we don't listen to others and accept others, we won't be heard or accepted. So thank you to the foundation for this award. I dedicate this to my deceased wife, Shari. I love you, babe. I was planning to use the stipend to buy a new hunting dog, but thanks to a new friend I made tonight, I'm reconsidering that." Knuthe winked at Petra Barnhouse in the audience, who blushed. "Thank you."

Resounding applause.

Candace appeared at Knuthe's side, taking his elbow and turning him to face a lone chair placed at center stage. Using that perfected gesture of hers, the open-palmed directive like that of dog handlers on the plastic turf of the Westminster Kennel club during exhibitions, Candace led Knuthe to understand that this was his special seat, and he was to take it. Knuthe had sat in plenty of folding chairs on daises in his day—every year at graduation, for one. There Knuthe sat with the trophy on his lap, a smile fixed to his face, and while Candace made closing remarks at the podium, Knuthe's mind drifted off. He thought of a marsh on some state land about 40 miles from his house where he often hunted quail. He looked forward to getting back there, his rifle across his chest or over his shoulder, stepping through the switchgrass. The sky was wide and open, a blue the color of the Oriental Avenue on the Monopoly board. He could practically see the land underneath his feet as he crossed a dry creek bed—but then he realized that his cinematic rendering had him shouldering the trophy in his hand. Where would he store this thing? He had to figure that out. In the wild, it was useless that's for sure. No quail could honor it. Any elk spotting him with it would level him just the same. No rattlesnake or scorpion would reconsider their attach either. The fact is only 25 of the nearly 1,500 varieties of scorpion deliver stings that can be fatal to humans. Even then, if you're healthy you'll just have convulsion and shortness of breath. Knuthe thought of himself convulsing on the desert floor of the American west, knowing that he wouldn't die, only suffer for a time, all the crude that had ever been extracted back in the ground underneath him, where it came from, because the biology standards for public school students in Oklahoma had been written to sensibly resemble reality, naming green energy as verifiably safer to a sustainable planet... after which, Knuthe guessed, someone made a time machine, went back, and prohibited it entirely. Hey, it could happen. Amused, Knuthe turned his head thoughtfully to attend, in thought and in consciousness, to the final words from Mrs. Winslow.

The End

You have chosen Hermann Donskoy as the winner of the 2018 FAIR award.

—24—

"...Hermann Donskoy!"

Delighted applause.

Donskoy did not move from his seat. He had turned his hearing aid off, to rest his mind, which was tired of absorbing new names and idle chatter, and he was also resting his eyes during Candace's introductory speech. His eyes were dry and stinging. But then an elbow jabbed him, and he found that everyone was looking at him, clapping, smiling. Either he was having a good but puzzling dream, or the improbable had happened. As quickly as he could he turned the hearing aid back on.

"Get up there, Hermann!" Merrill Roselli said. "You won! You won!" It was kind of like a role-reversal of Charlie and Grandpa Joe in *Charlie and the Chocolate Factory*, in the scene where the bar is unwrapped to reveal the gold foil.

As Donskoy sidled down the row, Candace spoke: "Hermann Donskoy served as a Morse Code high-speed intercept operator for the Army Security Agency during the Vietnam conflict, work the nature of which was protected by a 40-year nondisclosure agreement. In other words, the families of service members like Donskoy knew nothing of their true locations and duties until only recently."

Fillmore handed Donskoy the trophy and stepped backwards—there was no limelight, but out of the proverbial limelight. Donskoy held the trophy at arm's length, the only way anything came into focus for his aged eyes. He puzzled over the trophy's features, saw his name engraved at the base, and smiled at that. He regarded the triumphant, vaguely seraphic figure atop it holding the wreath. He stuck out his lower lip as if to say, "Not bad, not bad." Throughout, the audience applauded.

"Ladies and gentlemen, our 2018 FAIR award winner, Hermann Donskoy!"

The applause strengthened as Candace stepped back from the podium and gestured for Donskoy to take it.

"Thank you," Donskoy said, bending the microphone. Diminishing applause. "Thank you." He bent the arm so he could stand up straight. "That's better." He looked out at the audience, absorbing the reality of his victory. "It's a hell of a thing. My goodness. Thank you to the foundation, Mrs. Winslow, Joyce, and all the staff," He turned and issued a gravely obliging nod to the Winslows.

He set the trophy atop the podium and grasped its sides, attempting to assume something like the maniacal self-possession of Colonel Kilgore in *Apocalypse Now*. The attempt was a robust failure, given Donskoy's general doughiness and the chasm-like decades spanning between the present moment and the bellicosity of his long-gone soldiering days. "You know, I come from a big Catholic family," he said. "Fourteen kids."

Amused reactions.

"My father came from a family of 14 as well. You could say our family was a bit like the service itself. Dinner was, Get in line, plate up. Everything was regimented, and sometimes you were made an example of. In other words, for me childhood wasn't all it was cracked up to be. The army was my second family. There I found I could make an impact, not get lost in the shuffle. In '68 I left California for Saigon and was stationed at Engineer Hill on the mountain of Pleiku, home of the 330th Radio Research Company. If sitting in 115-degree heat with headphones on for 12 to 16 hours a day is your idea of a good time, you shoulda joined my company. Sometimes I would take my headset off and still hear the clicking of the code."

Reverential silence.

"We had all kinds of other fun ways to pass the time after

a full shift, such as manning a machine-gun tower for another 3 hours. This all happened in a time when you didn't expect recognition. We sure as hell didn't care if the men in our troop were brown, red, green or purple. If they could pass the 27-week training in Morse, they were a 330 RRC. If they did the work, they were one of us."

Uncomfortable silence. The silence of a crowd uncertain whether it is being criticized.

"Later, towards the end of my service, we flew missions in Operation Left Bank. Finding enemy radar and jamming it, so they couldn't lock on to our boys. What you got if you did your job right and saved a pilot's life was a thumbs-up. That was it. That was enough."

"Things are different now, I understand, and everyone gets a purple heart just for getting out of bed, and sometimes not even that. Nothing I can do about that."

A few reluctant chuckles and shocked muttering.

"I don't wish to seem ungrateful however. I appreciate this award."

Corrective, relieved, assenting muttering.

"I think it clearly demonstrates that old-timers like me could use a final salute before we fade into the sunset. The young ones, god bless 'em—I got 8 grandchildren—they might learn a thing or two about getting on in the world and bucking up. Don't get me started—I realize I wasn't invited here to preach to you good folks. So thank you to the foundation for this award. I dedicate this to my ailing wife, Judith. I plan to use the stipend to rejuvenate the coffers of the Hermann Donskoy Model Train Hobbyist and Single Malt Scotch Fund. Thank you."

Resounding applause.

Candace appeared at Donskoy's side, taking his elbow and turning him to face a lone chair placed at center stage. Using that perfected gesture of hers, the open-palmed directive like that of dog handlers on the plastic turf of the Westminster Kennel club during exhibitions, Candace led Donskoy to understand that this was his special seat, and he was to take it. There Donskoy sat, putting the trophy on the floor beside him and taking out his hearing aid. The volume dialed down, he watched Candace command the podium, while reaching his ears were her faint vocal sounds in a summative cadence. He began to relax into the chair, and his mind drifted off.

Vindication really was a sweet thing. Donskoy felt it in his solar plexus: just a warm, solid kind of feeling, a fullness like when your income tax refund check comes, and you know you're not being audited, and you're in the good graces of Uncle Sam for another year. The model train setup in Donskoy's basement truly was a consuming pastime of his. He understood that; he openly admitted how much he cherished it. To a lesser extent he understood that it served a complex psychological and emotional function in his life, as a repository for his experiences, traumas, loves and losses. In total, he had over 80 square feet of an imaginary landscape created, constructed atop three-quarter-inch plywood that he'd cut himself. It was all laid atop an old table and several construction sawhorses, accessible around the perimeter. He called it Margaretville. That was the name he'd painted on the miniature water tower standing on the outskirts of the village—a tribute to his ailing wife, Margaret, the one who stayed at home tonight and who would have no one else to contact if Donskoy were unreachable due to a confiscated phone. The area surrounding Margaretville was hilly: one big hill in fact, shaped very much like Engineer Hill on the mountain of Pleiku, Gia Lai, Vietnam. But then there were American town features such as a rail station, wooded areas, houses, farm animals, and so on. Incongruently, there was a radio intercept building and a guard tower. A mixed bag, this playground of Donskoy's imagination. In and around and through it all ran an eight-car train with a simulation Soo-Line diesel engine, hauling an unlikely mix of livestock and war supplies, through one tunnel, over one bridge, served by a full-service switching yard.

Now his natural thought was to incorporate the FAIR award trophy into the place, but in terms of scale, he realized, it'd look like the Burj Khalifa tower if he dropped it in there as is. He turned and looked at the vaguely seraphic figure, the lithe golden lady. Maybe break her off of there and stick her on the peak, something like that deal they have above Rio de Janeiro. Satisfied with that idea, Donskoy closed his eyes to rest while the misshapen, partial sounds (not words exactly) from Mrs. Winslow continue to play about the periphery of his internal headspace, sounds that belonged to another place and time and which he alone could never translate.

The End

You have chosen Christine Wong as the winner of the 2018 FAIR award.

—25—

"...Christine Wong!"

Delighted applause.

As Wong sidled down the row, Candace spoke: "Christine Wong is Creative Director of the Lesbian Theater Collective and an American immigrant. She recently directed a very successful production of Eve Ensler's *The Vagina Monologues*, a title which sends chills down the spine of certain corporate donors to theaters. She is the author of *Swimming Across the Pacific*, the award-winning play of a Chinese immigrant girl facing a fat-shaming culture. She founded the YLPC, the Youth Lesbian Playwriting Collective, which works with inner city Lesbian Asian-American youth, helping them discover the transformative powers of the dramatic arts."

Fillmore handed Wong the trophy and stepped backwards—there was no limelight, but out of the proverbial limelight. Wong looked at the trophy with suspicion, read its engraving, and regarded the triumphant, vaguely seraphic figure atop it holding the wreath. She kept her face expressionless as the audience applauded.

"Ladies and gentlemen, our 2018 FAIR award winner, Christine Wong!"

The applause strengthened as Candace stepped back from the podium and gestured for Wong to take it. She did.

She said nothing until the applause diminished. She set the trophy atop the podium and stood before the podium with her arms hanging at her sides. When the room was silent, she said, "Okay. I want to thank the foundation, Mrs.

Winslow, Joyce, and all the staff." Her shoulders described the symmetry of an isosceles triangle. "You know, recently I've been thinking about death. By recently, I mean tonight. Earlier this evening. Death as commodity. Death as product."

The further solidity of silence turning to pure silence. Attentive silence. Arrested, breathless silence.

"There is a saturation of death in the marketplace. Podcasts on death. TV series about death. Video games about death. Of course we've always had films about death. I think I will begin a new work in which death as a design concept leaps out of the death marketplace and into other retail environments. So our canned corn is no longer Del Monte brand canned corn, but Death Brand canned corn."

Tremendously faint laughter.

"Our undergarments are no longer by Hanes or Calvin Klein but by Gruesome Murder Brand Clothing. Perhaps our entire environment comes to encompass the death brand. Mass Slaughter Homes. Prefabricated, passive-solar homes at affordable prices, with all the allure and excitement of a senseless violence. This would be more popular than Shady Grove or Gladbrook Estates. The new 2025 Subaru Horrific Bloodshed all-wheel-drive SUV. We are not far away from this, I think."

Skeptical silence. The creaking of furniture under the shiftings of doubtful bodies.

"And that is a shame."

A welcome return to clear-thinking.

"It would be much better if everyone could find the appeal of life. Life is much more beautiful than death. Don't you think?"

"Yeah!" yelled Merrill Roselli, and his yell obliterated the silence of all those who assumed Wong's question to be rhetorical.

"Thank you, Merrill."

Tittering.

"However that is the future," Wong said. "That is just what's happening in my brain at this time." Wong's tone was always minorly incremental from baseline. Elation in her would be shown by a smile only as broad as the one most of us give the mailman. Severe anger came through, in her, as a nearly undetectable crinkling of the brows and pursing of the lips. Similarly, her present self-deprecating humor, her attempt to convey her experience of being powerfully over-taken by the concept of death-as-product, of being washed away on the winds of fresh creative impetus, was hardly per-ceptible. She wanted to be regarded as a consummate artist, experiencing this party and this night not as mere mortals do. But as usual, she felt misunderstood and like she had botched her moment. She blushed a little and laughed. "I better talk about the award. I appreciate this award."

Corrective, relieved, assenting muttering.

"I think it clearly demonstrates that theater remains the timeless art form, *the* transcendent art. The mirror to soci-ety. A way for us to understand and know ourselves. I want to thank my partner Jennifer. I want to thank my parents. Also Eve Ensler, who inspired me to write about whatever the hell I wanted to write about. And of course thank you to the foundation. I don't know how I'll use the stipend, and I don't believe it's expected that I declare my intentions or make a vow of charity. Thank you."

Resounding applause, tempered only by confused reac-tion to the defiant part of Wong's final statement.

Candace appeared at Wong's side, taking her elbow and turning her to face a lone chair placed at center stage. Using that perfected gesture of hers, the open-palmed directive like that of dog handlers on the plastic turf of the Westmin-ster Kennel club during exhibitions, Candace made Wong understand that this was her special seat, and she was to take it. Just a plain folding chair—jeez, talk about low-budget. Wong sat with the trophy across her lap like a dry umbrella, staring straight to the back of the room in an ap-parent impersonation of the Buddha. While Candace made closing remarks at the podium, her mind drifted off.

She shouldn't have doubted herself, she saw now. Her in-stincts had told her that the award was hers, that the dawn was finally nigh when this country recognized the Korean-

American population and its important contributions to the American arts landscape. Had it somehow been fueled by the childish taunts being lobbed forth and back between the U.S. President (Wong refused to sully her tongue or her synapses with his name) and Kim Jung-Un? Yes, possibly. These slurs of Rocketman and such undermined the serious importance that Korean-Americans like Wong feel about their role as emigrants and the seriousness of Korea's dysfunction and the important discourse that could be happening between the U.S and Korea, two countries who have both had north-south civil war. Imagine all that could be learned from each other. So, yes, possibly the award went to her, Wong concluded, as a move to restore some dignity to the identity of the Korean-American. If so, that was okay. Surely her selection still stood primarily as a signifier or her relevance as an artist as well as the to honor the voluminosity of her plights.

The End

You have chosen Merrill Roselli as the winner of the 2018 FAIR Award

—26—

"…Merrill Roselli!"

Delighted applause.

As Roselli sidled down the row, Candace spoke: "Merrill Roselli was Class President, class of 2012, at the University of Chicago. Xe was an organizer and activist of the Occupy Chicago movement in 2011, and served on the Office of LGBTQIA Student Life Advisory Board. Xe's also an author on Medium.com, where his articles regularly garner thousands of claps. He's thinking about running for office someday. Let's hope xe does."

This introduction was supplied by Roselli himself, and it used Roselli's gender-neutral pronoun of choice. Candace managed its use with grace and aplomb.

Fillmore handed Roselli the trophy and stepped backwards—there was no limelight, but out of the proverbial limelight. Roselli gaped at the trophy, holding it at arm's length like an animal that might sting. He wiped away a tear. He saw the triumphant, vaguely seraphic figure atop it holding the wreath, and was chagrined that it wasn't more androgynous. Throughout, the audience applauded.

"Ladies and gentlemen, our 2018 FAIR award winner, Merrill Roselli!"

The applause strengthened as Candace stepped back from the podium and gestured for Roselli to take it. Merrill did.

"Wow. Thank you." Diminishing applause. "Thank you. Wow, this is *amazing*. I wasn't expecting this. I want to thank the foundation, Mrs. Winslow, Joyce, and all the staff."

Light applause. Roselli smiled at everyone, then comported himself into the reflective, issue-driven person that he was. Setting the trophy atop the podium and grasping its sides, in the default pose of the aspiring politician, he said, " 'It takes a great degree of bravery to stand up to our enemies." Merrill paused ceremoniously, looking to the audience. "But just as much to stand up to our friends." Then he dropped the bomb on them. "Harry Potter and the Sorcerer's Stone."

Dispirited laughter mixed with groans—the groans of adults having been fooled into hearing sagacity in a children's storybook hero.

"I got you with that one, didn't I? Well, Harry Potter's words may come from a made-up place, but I think they are true of us in the world today. It *does* take a lot of courage to stand up to our friends. But why would I stand up to my friends? That's a question I've had to ask myself many times throughout my life." (In crafting his acceptance speech, Roselli had turned to the rhetorical tropes that were passable, even expected, of his SAT long-form answers in English Language Arts, and in college applications essays, and that had sustained him throughout his academic career, and into his journalistic ventures.) "In fact, I would argue that it's within the ranks of our closest friends where we need to be most diligent, to root out the hatred, bigotry, sexism, misogyny, homophobia, and xenophobia that me and my generation have made it our duty to eradicate from the landscape, come hell or high water."

Applause.

"Because it's easy to see the faults of our enemies. They're the ones who want to discriminate, judge, and even eliminate people that are different than them. These foibles stand out like sore thumbs."

A mass exhalation as if everyone had been gut-punched.

"But sometimes the sore thumb is on our own hand, or the hands of our friends. For example, maybe our family members use a negative gender stereotypes. Do we speak out about that, if it's from our own mother, father, grandmother, grandfather, aunt, uncle, sister or brother? Or maybe our boss thinks they're being racially inclusive, but they're really not. Are we willing to say something? Are we willing to lose our job for it?"

The sounds of uncertainty. The sniffing of uncertain noses. The keeper of a sniffing nose cannot attend to questions posed—he or she is occupied with sniffing, the really unpleasant experience of running snot or irritated sinus passages. Was this a rhetorical question even?

"This is the kind of bravery that we all need to find in ourselves now. Because even our enemies have friends, and so if everyone speaks up about intolerance and wrong-thinking in our friends, then we'll have found the bravery to speak up against all the negative forces, wherever they are found. Right? Anyway, ultimately, the goal is to all be friends anyway. That would be ideal."

"I want to thank the foundation again. I think this demonstrates that rooting out intolerance is the most important issue today. It has to be the starting point for going forward. We cannot continue down the path we're on. Only once we recognize our shared humanity can we progress and heal the wounds of this great country." (Here, Roselli was practicing for being a statesman.) "Thank you so much!"

Applause.

Candace appeared at Roselli's side, taking his elbow and turning him to face a lone chair placed at center stage. There Roselli sat with the trophy on his lap, a radiant smile beaming out of his face. While Candace made closing remarks at the podium, Roselli's mind drifted off. He thought of the many daises, County Fair platforms, stages, halls, auditoriums, and gymnasiums that he would visit throughout his future career as a politician. He could he really see himself on them all, waving, speechifying, debating, and raising the clasped hands of his loyal spouse (whoever that might be) as the balloons and confetti fall. His heart was up in his throat. Today was a great day. Today was the start of it all. Drawing in his lips and narrowing his gaze Bill Clinton-style, he looked down on the trophy that symbolized it all. It really wasn't right that the person on it was a woman. So what are we saying, Women aren't the ones to get awards? They're just the ones who congratulate the guys? As he started penning a Medium.com piece on the topic, he turned his head thoughtfully to create the appearance of attending, in thought and in consciousness, to the final words from Mrs. Winslow.

The End

You have chosen Joseph Hector Depace as the winner of the 2018 FAIR award

—27—

"...Joseph Hector Depace!"

Delighted applause.

As Depace sidled down the row, Candace spoke: "Joseph Hector Depace is a small business owner and proud American immigrant. He's the father of three. Coming to this country in the early 1960s, he and his wife Valerie lived and worked here in Minneapolis, Minnesota, for over 40 years. But the barriers to citizenship were great, and the biases even greater. In 2014, Joseph's wife Valerie died of symptoms which went largely untreated, due to a lack of adequate medical coverage."

Fillmore handed Depace the trophy and stepped backwards—there was no limelight, but out of the proverbial limelight. Depace squinted at the trophy's, seeing it poorly due to his outdated eyewear prescription. He saw an engraving that seemed to contain his name, and then a the triumphant, vaguely seraphic figure atop it holding the wreath. It made him proud, because it seemed patriotic, like Lady Liberty or something. Throughout, the audience applauded.

"Ladies and gentlemen, our 2018 FAIR award winner, Joseph Hector Depace!"

The applause strengthened as Candace stepped back from the podium and gestured for Depace to take it. He did.

"Thank you." Diminishing applause. "Gracias." The obligatory fussing with the microphone's height. Silence. "Dios mio, I'm so happy." He thanked the foundation, Mrs. Winslow, Joyce, and all the staff—and his thanks were met with applause. He grinned and nodded his head repeatedly.

Finally he set the trophy atop the podium and grasped its sides, the pose of the humble working class immigrant finally given his due. "You know, America is the land of the free. Sometimes this is a good thing, sometimes a bad thing."

Skeptical near-silence as of apprehensive people in chairs. The minute sound of muscles twitching, ready to defend a homeland. Was he going to bad-mouth America?

"Americans are free to do religion—whatever religion they want. Americans are free to have a family. Free to work. Free to get a education [sic]. So many wonderful things in the land of the free."

Here it comes.

"But Americans are also free to eat whatever they want. Free to buy whatever they want. Free to behave however they want. Thirty-one years I've owned a corner grocery, a bodega, in my neighborhood of Kingfield. When I first buy the place, it was 1965. I put in the things that I believe will be good for business. Fruits and vegetables. Okay, I'm buying bananas, apples, lettuce, carrots. Milk, cheese, and like this. And you know what, they sell OK. A few people are buying them. But over time I see, you know what is selling even better? Candy bars. Licorice. Gum drops. Bubble gum. Potato chips. Coca-Cola."

Assenting hums from the audience. The agreeable reactions of those who do not stand accused. It's always someone else who eats crap.

"And as the years go on, the lettuce is rotting, the bananas are going brown. They are not selling. Now, me, I'm a businessman. I got rents to pay, I have to put food on the table, yes? So I give the people what they want. Another cooler for more Coca-Cola. No more fruits and vegetables. I got rid of that. Instead I bought more cookies, more candies, and so on. You know how it is, you have seen the gas stations and markets in this country. Then, over the years, we are adding the cigarettes, many, many kinds. We are adding the glass pipes for marijuana. We are adding ice creams, and Slushie machine, and now we have the e-cigarettes and soon it's gonna be weed and who knows what! Maybe we're going to have cocaine right in the bodega. Ha ha. But today, this is where I make *all* my money—not much money, don't kid me!" Depace laughed self-deprecatingly. "I'm not a rich man, but this is where the money comes from. If it's bad for you, it sells good. It's just that simple. If it's good for you, I can't sell it."

"My wife, Valerie, she smoked. I said to her, Come on, honey, you gotta quit those. She tried, but she could not do it. She liked the McDonald's, the Wendy's, the Burger King. She was only 62 years old when she died. Because we had no citizenship, we didn't have no medical coverage."

Pained breathwork.

"This story has a happy part though. You wanna hear it?"

Most everyone saying, *Uh, yeah. Yes.*

"In 2105, with the help of my daughter, I took the citizenship exam, and I passed. I now have a social security number. I have a passport. I'm very proud to be an American, after living here so long. And I have full medical coverage. The premiums? Ay caramba. That is an issue for another day."

Laughter and applause.

"Thank you. But you know, I still have one thing on my mind. When I think about the freedom we all enjoy, I think of the freedom people have to do what they want. In my shop, I've been shot, I've been stabbed, I've been punched and kicked. People drive their car into the window. People smash the glass. They steal and rob me. How we going to get people to have freedom and use it right?"

Awkward, shifty contemplative restlessness. Wasn't this more of a philosophical problem, and an old one at that, to do with free will and morality?

"Well, maybe we solve that next year. For now, I think I should say thank you for this award." Depace put one hand on the trophy and regarded it affectionately. "I think it shows that a pathway to citizenship for immigrants is the most important issue facing America today. We gotta have the laws and policies that allow people to become citizens, if they want. I am happy to see that many politicians now are saying ICE should be finished. I agree. Like me with my wife

Valerie, I think if this country loses the immigrants, only then will it know what it has. Immigrants work hard. Immigrants pay taxes. We are not rapists. We are not 'bad hombres.'"

Depace seemed to flinch, as if feeling some ire flare up and squelching it.

"Okay, I thank you very much. Good night."

While the room filled with warm applause, Candace appeared at Depace's side, taking his elbow and turning him to face a lone chair placed at center stage. There Depace sat with the trophy on the ground beside him, a pleasant smile on his otherwise weary and ashen face. While Candace made closing remarks at the podium, Depace's mind drifted off. He thought of the shelf behind the register at his bodega. Which shelf could he clear to make room for the trophy? It would be nice to display it. Customers could remark. It could be a real conversation starter. But as he considered the different products he could relocate to make room—cigarettes, pipe tobacco, e-cigarettes—he began to envision a life back behind the register and to foresee a time when he'd need to dust the trophy just like he regularly dusted everything else. Could it be that the trophy would actually just sit there and age like everything else in his shop, including himself, without changing his life in any way? ¡*Joder*! If only Valerie were here, she would tell him it wasn't so.

The End

You have chosen Evonne Sorenstam-Finch as the winner of the 2018 FAIR Award.

—28—

"...Evonne Sorenstam-Finch!"

Delighted applause.

As Sorenstam-Finch sidled down the row, Candace spoke: "Evonne Sorenstam-Finch works in media relations for the Pittsburgh firm Janklow & Janklow. In 1992, at age nine, she was abducted in her hometown of Grand Rapids, Michigan. She was held captive for six years."

Audible gasping in the audience. Reedy inhalations of breath passing through throats constricted by disbelief and shock.

"At the age of 15, she broke out of the basement where she was held. Her captor was caught and jailed. Evonne was then married to MK Finch, perpetrator in the Carlow University Swim Team sex scandal. Evonne has worked through her experiences to find joy, peace, and happiness both personally and professionally. She is currently an advocate for holistic and homeopathic medicine and somatic cognition therapy, among other naturopathic modalities."

Fillmore handed Sorenstam-Finch the trophy and stepped backwards—there was no limelight, but out of the proverbial limelight. Sorenstam-Finch looked at the trophy in her hands and felt a tsunami wave of gratitude in her chest. The trophy's features, its engraving, and a triumphant, vaguely seraphic figure atop it holding a wreath, appeared doubled and wavering through her tear-filled eyes. Throughout, the audience applauded.

"Ladies and gentlemen, our 2018 FAIR award winner, Evonne Sorenstam-Finch!"

The applause strengthened as Candace stepped back from the podium and gestured for Sorenstam-Finch to take it. She did.

"Wow. Thank you." Diminishing applause. "Thank you." She adjusted the microphone's height and took a deep, calming breath and silence settled across the room. "I'm really honored." She thanked the foundation, Candace, Joyce, and the staff, and light applause rose up again. Finally, she set the trophy atop the podium and took a folded slip of paper from the pocket of her dress. "I would like to read a quote from the Buddhist writer Pema Chodron." She unfolded the paper and held it before her. " 'The most fundamental aggression to ourselves, the most fundamental harm we can do to ourselves, is to remain ignorant by not having the courage and the respect to look at ourselves honestly and gently.' "

She looked up, anticipating a response. She got one. It was not, however, the response she expected, of savoring nods and assenting hums. Every member of the audience had their neck craned in a bewildered way. Their faces showed perplexity, as if they'd heard a Zen kōan too complex to parse.

"Is that true?" some at the back muttered.

"But *others* harm *us*..." someone else remarked. "That's way worse. Way worse."

Sorenstam-Finch continued: "Yes, Chodron's ideas are radical. But take me, for example. I'm someone, on the surface, who has endured harm by others. Many of you know my story. I was abducted when I was nine years old and held captive in a basement for six years. My captor harmed me greatly. He was cruel, manipulative, violent. He stole my life from me—for a time. *For a time*: I want to clarify that. Later, I was married to a man who—again, you may know this story as well—" she laughed a little. "I'm famous for all the wrong reasons."

Appreciative laughter.

"Later, my husband, harmed me through his deceit and betrayal, his inappropriate behavior. He was controlling of me, abusive, manipulative, and cruel." She paused to let the gravitas of her experience sink in. "And yet, I truly believe that I did more harm to myself than these people did to me. In the years both before my captivity and after it. As a young girl, I was very cruel to myself. I hated the way I looked. I hated my height, my long bony arms and legs. I hated my goofy face. I called myself Lizard. I convinced myself I was stupid, because I was not at the top of my class. I treated myself carelessly, including putting myself in a position to be harmed, by walking alone in bad parts of town, quite often. I seemed to feel that I deserved ill-treatment. I expected bad things to happen to me, because they felt warranted."

"Later, as an adult, after both of my traumatic events, I did not treat myself *gently*, as Pema Chodron suggests we should. I continued, for a time, to berate myself for my choices. I continued to believe that I was cursed and deserved these outcomes. That was not a gentle way to help myself after what I'd experienced."

Tumultuous stirring as of those stumped by a frustrating puzzle.

"Turning, then, to the broader experience of women in 2018. It was last year that the #metoo movement began, with revelations about Mr. Weinstein and the sexual abuse and rape he perpetrated. What I understand about what these women went through is that they—many of them—blamed themselves. They walked into it. The invited it. It's all they deserved. None of which, of course, is true. It's not what they deserved. Because they wanted to act in films, they didn't deserve to be sexually violated."

"The #metoo movement has been amazing. It's a long-overdue revelation. It was high time that the abuse of power in professional environments be ended. It was high time that any type of sexual predation be spoken out against—whether male-on-female, male-on-male or any other combination. It's 2018. Civilized society ought to have condemned sexual violence of any kind centuries ago. Okay, better late than never, right?"

Applause.

"However, I want to speak to the attitude of

condemnation that many #metoo proponents wield. Many women are seizing on this movement to vilify. I'm not talking about whether the scope of accusations is too wide-ranging—whether a particular behavior is egregious enough to be included in under the hashtags aegis. Nor am I talking about whether #metoo makes too sweeping an indictment by naming men in general rather than offenders only. I'm talking about the tone and attitude of the direct accusations. The accusations are just when founded in fact. The call-outs are just. But when someone stands accused, how are they treated? How is the situation handled? What do the victims wish for? Do they wish for their own healing and the healing of the perpetrator? Or do they wish for their own retribution and the concomitant *suffering* of the perpetrator?"

Agitated creaking of folding chairs. A range of disquieted vocalizations. Throat-clearing, anxious cheek-clacking. The mutterings of the cornered prey.

"Thich Nhat Hanh has many words on this issue, in his book *Anger: Cooling the Fires Within*. He's a very wise man, and his teachings have been instrumental to me in my healing journey. He says, 'When you do something in retaliation, your anger increases. You make the other person suffer, and he will try hard to say or to do something back to get relief from his suffering. The result is an escalation of suffering on both sides.'"

Impatient silence.

"An escalation of suffering on both sides," Sorenstam-Finch repeated. "I propose to all those out there who have been victimized, men *and* women, victims of sexual violence and other forms of violence, consider this. Consider whether you want the result to be resolution and peace, or you want the result to be increased suffering on both sides. If you really want to treat yourself gently and honestly, then you should chose less suffering for yourself, and that means not choosing to seek retribution. Not choosing to inflict further suffering on the other side."

Tepid, uncertain, even fearful applause. Obligatory applause that seeks to usher the speaker to a conclusion so that the applauded sentiment can be forgotten and even re-tracted in spirit.

"The certainty with which victims feel that their perpe-trators haven't suffered *anything*, while they have suffered greatly, is an illusion. Think of my captor, Warren Dudzic. He was in his late-twenties. He had never been married or had a girlfriend. He lived alone. He was lonely and craved com-panionship. But he felt he was undesirable. In fact, he was so certain that the only way he could obtain the company and human connection that he craved, was to take it by force. Which he did. Choosing me. He must have suffered greatly. Imagine being driven by loneliness and a feeling of inferior-ity so powerful that the option of *stealing a human* occurs to you, and as you continue to suffer, you consider this option, and it comes to seem like a viable one, and as you continue to suffer loneliness, you eventually act on it. That is very great suffering."

Aghast, uncomprehending silence. The silence of those feeling judged for their own limited viewpoints, for their selfish seeking of recognition.

"A similar thing was true for my husband. We know that homosexuality is not a disease contracted by airborne vi-ruses or anything like that. It's genetic. Homosexuals are born with their sexual preferences. My ex-husband MK felt homosexual urges from a young age, when puberty set in. But, as a member of Christian family, living a homosexual lifestyle was not an option that was available to him. His local parish priest spoke against it as sinful. His family condemned it in public figures. They called it abhorrent and so on. MK was so conditioned to revile homosexuality that he reviled it in himself, and he did everything he could to deny it and sat-isfy his family and church, so he could be accepted by them, including entering into a heterosexual marriage. When the repression of his natural desires grew too much to bear, he acted on them inappropriately. MK suffered greatly."

Chilly, resentful applause.

Sorenstam-Finch looked in bewilderment over her shoulder to Joyce Winslow, who all but shrugged helpless.

With the index finger of one hand, she made a forward-rotation movement suggesting 'wrap it up.'

"Well, in conclusion, I appreciate this award. I think it clearly demonstrates that the safety of women, the equality of women, the rights of women, and indeed the safety, rights and equality of all sentient beings, is the most urgent need for American society. I plan to use the stipend to open a holistic naturopathic wellness and after-school center in my home neighborhood of Troy Hill. Thank you very much. Namaste."

Downright angry applause at the insolence of this uppity woman.

Candace appeared at Sorenstam-Finch's side, taking her elbow and turning her to face a lone chair placed at center stage. There Sorenstam-Finch sat with the trophy on her lap, a serene expression on her face. She felt gratified, but to a degree that surprised her, she noticed no euphoric feeling of vindication. Perhaps because she worked to prevent such a feeling from arising. A million thoughts rained down upon her mind about what this award meant—that she was special, elevated, more worthy, even divine. She mentally popped each of these thoughts as if it were a soap bubble floating above her head. *Pop, pop, pop!* She drew long, full breaths through her nose, noticing the point at the entrance of her nostrils where the air entered. This simply confirmed that she was in the room with the air. She wished to be present while Candace made closing remarks at the podium. She turned her head and listened, and was able to catch caught most of it and to appreciate her insinuation that the race for next year's prize had just begun.

The End

You have chosen Jeong-Hwa Pak as the winner of the 2018 FAIR Award

—29—

"...Jeong-Hwa Pak!"

Delighted applause.

As Pak sidled down the row, Candace spoke: "Jeong-Hwa Pak was formerly research scientist at Pyongyang University of Science and Technology. He was jailed for speaking out against North Korea's nuclear weapons program. He now lives in exile from his home country and is a writer and activist on the issue of nuclear non-proliferation."

Fillmore handed Pak the trophy and stepped backwards—there was no limelight, but out of the proverbial limelight. Pak bowed deeply several times at Fillmore, before even looking at the trophy. Once he did regard it, he did so with apparent succor, smiling especially at the triumphant, vaguely seraphic figure atop it holding a wreath. Throughout, the audience applauded.

"Ladies and gentlemen, our 2018 FAIR award winner, Jeong-Hwa Pak!"

The applause strengthened as Candace stepped back from the podium and gestured for Pak to take it. He did.

"Thank you." Diminishing applause. "Thank you very much to the foundation, Candace, and everybody." Silence. "I'm very honored." His head continued to make small bows. Finally, he set the trophy atop the podium and grasped its sides, the default pose of the socially-conscious man of letters. He looked up. "Sixty-four thousand, four hundred forty-nine." Pak paused, looked inquisitively from audience member to audience member. "What's that? Anybody know? It happened in 1986." Some muttering in the crowd. "Yes, I think I hear someone say it. That's the number of nuclear weapons we had at one time. That's the most we ever had. Sixty-four thousand nuclear weapons. In 1986, that was the global nuclear stockpile. Now, we know that together 'Little Boy,' dropped on Hiroshima, and 'Fat Man,' dropped on Nagasaki, together killed somewhere around two-hundred thousand to two-hundred fifty thousand people. Maybe even more. That means, all those bombs have the potential power to kill 7.8 billion people. Guess what. That's more than enough to kill every living person on planet Earth. And in case you think I'm exaggerating, this does not even factor in the increased power of today's weapons compared to that of 1945. Today's B83 bomb is 1.2 megatons. That's 80 times more powerful than Fat Man."

"Now, the global stockpile has come down since the nineteen-eighties, thank goodness. But it's still over ten thousand nuclear weapons.

"By the way, maybe you notice I don't call them 'nukes.' I call them nuclear weapons. Nukes I don't like, because it makes them sound cute, like a puppy. They're not cute. It's like saying troops. The army wants the news to report, ten troops killed today. They don't want the news to say ten *men* killed. They don't want the news to say ten *persons* killed. It's the same with nuclear weapon. It's a deadly weapon. Let's not forget that. Let's not call them nukes. Nukes is too cute. It's almost delicious like cucumbers. That's not right."

A few chuckles.

"So, I was saying, the stockpile is lower. Six times lower than 1986. But each weapon is dozens and dozens of times more powerful than the first nuclear weapons of 70 years ago. Now, why do we have the capability to end the existence of the entire human race? What a foolish thing it would be to do that. What would be the point? If it happened, and aliens came to earth much later, they would look and say, Hmm, I guess they did it because they couldn't get along. I guess they did it because they all wanted the most power and no one would give up their power."

Pak yearningly scanned the audience, and saw many

affronted, self-assured visages. They themselves, they in particular, were not the obstinate, power-hungry ones.

"How foolish. Right? Oh my gosh, we're going to be the embarrassment of the universe. 'Those guys wiped themselves out, and ended life for millions of other creatures by poisoning the earth.' Oh, dear. Do we really want to go down in history as the laughing stock of the universe?"

The sounds of moderate dissent. The sounds of bodies saying, No, obviously not.

"I think John Lennon picked exactly the right word when he wrote 'Imagine.' Such a beautiful song, Imagine. Right now we have to *imagine* a world with no nuclear weapons. Not a single one. I think if we imagine it, that is the start of making it a reality. If we don't imagine it, why are we going to make it happen, because it's not in our minds if we don't imagine? See? In that way, imagine means to really want it. We have to really want it."

"I do. I hope you do to."

Heartfelt silence. Affirmative humming. Inhalations of the profound.

"Thank you for this award. I think it really demonstrates that denuclearization is the premier issue of today. I think when we have arms for deterrents, it sends a message to other countries of threat. And I think, how can we stop having refugee crises everywhere, how can we have safe lives for immigrants, when we hold nuclear weapons? It sets the tone for everything."

"I will donate the cash prize to the Dag Hammarskjold Fund for Journalists. Thank you."

Applause.

Candace appeared at Pak's side, taking his elbow and turning him to face a lone chair placed at center stage. There Pak sat with the trophy on his lap, a mild look of gratitude on his face. While Candace made closing remarks at the podium, Pak's mind drifted off. He thought of a nice bowl of bibimbap, with plenty of pickled vegetables like his mother used to make.

The End

You have chosen Gabrielle Rauch as the winner of the 2018 FAIR Award

—30—

"...Gabrielle Rauch!"

Delighted applause.

Rauch rose from her seat. As she sidled out of the row, Candace spoke on: "Gabrielle Rauch's son Ryan Rauch was slain in the 2018 Brenton, New York, Blowgun Massacre. Ryan was a sophomore, 15 years old, an A student. First chair trombonist in band. He was preparing for his confirmation at church, where he enjoyed volunteering. He played soccer, and loved tacos and the music of Taylor Swift. Gabrielle has become a leading spokesperson for blowgun regulation reform."

Fillmore handed Rauch the trophy and stepped backwards—there was no limelight, but out of the proverbial limelight. Rauch beheld the trophy with cosmic wonder, unable to read its engraving, so full was her heart with the holy spirit. She regarded the triumphant, vaguely seraphic figure atop it holding the wreath, and drew her lips inward as of one fighting back the lip-trembles of weeping. Throughout, the audience applauded.

"Ladies and gentlemen, our 2018 FAIR award winner, Gabrielle Rauch!"

The applause strengthened as Candace stepped back from the podium and gestured for Rauch to take it. She did.

"Thank you." Diminishing applause. "Lord have mercy." From the interior pocket of her red blazer, just under the "Enough" and "Policy and Action" buttons, Rauch withdrew a sheet of paper. She unfolded it and spread it flat atop the podium. She wore reading glasses on a chain around her neck, and now put them on. Her chin high with dignity, she closed her eyes and stood silently—saying a prayer. Her hair was auburn and styled in a quite passé fashion—a helmet-like coif that rose off her forehead into curling crests and from there flowed back in an array of uncannily syncopated barrel-rolls of hair that fell down her neck to her shoulders. It was a "do" that alluded to the complexity of the Holy Trinity.

She set the trophy atop the podium and grasped its sides in the same manner that Father Delbonis, parish priest of St. Ann's Catholic Church back in Brenton, did at the lectern every Sunday morning. Father Delbonis had in fact baptized Gabrielle, way back in 1964, and being 75 years old now a lectern looked more like something that could helpfully blunt his fall, a medical safety device, than a fixture in any fire-and-brimstone kind of scene. Nonetheless, he was a man of greatly inspiring faith, and it was a trait Rauch never expected to match—only "hem of your garment" etc.

Feeling Christ in her bones, she announced in a loud, clear tone: "Sixteen."

Pause.

"Sixteen lives."

Turning her head this way and that.

"Sixteen lives were lost at Edison High School, in my hometown of Brenton, New York, back in February. Hundreds of others, like me, were left grieving. They include mothers and fathers, sons and daughters. They include spouses of the teachers and Edison's facilities manager, Mr. Carl Lange. Also community members, church members, coworkers and friends of those killed. Brenton is a small community, fewer than ten thousand people. We all knew these victims. Everyone in Brenton is deeply impacted by the loss of these lives. Every one of us. We are bereaved. We are devastated."

She paused again, her head twisted into the suggestion of bewilderment. "What was it for?"

Rauch asked the question in the earnestly beseeching tone she had become known for in the many media appearances she'd been making since early summer. The in-home interview with Byron Pitts of ABC's *Nightline*, in particular, in which Rauch sat beside her husband Thomas, frequently dabbing tears but also valiantly excavating herself from several cavernous pits of self-absorbed grief to answer Pitt's questions and posing equally salient questions back to Pitt. Questions that America needed to answer.

The breathless silence of the reverential. The breathless silence of an entire group thinking, uniformly, "It was for *nothing*, obviously, and that's *bullshit*."

"It's tested my faith, people. I confess it. That this could happen in a country whose flag my husband Tom and I have flown on our front porch all our lives. A country I love. It's tested my faith. *Oh, yes*." Momentarily, Rauch's characteristic probing intellect was replaced with beginnings of spiritual abandon—that free-wheelin', tell-it-like-it-is, testifying spirit. She stopped just short of "Mmm, child!" and "Lawda' mercy!" Yet a surging wave of it drove her eyebrows skyward.

Regaining an even temper, she announced, "If I may, I will read briefly from the Good Book." She peered down her nose at her notes. "The bible says: 'Consider it all joy, my brethren, when you encounter various trials, knowing that the testing of your faith produces endurance.' " Looking up, speaking bluntly now: "Okay, well, I consider myself to have increased my endurance. I've got all the endurance I need now, Lord, thank you very much."

Nose-breath laughter, restrained by empathically felt bitter pain.

"I trust my boy, my dear Ryan, is with Jesus now. I know he is. You see, this *massacre* has not shaken my faith in God. Oh, no. It's shaken my faith in the *people* of this country, especially its leaders in government. It's so-called leaders, I might add." Honestly, now Rauch was nearing Dr. King territory with her climbs to pitch and her resumptions in the lower registers, with her emphases and punchy declaratives.

Slight murmuring and the sound of cushion foam expanding and retracted and a few metallic clicks of chair legs flexing, as people shift in their seats, recognizing that they themselves are *people* and they had voted for the so-called leaders being implicated. Perhaps they were faulty people as well. But, no, that couldn't be.

"But let's talk momentarily about the individual, shall we? That word is similar to *infidel*, I've noticed. One who acknowledges no religious belief. Hmm. America affords us freedoms, our cherished liberties. We can do *whatever* we like, *whenever* we like, within the bounds of the law. So how is it that people make the choices that they do?"

"Let's take Mr. Hartigan, for example. That fateful February morning, —" Oh, yeah, she said that—"he choose to get up, don a trench coat, and *fill* its pockets with poison darts. He then packed his Terminator brand blowgun, bought at Cabela's in Albany, in his car, and chose to drive himself to Edison High, where innocent children sat in classrooms and played floor hockey in the gymnasium, where teachers were working to make the students' lives better, as well as put food on their own tables."

"Now, what, I ask you, drives a person to this? I admit, I have struggled greatly to understand. It defies all reason. It defies all logic. It even defies human nature, as I see it."

"Is one man capable of deciding that people should die? Is one man able to remove his own sight to such a degree? To blind himself so entirely to all sense of right and wrong?"

Rauch shook her head, refuting.

The sound of scalps being scratched by fingernails.

"Which is why I want to take this opportunity to address Djink Greeley's remarks. People have been asking me ever since he released his statement whether I agree. Now, I don't know Mr. Greeley. I understand he wants humans to leave earth and go live on Mars. I don't necessarily agree with that. The bible talks about heaven on earth, not heaven on Mars. But frankly, I'm inclined to agree that the Brenton Massacre was orchestrated. By who, I don't know. I have no evidence. But it fits the NRA's purposes just perfectly. A little too perfectly. Y'all have heard their slogan, I know you have." Here Rauch borrowed some of the folksiness President Obama often adopted in speeches. "They've been hiding it for years:

Guns don't kill people, they say; people do." Rauch was experiencing bouts of self-conscious about her speech: the uncharacteristic use of "Y'all" came as a counterbalance to the feeling that she was out of her element giving political commentary and that her true identity was a rural stay-at-home mom. She heard herself say *y'all* and thought, What the hell was that? Now she just tried to make her point plain: "I think it is in their interest to have the attention drawn away from guns and the dangers of guns. And now it has been, right?"

"At the same time, I'm not really interested in being on a government watch list any more than I already am, so I will stop short of asserting that the White House is involved or the FBI or the pentagon or the Department of Homeland Security. I don't know. But I think Greeley's call for an investigation is appropriate. In fact, *he's got* millions of dollars—why doesn't he fund an independent investigation? That makes sense to me."

Relieved laughter and strong applause.

"Thank you. Going back to my faith, I want to say that every day I pray to the Lord that he sheds the light of his wisdom on our congresspeople and senators, that they may see: We cannot have blowguns for sale without the same background checks, ID laws, and waiting periods that we have for firearms. If Brenton has proven anything, it's that these weapons are just as deadly, and it's our moral obligation to protect our children. I hope to God that that number I cited earlier stays exactly where it is in my lifetime—and in yours. I pray that the body count of lives lost to blowguns stays 16 forever. Hashtag forever sixteen."

"Thank you for this award. The twenty-five thousand dollar prize is going, in full, to the Ryan Rauch Tacos for Heroes Foundation. We're making literature and getting the word out about blowgun law reform, so that there will never be another Brenton Massacre. Thank you."

Applause.

Candace appeared at Rauch's side, ushering her into a designated chair, as anointed, it seemed to Rauch, as the cathedra in the sanctuary of St. Patrick's in New York City, which Rauch always toured when visiting the Big Apple. There Rauch sat with the trophy on her lap, a reverent smile on her face. While Candace made closing remarks at the podium, Rauch's mind drifted off. She was quite overtaken, it must be said. With the feeling in the room, with her strong sense that Ryan was present in spirit. Gentle tears of gratitude streamed down her face, and she gloried in the righteousness of her Lord and Savior Jesus Christ. Then, most beyond her control, she found herself reviewing the contents of the dry good cupboard at home and making a mental list to pick up some of those potato sticks. What are they called? They're like potato chips but come in a cannister, and are thin and flat, like a dry noodle. Anyway, her husband liked them on top of the casserole that she planned to make Sunday. It wouldn't hurt to get more cream of mushroom soup as well. Campbell's has a low-sodium one now; she could sneak that into the casserole without Thomas knowing.

The End

You have chosen Johan Damgaard as the winner of the 2018 FAIR Award.

—31—

"...Johan Damgaard!"

Delighted applause.

As Damgaard sidled down the row, Candace spoke: "Johan Damgaard is an international storyteller. His TED talk 'We Are Made of Stories' has received over 2 million views on YouTube. His Podcast 'I AM STORY' is currently ranked number 7 on Podcast Industry News' monthly So Hot They're Dangerous list. Damgaard is a thought-leader in the emerging fields of Story Psychology and Story Healing. He has partnered to create life-altering—wow, this is really boastful. Uh, life-altering content with Deepak Chopra, Eckhart Tolle, and Tim Farris."

Fillmore handed Damgaard the trophy and stepped backwards—there was no limelight, but out of the proverbial limelight. Damgaard took it in one hand and without endearingly studying the trophy's features, raised his arms in a V for Victory over his head. So broad was his smile, so brightly burned his ecstasy, it would not have looked out of place for someone in a pit crew jumpsuit to spray champagne on him. However, the audience's applause seemed to wane the more Damgaard let his pride radiate, revealing its outsized strength.

"Ladies and gentlemen, our 2018 FAIR award winner, Johan Damgaard!" Candace Winslow said, subdued in deliberate counterbalance to Damgaard's display.

Candace stepped back from the podium and gestured for Damgaard to take it.

"Thank you." Diminishing applause. "Thank you." The

obligatory fussing with the microphone's height. Silence. "It's a pleasure and an honor."

He cleared his throat, which felt mucky, like he'd swallowed a gob of dry peanut butter. He set the trophy atop the podium and grasped its sides, in the pose of the sage intellectual. "Stories are in our DNA," Damgaard intoned. "They are literally encoded on the strands of deoxyribonucleic acid that wind in a double-helix around each other like the very serpent that tempted Eve in the garden of Eden—which is the setting of one of our earliest and *juiciest* stories."

The reluctantly pleased groans of an audience who "sees what you did there" with the juice of the apple and the interconnectedness and the layers of meaning.

"Stories are everywhere. We cannot spend a day on this planet as humans without stories, whether hearing a story, seeing a story, telling a story, or *living* a story."

Thusly, Damgaard went on, pilfering the best schlock about stories from his insanely lucrative lecture series and mail-order compact discs (for seniors and low-income people not equipped with digital gadgetry) "The Stories Our Bones Tell." He also dragged in a bunch of historical data such as dates of cave inscriptions in France, and the curious fact that the word "lox" was recently deemed by scientists to be the only word in the English language that looks, sounds and is spelled the same, and crucially which *means* the same, as it did 8,000 years ago by Indo-European tribes on the veldt of what is now Austria. (Parts of this he made up—no one would look it up.) He recounted a Native American origin myth about the moon and a fox. He cited Russian folktales and Japanese scrolls from centuries-gone dynasties, all in the name of forming this giant rubber-band ball of an idea, which he then set on the proverbial desk of the audience's consciousness, where they could stare at it and see its many colorful components and regale in its unquestionable....facticity: the idea that stories have been around a long time and serve a function in not only our emotional lives but in the evolutionary lives of us *all*.

Damgaard's oratorical tic, which he repeated frequently,

was to emphasize words with the "short" sound of the vowel *a*. Such as *all*.

And there it did sit, the rubber-band ball, and lo, the audience did stare, many of them wondering, *Okay, what then? Are we all supposed to become storytellers? You've got the market cornered; there's nary a dime to be made!* Often with these TED-talk-style trends, many in the audience observed, you take the thesis to its natural end, and the impracticalities sink it, defrocking all the breathy vicissitudes: to wit, a society whose every member attends to the supreme importance (as asserted) of stories becomes functionless, or non-functioning, as each individual decamps from the onerous tasks of banking and train conducting and food prep to wax eloquent around the campfire, or wherever one is inclined to wax.

Such was the feeling in the Winslow townhome on this otherwise splendid evening.

Damgaard also roped in more personal lore, such as the *gerlaap* tree bit that he had just told to his young female companion earlier on the couch (it was fresh in his mind); also the story about his father's interminable project of digging up the yard in search of treasure (no luck); and the story about the time Damgaard rafted down the Amazon for months with only a few cans beans and a wind-up Victrola (this tale borrowed liberally from a Werner Herzog film). After a considerable period, Damgaard concluded.

"So, I ask you: What is *your* story?" Here Damgaard looked to the audience accusingly. "What stories are encoded on your DNA? Will you let others tell you what your story is, or will you be brave enough to write it yourself?"

Tepid applause, during which Damgaard spotted Joyce making a finger-cracking gesture at him and wearing an apologetic grin.

"I appreciate this award. I think it clearly demonstrates that our stories are the most valuable treasure we have, and the most precious gem we can mine; the most nourishing food we can ingest."

Candace appeared at Damgaard's side, taking his elbow

and turning him to face a sad and insufficient chair placed at center stage. There Damgaard sat holding the trophy, a smile fixed to his face. While Candace made closing remarks at the podium, Damgaard's mind drifted off. He thought, *Note to self: talk to Pilcrow, see if we can up ad rates on the podcast, in light of this award.* Nolan Pilcrow was his general manager and Producer of I AM STORY. Damgaard thought: *Note to self: Oprah collab?* He thought: *Doesn't Branson own an island or two? If I can get a cut rate on some huts, we can stretch the margins...*He thought: *Weekend Retreat Series: Stories in the Caribbean.*

Putting these brilliant ideas aside, Damgaard turned his head thoughtfully to attend, in thought and in conscious-ness, to the final words from Mrs. Winslow. But all he saw and all he heard was Muhammed Ali, bouncing in the ring, dressed in his trunks, his incredible physique on display, jab-bing out at Damgaard, saying: "I am the greatest. I am the greatest. I am the greatest."

The End

You have chosen to delay the award ceremony.

—32—

In the kitchen, Candace found her purse in the cupboard where she'd stashed it. She checked her keyring, found the key she believed went to the pantry, and tested it in the lock. It worked. She locked the room. The catering staff saw her, so she met their suspicion head-on. "Yes," she said from the center of the room. "I've locked the door on him. It's for his own safety. He's out cold. If any of you hear a disturbance, *do not* let him out. Alert Jerome or me or Joyce. Understood?"

The caterers assented, variously. *Okay. Sure. Yes, Mrs. Winslow.*

"Thank you for your discretion. Where's Jerome? Jerome!" She unlatched the swinging door, and pulled it open to meet a wall of bodies—partygoers, oh-so-hopeful hopefuls. The conversational roar that wafted into the kitchen was thunderous. Braving into this sensory tempest like an intrepid explorer into an arctic headwind, Candace drew the door shut behind her. She wove through the room wielding a polite smile as a machete. There were no seas of humanity anywhere. "Hello! Hello! You made it! Welcome." Everyone tried to arrest her, bend her ear. Would the ceremony start soon, they all wanted to know. "Mrs. Winslow," they said. "Mrs. Winslow." "Excuse me," she pleaded. "I'm sorry. Urgent business... Patience, please. Thank you. Pardon."

She found Jerome in a tense-looking conference with Joyce, his arm draped on the fireplace mantel. They looked like a couple of 17-year-olds at the drive-thru after a sock-hop. Pulling up on them was like getting tossed by a wave onto a small beach. The shelter of two confidantes in a sea of... what we're they, exactly? Less like barnacles than the rest. As much as Candace loved the foundation and believed in its purpose and mission, one did come to feel like a constant sow with all the squealing piglets hustling for a teat.

"There you are!" Candace said.

"Where you have been?" Joyce said, stepping away from Jerome. "We were looking for you."

"Looking for me? You're standing here in a huddle. Never mind, I don't have time to argue."

Joyce brought her Givenchy wristwatch up to face-level, giving everyone at it a look, really, in these tight quarters. "What about the ceremony? The natives are getting restless."

"Natives? Is that the best choice of words, Joyce?" Jerome said.

"Relax. It's a figure of speech."

"It's derogatory," Jerome sarcastically stated.

"Well, the natives will have to get *more* restless, because—Oh!" Candace pulled out her buzzing phone.

If the text message is from the already selected winner— a white male novelist—announcing he's on his way, go to page - 178 -.

If the text message is from the already selected winner— a white male novelist—saying that for reasons of political impact and societal impropriety; on the advice of his agent; and to keep from committing career suicide, he has declined to accept the award and will not be attending, go to page - 191 -.

You have chosen that the white male novelist is on his way.

—33—

"Thank god! He's on the way! All right, let's do this," Candace said. "Here we go. Attic first."

Weaving in reverse. Parting parties with a wedge-like hand proffered like the splitting head of a maul, like a travelling karate chop. Pardon, pardon. Thank you. The anticipatory eyes, so multi-hued, expectant, and some eyes obsequious even at this late moment. Too late to sway the decision, surely, but worth a grin. What isn't worth a grin, when a grin costs so little?

Jerome went to the attic; the two women guarded the stairs. He emerged like a boy sent in a church to steal the communion chalice.

"Come on! Come on!" Candace barked from the bottom of the stairs.

"Do you want me to drop it?" Jerome snapped.

They went to the banquet room, still closed off to the parlor, entering from the kitchen. Candace stood before the podium, and Jerome and Joyce manned the French doors leading to the parlor. Curtains over the doors kept the candidates from reacting too excitedly. Otherwise, it might have been like one of those photos of Black Friday shoppers—faces against the glass, clamoring. Jerome paused with his hands on the doorknobs, turned back to Mrs. Winslow, who issued the confirming nod.

"Come on in, everyone," Joyce said, taking a sentinel's post at one side, waving everyone in with a regal fluidity of her arm, like a princess in a processional through Hyde Park. Jerome took the other post, crossed his hands at his waists, smiling and said, "Welcome. Time for the big show." He felt like a funeral director—once they were in, he'd go leap in the casket.

Buffalo stampeding across the South Dakota badlands. The wildebeest on the African savannah. So the guest-candidates for the 2018 FAIR award rampaged into the rows of chairs arranged in Mrs. Winslow's opulent townhome, dropping their asses into seats as if music would stop any moment, eliminating them from the game.

Lenore Happybones, Cassandra Mande, Evonne Sorenstam-Finch, Juan Ramirez, and several others sat in the front row. Santos Gougoutris, Petra Barnhouse, Andrew Knuthe, and several others sat in the second row. Johanna Sturludóttir, Johan Damgaard, Damgaard's young female companion, and several others sat in the third row. Avi Sobol, George Opfell, and several others sat in the fourth row. Gabrielle Rauch, J. Pak, and Charlie S. sat in the fourth row. Lamond P. Jackson, Merrill Roselli, Christine Wong, and Hermann Donskoy sat in the fifth row. Joseph Hector Depace, Balooja Inamdar, and several others sat in the sixth row, with Darla Emmenberg parked at the row's end. The architects Charles Knott and Boris Czecknik, along with several others, stood at the back. Joyce Winslow sat in a chair beside and just behind the podium. Dozens of others filled in the gaps and other chairs, clutching, in spirit, their plights, injustices, and iniquities, the precious transgressions they had endured.

As the guest settled, Candace's phone buzzed. She slipped it from her pocket for a glance. *Moments away.* "Oh, thank god," she said. She caught Joyce's eye and gave an excited thumbs up that could only mean one thing. The same to Ardizzone, who made a visible exhalation.

"Ladies and gentlemen," Candace said at the podium. "Thank you so much for your patience this evening. How wonderful to see you all here for this momentous occasion."

A reverential hush inflated the room, pressing outwards on its walls, depressurizing its center. Candace reached under the podium and produced a sealed envelope.

"Twenty-eighteen has been a hell of year."

Agreeable chuckling—a dispersal of anticipatory tension.

"And selecting our award recipient was not an easy process. It never is. We, the foundation staff, work with the advisory board, from a pool of 300-plus candidates and applicants. And I want you all to know, the so-called 'process of elimination' doesn't apply here. No one is eliminated. The foundation is not in the business of eliminating anyone. In fact, we *can't* do that. We cannot eliminate you. All of you will go on, continuing to be strong and valiant and determined and worthy, as you all are. The award recognizes one; but we are all one. At this time, on this point, I'd like to quote—"

Just then thunderous shattering of glass shook the room, followed by the sound of a heavy thud as of a body hitting a parquet floor topped by an authentic Persian rug. Everyone squealed and screeched and roared in terror. Ardizzone was right there at the door.

"It's Mr. Leyner!" he said.

"I'm in!" came a sturdy male voice from the parlor.

"Ladies and gentlemen," Candace said, tearing open the envelope, "our 2018 FAIR award recipient, Mr. Mark Leyner!"

In strode a man of 60, reasonably fit though perhaps bearing the physique of one who spends too much time in a chair; dressed in maroon Barbara Napoli jeans, a slim-fit Paisley dress shirt by Eton, and original Air Jordans (not the reboots); shaking glass shards and other debris from his hair, brushing detritus from his clothing.

"Fillmore!" Candace barked, off-mic, to Hollis Fillmore, in the front row, waving him up.

Back on mic, as Mr. Leyner walked to the front of the room, waving at the bewildered audience, Candace spoke: "Mr. Leyner is the author of the novels *The Tetherballs of Bougainville*, and others. It is primarily for his novel *The Sugar-Frosted Nutsack* that we recognize him today. TSFN, as it is known, is a work which elevates the working class hero Ike Karton, an unemployed white male butcher in New Jersey. Mr. Leyner has also endured illness recently, and thankfully, prevailed."

Applause ranging around 88 degrees Fahrenheit, in other words far from boiling.

"Ladies and Gentlemen, to present the award, last year's recipient, Hollis Fillmore!"

Leyner reached the front of the room, and Fillmore handed him the trophy and stepped backwards—there was no limelight, but out of the proverbial limelight. Leyner endearingly studied the trophy's features, read its engraving, regarded the triumphant, vaguely seraphic figure atop it holding the wreath, and smiled in wonderment. Throughout, the audience applauded.

"Ladies and gentlemen, our 2018 FAIR award winner, Mark Leyner!"

The applause strengthened as Candace stepped back from the podium and gestured for Leyner to take it. He did.

"Wow. Thank you," Mark Leyner said. Diminishing applause. "Thank you." The obligatory fussing with the microphone's height. Silence. "Wow, I'm really.... I wasn't expecting this. I want to thank the foundation, Mrs. Winslow, Joyce, and all the staff."

He set the trophy atop the podium and grasped its sides, the default pose of the sage novelist. "You know, it's an unprecedented time in America, a frightening time, a surreal time. Things are happening that should really only happen in novels by people like myself, who some call satirists. It's to the point that I feel my job security is threatened. I really can't think of things more absurd than what I read in the news every morning."

Subdued laughter.

"But seriously, folks, this award is wonderful." This Leyner said in the practiced obsequiousness of a man who has been giving readings and lectures, to either book lovers or medical professionals, for his entire career. A man who knows the strategic value of flattery. "I remember the meeting I was having with my agent when I learned I had been nominated for the 2018 FAIR award. My agent and I were in his 22nd Street office, cutting a savage swath through a laundry list of obligatory topics. How to minimize the tax burden on my considerable royalty income. Which venues to read at, which literary magazines to grant interviews to, et cetera. My agent told me that I'd been nominated for an award with the Foundation for the Advancement of Inclusivity and Recognition. I thought, That's odd."

"Certainly I'd noticed a movement afoot in multicultural literature. Starting in the late eighties, with books like *The Color Purple*. Not that there weren't writers of color before that. There were. Many. And important writers. Ralph Ellison. Zora Neale Hurston. Writers I admire and enjoy and who are important to the American canon of contemporary literature. But the early nineties was a time when I was active and closely involved with the publishing world, in particular with what was known then as the Big 6 (later, the Big 5). This was a time when we started to see an broadening of the cultural perspective. Readers had been reading for decades from the points of view of white male narrators, following the adventures of white male protagonists, whether heroes or antiheroes. Think Shakespeare to Dickens to William James to Hemmingway to Updike, and tens of thousands in between. In the literary orchestra, the white male had been seated in the first chair of every section, whether novelist, poet, dramatist, essayist. De facto, so it seemed. Again, many shining examples otherwise—Langston Hughes, August Wilson, Toni Morrison. Thankfully. Yet—and we know this now, this is not new information for you all especially, I'm simply creating context—the late nineties and aughts saw a further expansion of literature's cultural purview: Rushdie, Arundati Roy, Orhan Pamuk, Bolano, Khaled Hosseini. And now I elide a great many names and cultures who have been welcomed into the family of world literature and American literature in the intervening years, leading up to our present year, when a look at the new releases table is no longer like peering into a microscope aimed at a slide of homogenous white cells. Say, skin cells, for example. Now the new releases table is noticeably absent of John Irvings and David Foster Wallaces and Johnathan Franzens, and so on. Not that it's totally devoid of white males. But there are far fewer. Mr. Philip Roth has left this world. James Salter as well. Reading author names on the new release table more often than not requires some phonetic trial-and-error. Which is marvelous. Truly. Don't mistake my tone for anything but sincerity."

"And so what was I, Mark Leyner, a white male, doing with a nomination for an award about inclusivity? In my work, I've made infrequent reference to race, and with its regular inclusion of brand names and celebrities, my work appears to champion, if it champions anything, the grotesqueries of American consumer and celebrity culture, the nauseating and regretful preponderance of which we can credit, to some extent, to white males who conceived of the industries that dominate our landscape and the white males served by the gross excess of products and consumption. My novel *The Sugar Frosted Nutsack* in particular, with its hero Ike Karton, a wife-beater-wearing New Jersey Italian-American, offers little in the way of earnest tribute to the wonders of the multi-multi-ethnic mecca just across the waters of the Hudson from Ike's turf—meaning, New York City, duh. So. Had the publishing world and the literati whose tastes and thinking are guided by its output come full circle? Had the *entire* multi-national, racial gamut been run? Had all the valuable and previously neglected stories from around the world been gobbled up and spit out so that now what we had was a truly, authentically multi-hued flow of artist works representing all possible nations and ethnicities, exposing and embracing the views of every culture that had ever lived? The Albanian genocide? Had that been covered? What about those patches of Somali immigrants in frigid Minneapolis? Australian aboriginals trying to get into Adelaide community college and find equality and love? It seemed improbable that the world's supply of interesting subcultures and obscure transnational mixes had been exhausted. Why, then, was attention being turned to me, a white male American with Italian roots, when a look at the timeline of literature's cultural foci (vis-à-vis ethnicity of protagonists, narrators, authors) forecast that the attention should not really return to me and my ilk until approximately the year 2240, perhaps beyond. To find the answer, I had my agent contact the man who nominated me."

Leyner drank from a glass of water. The audience was motionless in disbelief and confounding agitation, many of them harboring thoughts of running forward to the podium and conducting a FAIR-award equivalent to Kanye West's raid on the mic during Taylor Swift's acceptance speech at the 2009 MTV Video Music Awards show.

"That man, I was told, was Paul Treeley. Naturally, I googled him. An obscure writer. Lives up in the Hudson Valley in a remote part of the Western Catskills. Founder of a collective called Synthetic Prophetic, about which little is known. Apparently an old-school kind of aesthetic clique, such as those formed by the Dadaists and the Algonquin Roundtable. This struck me as potentially problematic, as such outfits are usually congealed around some perceived malignancy. Yet their perceptions are not always so clear nor their intentions free from bias. I entered into conversation with Treeley cautiously."

"Shortly, we arranged for a video conference. Now, many of you may be wondering, and so I'll tell you—Treeley's mother comes from Trinidad, and his father is French-Canadian. Just by way of curiosity. That's settled. He is light-browned skinned with curly black hair—what is clearly regarded as the hair of a black man. It is the kind of black man's hair that is styled in taut ringlets that stand up from the scalp—that is, black hair that seems to be particularly appealing to the curators of stock photographs of the type that get placed in college brochures and on billboards beside America's highways. Anyway, in our discussion Treeley revealed to me that the driving ethos of his collective, Synthetic Prophetic, is the restoration of the literary arts to precisely that which they are named, the *literary* arts. As opposed to what? you might say. This was my question as well."

Deeply restless sounds of all manner of clothing ruffling, fingernails being picked, toes being tapped, sock elastic being snapped.

"As opposed to a kind of popularity contest in a game of identity politics. Mr. Treeley's feelings on the matter is that while multicultural literature is a great thing, what he calls 'identity politics' has become the driving force behind the literature vis-à-vis literature sales: that is, the reason writers are writing, the reason the people in publishing are publishing what they are publishing. He and his small band of acolytes would prefer that literature attend more closely to matters of artistic form and expression. On the one hand, this is nothing very complicated: his wish is that works be judged on the merit of those features of literary arts as described in English Language Arts textbooks for ninth through twelfth graders. Poems for their use of imagery, assonance, dissonance, allusion, onomatopoeia, etc. Novels for their themes, characterization, description, voice, tone, diction, imagery, etc. Treeley's aesthetic—his idealism—is in this sense, classical."

"But, he also yearns to see the rise of literary artists who grow the novel in directions that evolve it as a species, so to speak. The problem, Treeley told me, is that—well, actually, I should clarify, Treeley says it's not a *problem*, per se, it's simply his preference and the preference of those in his collective. And so the *preference*, as he sees it, is that novels and short stories, poems, plays, and other prose works do not very much presently act as expressions of the capabilities of the form itself. They are not exemplars, pushing boundaries so to speak, and existing in relationship to previous works in the sphere of literature. What he have now, Treeley says, instead, is an entire form, the novel in particular, mired in one ideation, not growing, not advancing. Again and again we see realist novels detailing a protagonists' struggles for freedom and individuation, escape from oppressive governments, escaping from strict religious and cultural norms, not always but often into the supposedly welcome arms of America, Where Results Vary. Hey, maybe that should be on the dollar bill rather than *E plurubus enum*. An unofficial slogan: America, where results vary. Anyway, on the sentence level, Treeley contends, novels are aren't always composed with much originality or verve for linguistic exuberance. They are plainly told, and rather droll."

"Says Treeley. Believe me, I never would have come here tonight to serve as a mouthpiece for some racist piece of shit. I don't believe Mr. Treeley is a racist piece of shit. If he's a purist of any kind, it's on an artistic level. That is, he's an aesthete. Which may mean trite and pretentious. But not necessarily. I really don't know him well at all. But the accusation we often can, and often do, levy at such individuals is a charge of offensive superiority."

"But to summarize his views a little further, as they connect to my nomination: Novels, Treeley asserted to me in a jittery, coffee-fueled rant via frequently-cutting-out video conference (where he lives, only satellite internet is available), ... novels are presently resting on their proverbial haunches and doing what novels have always done. At the thematic level, they bear similarities to each other. They don't often seek to use language in an original way, but often employ stock phrases and even stock feelings—stock feelings of alienation, craving for restoration of dignity, fulfillment of healthy national identify, reconciliation of national identity conflicts vis-à-vis immigration status and the oddities of American culture. All of this Treeley regards as *kind of Okay*—the works are strong and offer moving accounts that reach people and probably widen people's views and expand knowledge. But as art works, they do not 'move the ball.'"

"Now, I asked Treeley right away whether his position wasn't simply a case of sour grapes. It struck me that his geographic remoteness might parallel an aesthetic remoteness. That is, he seemed like someone who lived on the outskirts of mainstream acceptance. From what he explained to me about his past, I understood he had labored for a nearly a lifetime to cultivate his craft, refine his art, but he had not seen his name in a catalog of the Big 5, or ever graced the New York Times best-seller list. So was his stance a bitterly affronted one? To this question, he answered, 'Only God knows.'"

"As right or wrong as Treeley's viewpoint may be, it does offer a foundation for the reasons he nominated me for the 2018 FAIR award, and I do feel compelled to share with you those precise reasons. To that end, I'd like to read a portion of the nominating essay Treeley submitted to the Foundation and which I asked him to provide to me. This will enable me to disown, to some extent, the onus of receiving the award. And I have to say, when a fringe figure such as this speaks admiringly of your work, it can be a disquieting feeling. This was the first and only time I felt any kinship with J.D. Salinger; I imagined this is what he felt like when he learned that Mark David Chapman was carrying a copy of *Catcher in the Rye*."

Wary muttering veering close to an eruption.

"Chapman of course was John Lennon's assassin. Ahem. And here I quote. Mark Leyner's novel *The Sugar-Frosted Nutsack*, also known as TSFN, performs the ultimate act of inclusivity. On page 1, a trio of cheerleaders in a terrarium wears t-shirts saying "I Don't Do White Dudes." This necessary disclaimer serves to align the work with the feelings of contemporary readers: book buyers do not currently *do* white dudes either. This is a Trojan horse, of sorts, however. No sooner does TSFN refute the appeal of white males than it elevates a white male protagonist, Ike Karton, an unemployed butcher, to heroic status through sheer audacity of style, through linguistic wizardry, vast cultural scope, far-reaching and arcane but salient references (cultural, musical, filmic, historical), scalpel-like insertions of lacerating prose, etc."

"Slipping through the publishing world's aesthetic gates, so to speak, TSFN shines the proverbial artistic mirror on the current ethos of American elite liberal society. Most interestingly, TFSN, traces a history of the universe that characterizes the Gods who formed it (the universe) as total assholes. And here I quote, strangely, from my own work, p. 21-22:"

"Gods are self-important. They tend to have ADD. They love to fuck with your head. Because they're immortal, they tend to be late all the time. And because they're omnipotent, they usually exhibit a complete lack of empathy. They are narcissistic and furiously self-absorbed. If they want to have sex with you, it doesn't really matter to them how you're feeling or what you're going through."

"That sounds exactly like the type of behavior that would be vehemently condemned in any present-day professional or social arena. People who do *anything* with someone *without caring how they feel* are currently regarded basically as criminals, unfit for society. Having sex with them would be the ultimate act of disrespect (or 'dissing'). And this is how our gods behave. In other words, TSFN radically supposes that if man is made in God's image, then man is not inherently empathic at all, which suggests that our current institutions are pressing on us behavioral requirements that are a perversion of unnatural drives. Which sounds shockingly like support of racist redneck BS that labels any call for equal rights as 'political correctness.' But that's not what Leyner's work supports.'

"In an age when people seem to aspire to a kind of perfect expression of tolerance and understanding for other cultures, creating a kind of Vlade-Divac-like flopping culture of outrage when any marginalized person is spoken of in a manner anything but utterly reverent... TSFN lays out, in grotesque and irrefutable detail, a scenario in which the Gods who created our universe would never have been capable of such compassion, inclusion, etc., and so we are begged to consider the potential folly of today's cultural climate and its demands on literature."

"But the genius of TSFN is that throughout the work that presents such an argument, Leyner continues to beguile readers with action and characterizations that align with the multi-cultural drive in the publishing industry. For example, the character Mi-Hyun, a 29-year-old florist shop employee. Mi-Hyun (obviously Asian-American) is physically enlarged by the god Bosco Hifikepunye to the height of 50 feet, symbolically empowering her as a minority figure on the American landscape. She even inserts the corpses of Vladimir Lenin and the cryogenically preserved head of American baseballer Ted Williams into her ass—the kind of treatment of white dudes that reading audiences can't get enough of right now. But in the case of TSFN, it's all in the service of a greater cause: the exploration of the complex hero, Ike Karton, a man whose lewd Italian breadcrumb mandala is eaten by sparrows—nature symbolically debasing his Italian-American heritage, because it is not as ethnic as that of others."

"In fact—" and here I'm skipping ahead, "In choosing the New Jersey Caucasian Ike Karton as its protagonist, TSFN performs the ultimate gesture of inclusivity and recognition by painting a deeply humanizing portrait of the single most vilified figure on the present-day American landscape: the male white. The white male is the only figure on the American cultural landscape presently more repugnant than the rich white male in power. Even serial killers are more admired—for at least their heinous acts are understood to be some profound derangement or psychosis by which they are helplessly compelled to kill. Ike Karton is not deranged; he's a guy who sensibly puzzles aloud like the rest of us about what he should have for breakfast, when he doesn't feel like something "*breakfasty*." Yet with his declaration 'I may have to kill somebody or fuck someone today, but if I do, I'm doing it for you guys [his wife and daughter]" Ike epitomizes the kind of power-by-force, the entitlement to power, the senseless use of violence, and the sexual profligacy that is so abhorrent today, and which countless Americans spend their time speaking out against (exclusively in others—never themselves) online."

"For this profound accomplishment and its contribution to the arts, I hereby nominated the author of TSFN, Mark Leyner, for the 2018 FAIR award. Signed, Paul Treeley."

"So there you have it."

The sound of extreme ire being physically repressed in the bodies of dozens and dozens of people: the sound of teeth grinding, of optic blood vessels popping, of knuckles cracking as fists are clenched.

"I gratefully but with some trepidation accept this award. The generous cash prize comes at a timely juncture, as I'm presently redecorating my basement man cave. I've always wanted an original Degas sketch of a ballerina. They're just so beautiful, and I think even a small one would look great behind the Tiki bar. Thank you! *Buenos noches!*"

Leyner left the room, with the trophy in his arms, crossed into the empty parlor, mounted the sash of the broken window through which he'd entered, took hold of the vinyl rope he'd swung in on, and was whisked away as the helicopter it was attached to alit from the roof of the Winslow townhome.

The End

You have chosen that the white male novelist declines to accept the FAIR Award, on the advice of his agent.

—34—

"Oh, shit," Candace said.

"What?" Joyce asked.

"He's not—" The phone continued to buzz.

"Don't even," Jerome said.

Candace threw her head back in despair. Then read the texts, conspiratorially: "...'On the advice of my agent, I regretfully *cannot accept* the award. ... In 2018, white male writers are basically somewhere above the paramecium and just below—' What is that word?"

She showed the phone to Jerome.

"Eukaryotes?"

"...'Eukaryotes when it comes to public opinion.' What is he talking about?"

"He used to be a doctor," Joyce clarified, despairingly.

"God damnit." Candace, skimmed on, as new texts arrived: "...'would cause too much of an uproar... intolerant, hypocritical masses...' et cetera, et cetera. Well fuck me with a chainsaw!"

"What do we do now?" Jerome asked, a panicked look on his face.

Joyce was clutching her temples as if fending off a migraine.

Candace stuffed the phone in her cardigan pocket and looked around. "Okay, composure. Let's reconnoitrer in the kitchen."

Weaving in reverse. Parting parties with a wedge-like hand proffered like the splitting head of a maul, like a travelling karate chop. Pardon, pardon. Thank you. The anticipatory eyes, so multi-hued, expectant, and some eyes obsequious even at this late moment. Too late to sway the decision, surely, but worth a grin. What isn't worth a grin, when a grin costs so little?

Again, everyone tried to arrest her, bend her ear—and Joyce's and Jerome's ears as well. The ceremony, was it starting soon, they all wanted to know. "Mrs. Winslow," they said. "Mrs. Winslow. Excuse me, Joyce, Joyce." Each of them uttering placating vagaries—"Very shortly...Patience, patience....Finishing touches...Moments away...Thank you, thank you"—they all reached the kitchen door as if in a processional conga line, minus the hands on hips (except for Jerome's hands imaginarily on Joyce's hips).

Candace, leading the pack, knocked on the bolted kitchen door. "Candace here," she sang into the crack. The door immediately opened. They charged in, Candace saying, "Jesus H. Christ on a popsicle stick, what kind of novelist—"

A scream from Joyce, cut short.

Candace and Jerome spun around to see Joyce detained in a half-nelson by Monti Taylor, one hand over her mouth, the other wielding a kitchen knife at her throat.

"Well, this day just keeps getting worse and worse!" Candace said.

"Don't move," Taylor said. "I *will* splay her pretty throat like a... like a..."

"Filet?" Jerome offered.

"Phones," Taylor said. "Both of you. In that bin."

"Fuck me, Monti, this is the new iPhone!" Candace said.

"I need mine for work," Jerome pleaded.

"Motherfuckers, I'm not joking! In the bin!" Taylor gestured at the trash can.

Candace and Jerome pitched theirs. "Where's yours?" Taylor said, groping up and down Joyce's dress.

"Watch it there, handsy," Candace said. "That's my daughter."

Taylor located a pocket, drew Joyce's phone out and tossed it in the trash.

"How did you get out even?" Jerome asked.

"A couple of lovebirds came looking for a place to make out," Taylor said. Candace and Jerome looked at each other, wondering who. "You'll have plenty of time to catch up with them. Come on—in the pantry." With the knife he, *swish swish*, motioned them across the room.

"Monti, what's gotten into you?" Candace said, crossing the room. "What would your father-in-law say to this?"

"You must have missed a tennis match, Mrs. Winslow. Me and Gail are divorced. I don't work for Hanwell anymore."

"Lucky you. Opening your own shop? I'd be happy to give up Hanwell Merc for somewhere with better prices."

"Can the sycophancy!"

He took his hand off Joyce's mouth to fetch the pantry key from his pocket—Joyce screamed. He clamped it shut again.

"Nice try, babe," Jerome said.

"Babe?" Candace snapped, glaring at Jerome.

"Did I say babe? I meant, uh, Gabe! I should text Gabe."

"ur mop exxing ae!" Joyce yelled, thoroughly muted.

Taylor fumbled in the lock, kicked the door wide, wielding the knife.

"Mrs. Winslow, I can explain," Evonne Sorenstam-Finch said. She and Juan Ramirez were in there.

"What are *you two* doing?" Candace said.

"I thought it was a restroom?" Evonne said, unconvincingly.

Taylor laughed. "Ha ha. They crashed in here, lips locked. She was groping in Juan's trousers," Taylor laughed sinisterly.

"Oh, brother," Candace said.

"*Lo siento*," Ramirez said, eyes lowered in shame.

Tara Voss and Michael Dulka got up off the floor at the back of the pantry.

"He forced us all in here," Dulka said.

"We tried to stop him," Voss said.

"All right, all of you, in there. Let's go." Taylor waved the knife in little flicky, flicky motions. Candace and Joyce stepped in.

"Are you okay?" Candace said to Tara and Michael.

Jerome lingered in the doorway.

"Move it, pretty boy," Taylor said. "Do as the knife says." He jabbed it in Jerome's back.

"Watch the suit!" Jerome proceeded warily.

"Thaaat's it." Closing the door to just a crack, Taylor pressed his face in the crevice. "There's plenty of rice to eat. But you know what happens to birds when their bellies fill up with rice?" He laughed maniacally, slammed the door shut, while making a world-class Hollywood explosion type sound, complete with puffed cheeks flapping.

"What happens?" Jerome said.

"Si, what happens?" Ramirez said.

"They explode," Tara Voss said drearily, slumping back to the floor.

—35—

Monti, the kitchen to himself, raided the wine rack, opting for a Penfold's reserve Shiraz (an Australian vintner). He rummaged violently through drawers, eventually locating a corkscrew. He found himself whistling AC/DC's "Back in Black." No wine goblets in sight, but Pilsner glasses, so he poured a tall one. Then feeling completely despicable already, he fished the phones from the trash, identified Joyce's, and pulled up a stool to the kitchen island, imbibing the Shiraz (stonkin'), and scrolling through Joyce's camera roll for provocative selfies. Nothing risqué, just woman-about-town stuff—along the waterfront, theater, dining on a boat. "Classy," Monti said. He opened up Spotify and got some AC/DC going, turned it up, set the phone down.

"We hear you out there!" Ramirez yelled.

"You're in big trouble, Hanwell!" hollered Jerome.

"It's Taylor!" Monti replied. "Monti Taylor! I told you, divorced that cow." He remembered his weed vaporizer in his jacket pocket, got it out, powered it up, and started taking giant draws, one after the other, coughing violently, doubled over, eyes watering, soothing his throat with vino. AC/DC's one ballad, "Ride On," came on. No, no, no, he skipped ahead. The sinister guitar licks of "Hell's Bells" started up.

"That's more like it," Monti said. He shuffled around the kitchen bobbing his head.

Out in the parlor, guests continued to arrive. The Winslows were indisposed, it seemed, so whoever stood closest to the door served as impromptu host or hostess, welcoming newcomers. Ronald Worthington, of Omaha, Nebraska, arrived. His nine-year-old son, Ronald Jr., black like Ronald and armed with a water pistol, had been fatally shot by police. Abagail Dahl arrived—relieved of duty by her employer, a medium-sized insurance agency in Asheville, NC, when it was discovered that she identified as a sexual submissive, and had willingly (open to interpretation) entered into a BDSM relationship with her boss, a white man who happened to identify as a "dom," to use the lingo. In other words, she was victimized by being unfairly fired after being falsely identified as a victim of a sexual predator. (The boss was fired too—their lawsuit thrown out of court).

The Winslow townhome was getting noisy and hot. People began to feel that the amount of personal space available to them was noticeably insufficient. The distance from one person's eyes to another's as they spoke, visiting, was for some, not great enough to allow for focusing—older people, mostly, people who held medicine bottles at arm's length under a lamp in order to read the dosage directions. Some guests noticed that they could smell a person's breath, they were standing so close—or their perfume or cologne, or, because of the growing warmth of so many bodies, their underarms. Yet, rather than discomfort, everyone grew in animation and excitement, a pleasant and gratifying sense of cohesion, belonging, and unity. What a great number of excellent people there were! How marvelous to have such a diverse body in attendance—all the wonderful faces and manners of dress, the backgrounds represented. Southerners, northerners, east-coasters, west-coasters. There was a Danish storyteller, and a Korean political dissident—maybe even a French chanteuse!

"It's terrible what's happening with these guns, these blowdarts, everything," said Santos Gougoutris. "Whatever happened to turning the other cheek? Have these guys heard of Matthew five thirty-nine?"

"But it's not every plane, have you noticed that?" said Chief S., a believer in the conspiracy theory that chemtrails from government aircraft had been dropping brainwashing chemicals on the American populace since the Truman era. "747, 737, DC-10, DC-9, these commercial planes, you see them all the time—no trails. When you see the trails, they're way high in the sky, so you can't read anything on the plane.

Not even drones can get a photograph of them."

Darla Emmenberg was talking to Lamond P. Jackson, and incredibly nervous about it—about him, a very impressive figure. "I watched all four seasons of Dead Ringers in, like, a weekend. And then Morgue Bandits I couldn't get into, I watched, like, some of Season 1, the main guy was cool, but it just didn't grab me, but Corpse Parade was awesome, have you seen that, it's on Hulu, it's about this guy who keeps dreaming that he's dead, but then he wakes up one day, and everyone *else* is dead and he has to figure out why..."

"Galveston and the islands," George Opfell said. "Wildlife. But landscapes too. For a time there, I was driving out to west Texas. The ranchland and everything is very scenic, as you can imagine. But I've got this neuropathy in my foot, so driving is a pain..."

"Not every Muslim woman does," said Balooja Inamdar. "I personally stopped wearing the hijab about ten years ago. At a certain age, you feel you are not tempting men or causing corruption in their minds." She laughed, cueing the Americans that the religion they assumed everyone who practiced an extremist form of, was actually taken somewhat lightly by some of its adherents, just as you find with some American Christians. "Tell me," she said, "changing the subject. I hear this term 'cafeteria Catholic.' Can you tell me what it means?"

"What do you think?" Lenore Happybones said. "Honey, you asked! No, they're gone! Long gone! Did you know there's such a thing as fake testicles? Testicular implants. For men who lose one to cancer or anything else. Nothing more emasculating than the sight of a deflated sack! Can you image? Just put an avocado pit in there. Or bigger—a baseball, why not?" She was somewhat drunk. "Actually, a nurse asked me on the operating table if I was getting implants. She didn't know. They just have a patient on a gurney with an order to shave and iodine swab. Maybe later they think I'm going to upgrade. Well, because they do the other reconstruction in stages. So to them, there's no difference. I just said, No. I couldn't say anything sassy, I was already going under, Dilaudid or something killer."

People began to speculate about the delay.

"...must have been an incident of some kind," Gabrielle Rauch said. "They passed through a while ago. Haven't seen them since..."

Andrew Knuthe was backed into a corner, his arm up against the cool glass of a window looking onto Washington Avenue. He was happy to be talking to Petra Barnhouse about their mutual states of unplanned widowhood and widowerhood; about the pleasures of hunting, the silent woods at dawn; how native Americans put every part of the hunted elk to use; and he was enjoying listening to Petra, this diminutive but powerful woman, about acclimating the body to a meat-free diet, good sources of protein, the variety of lentil-pastas and chickpea-pastas available on the market these days; about the relative ease of a drive from Snow Shoe, Pennsylvania, to Tulsa, Oklahoma. Oh, yeah, easy. Probably do it in a day, Knuthe agreed. Knuthe had said he'd be interested in seeing Barnhouse's well water firsthand, and she had said she wanted to see him in the classroom, teaching in action. There was an electric energy, some kind of symbiotic thing that was increasing blood flow to their hearts. They both felt inflated—rising, increasingly lighter. Knuthe was growing more handsome. The degree of Barnhouse's resilience and fortitude was dawning on Knuthe, to have handled what she'd experience that way and made of herself what she had. Her smile warming, her eyes growing greener, more flirtatious.

Joseph Hector Depace happened to be near the front door when it opened.

"Sorry we're late," said Lewis Bradley-Brown, a district manager of Staples, the office supply store, a former marathoner, girls' soccer coach, and victim of medical malpractice. Bradley Brown was scheduled for the ultra-sound destruction of some kidney stones, but left-turn, right-turn, 3A, 3B, the doctor came in and amputated his right leg below the knee. Bradley-Brown had a prosthesis now, the cool springy kind, concealed behind his dress slacks. He was back to marathoning and coaching. There'd been much feel-good coverage on the local news network and in the papers, (Huntsville, Alabama) about his ordeal, and in the end a hefty malpractice settlement, so no one believed he was a top contender for the FAIR award, having been amply compensated and widely recognized already. But here he was, squeezing into the fete, in full swing.

"Did it start at nine?" Bradley-Brown asked.

"No, like, 6 or 7, I think," Depace said. "We had dinner already. It was very good. But you didn't miss the ceremony yet."

"Marvelous. I'll just have a cocktail." Bradley-Brown angled into the crowd.

At one point, Christine Wong started yelling to no one in particular, "What the hell is going on? Are they going to give out the award, or what? Where are the Winslows?"

No one answered her directly. People looked sheepishly away. Rosalind Duffy, standing nearby said, vaguely in Wong's direction, without meeting her eyes, "They're probably setting up right now. Just remember, patience is a virtue."

At that moment, the door opened, and Claire Raney came in, her emotional support dog, Nicknack, a King Charles Spaniel, on a leash at her side.

"Are we just going to keep letting people in all night?" Wong cried.

"Excuse me?" Claire Raney said. "I have an invitation. I'm a guest-candidate just like you."

"Yeah, Christine," Merrill Roselli said, seeming to basically fly, aeronautically, across the room the very moment this triggering and disrespecting situation arose. "She has a right to be here. What's your name?"

"Claire," Claire Raney said.

"Claire has a right to be here, Christine. Welcome, Claire. I'm sorry, some of us are just a little on edge. Come in, won't you? Come in. I'm Merrill."

Wong issued a blunt, terse apology and barreled away, through the crowd to the other side of the room.

And so the fete continued, many people now offering placating aphorisms and nervous looks about the room as if trying to visibly gauge growing tensions, the consensus being that despite the agonizing anticipation, despite the confusion about the failure of the ceremony to commence, despite the lack of explanation or announcement from the Winslows about the programming time snafu, despite the mounting feeling of ominousness, the fearful suspicions arising in some that something had gone wrong behind the scenes, despite all this, the consensus was that all would be revealed, patience pays, and one must not rock the boat. The concomitant forces of conformity and propriety that kept everyone (accept for Wong's outburst) from speaking up or acting out were very strong. And above all, as many remarked, people were still arriving.

"Why are they coming at this late an hour?" Hermann Donskoy asked.

"Yah, if the presentation was on time, these people would have missed it," said Johan Damgaard.

"It doesn't matter," said Avi Sobol. "The fact is, they are arriving. When the Jews left Rephidim and journeyed to the desert of Sinai, they were of every sect, and they camped beside the mountain as 'one people with one heart.' So it should be today."

Denise Underhill asked Cassandra Mande, "Was there a miscount, a miscalculation? Were too many people invited?"

"Too many people? No, definitely not." Mande said.

Johanna Sturludóttir was there as well. "Everyone invited is a qualified candidate, no question. Anyone who walks through that door could be the winner."

"People, we cannot turn anyone away," said Jeong-Hwa Pak. "That's tantamount to persecution! Besides, imagine we refuse someone, only to find out they are the winner. Shame on us."

"What would Jesus do?" Santos Gougoutris said. "That's a no-brainer!

George Opfell said, "The moment we turn someone away, we become just like *them.*"

Who George meant exactly was not clear. Different ideas of *them* occurred in the minds of different people. The one percent. The unenlightened. The Turks. Slave-owners. People historically gone in time, who were not as evolved as *us*. Bigots. Oil companies executives. Incompetent doctors who saw off your leg without so much as a blinking an eye. Directors of ballet troupes who only liked tiny tits. The NRA.

The fete resumed in a spirit of collective rebellion, or determined adhesion to principle anyway. As a group, united, they were rebuking the mores and wrong-thinking of their enemies; acting on clear principles, they were untangling the hypocrisies of the world's problem-causers. They continued to visit, savoring the virtuousness of their big, open hearts, of their unjudging eyes, reflecting to each other the correctness of their jurisprudence. They felt satisfaction at the multifarious sources of their aligning good will—coming from the Koran, the Torah, the Christian bible, the teachings of Buddha, the Universal Life Church, secular humanitarianism, scientific eco-warriorism. Many hairs stood on many ends. The refreshing sweat of the chartable dewed upon many hues of skin.

"Scoot over, please," Gabrielle Rauch said to Johanna Sturludóttir.

"I'm already standing on the lamp," Sturludóttir said.

"Every inch counts," Darla Emmenberg said cheerfully. "It's for a good cause."

Still, piano music continued to play, though it was masked by the noise of conversation. Jeong-Hwa Pak, who had studied and played cello as young man, heard some passages, or detected some moods he recognized. It was Chopin. It was the Nocturne in E-flat Major, Opus 9, No. 2.

"You're not claustrophobic are you?" George Opfell said to him, trying for a joke, as he shuffled closer to Pak.

"I was just listening to the music," Pak said.

"Cheers," Opfell said, moving his wine glass an inch to clink Pak's. They both clutched their drinks at the sternum.

Hollis Fillmore was standing near the kitchen door with Wendy Friedmann, a new arrival (failed brakes in a Toyota

Camry, prosecuted for manslaughter, not her fault, re-deemed by evidence of failing parts, the testimony of astute scientists, ruling overturned on appeal).

"I can hear music in there," Fillmore said. "Rock music." His ear was to the door.

"Oh, yes," Wendy said. "How unusual." Wendy pressed the door, testing it. "Locked," she observed.

"Then I won't be in anyone's way," Fillmore said, leaning tight against the door, to maximize space. He smiled victo-riously.

The denser the scrum became, the giddier the sense of camaraderie. People were laughing, wiping sweat from their brows.

"We're a happy bunch of sardines," Johan Damgaard said.

For many, the conception arose that the stultifying heat, the torpid staleness of the air, and the mounting feeling of physical constriction were kinds of hardship in themselves. They felt tested, and so because of their dispositions, their belief in the virtuousness of tolerance, their fortitude rose to the test, and they endured it. A kind of exhilaration swelled in their hearts. They felt noble. They imagined them-selves to be an elite delegation having specialized capabili-ties like green berets or navy SEALS. A foreboding aura of historical significance shot through the occasion, and they saw the scene of their many heads and shoulders, in their diverse costumes, pressed into the Winslow town home, as one sees a black and white photograph of Selma, AL, in a textbook. Or the '68 Democratic convention. Or any other number of catalyzing moments intoned in sepia. They had no placards, but they had their indomitable conviction. They were not recognized in the moment, but they *would be seen.*

At the same time, a perverse kind of psychological phe-nomenon began to happen in them. The pique generated by oxygen deprivation and body temperature increases, the profound feeling of accruing importance and mounting ten-sion, led each to believe that some personal transformation was imminent. When one labors for hours hiking a moun-tain, they do so because the reward of the peak awaits. There is no precedent for a grueling ascent *without* conquest; thus, given the event they were at, what climax, what summit could await them, but the reception of the award itself? Each person began to believe in the certainty that they were the destined recipient of the 2018 FAIR award. A thrilling prospect. Could it be? There was baselessness to this fact, however; but they did not want to relinquish the tantalizing anticipation of reward, and so, without realizing it, they began to speak in ways that rationalized the inevitability of their own success. Which largely meant describing reasons that others would not, could not, ascend.

"I kind of think the fracking thing has passed as an issue, don't you?"

"The mid-east crisis has gone on *so* long. The six-day war, '67. That's fifty years ago now! And it's awful. But, let's be honest, to award either side is to *take* sides. Plus Netanyahu is under investigation now for fraud..."

"This BDSM stuff—sorry, no way. Perv out on your own time. Your own dime, for that matter."

"They're private institutions, that's the thing. If they want to admit only whites, they can. Show me the law that says 8% or whatever *has to* be Asians. Harvard probably gets sick of reading a million applications from Asians."

"We're a news-saturated culture. Headlines are reality. The facts of law. The Supreme Court. The stuff of storybooks is old news. That's nice that he makes a living at it, but what he does is not *that* relevant."

"My own feeling is that we're kind settled on the Latino immigrant issue. Obviously, it's inhumane to shoot 'em down at the border. It's inhumane to separate the children and lock them up. The port of call laws are archaic. You know what I mean? God bless him, God bless them all, but I don't see like, Mr. Depace, for example, getting the award. So you have diabetes as well? Yeah, well, you can avoid that with a proper diet."

"He *is* charismatic, I'll give him that. But I read some of his articles online the other day. You shouldn't buy Happy Meals when the figurine toy is a superhero, because that's creating false expectations on males. That's real sensitive and all, but can you imagine this story in Reuters? FAIR award winner is a hyper-liberal. It looks bad. I just looks bad."

"The name says it all: *natural* disasters. They're natural. So your house was ruined in a flood? Talk to Noah. Cry him a river, pun intended. I get the idea that because it's connected to global warming, we're supposed to see it as topical, but I don't buy it."

"Fred Rogers was bullied; did you know that? Mr. Rogers. I saw it in that film about him. Fat Freddy, they called him. And he *was* a chubster, too. They showed a picture. But look what he made of himself. Maybe bullying serves a sociological purpose. I'm just sayin'."

—36—

"Red red wine make me feel so fine," Monti Taylor sang, tottering across the kitchen with a glass of Montepulciano in his hand. He had finished the Penfold's Shiraz. "You keep me rockin' all of de time." He paused, striking a pose that felt to him like dancing: one foot slightly raised, glass lofted high, head dropped. Surely Bono had struck this pose on a poster. Wine sploshed out of the glass into his hair.

"Darling, I'm pecking," he said, opening the refrigerator. "I mean puckish. Rustle me up a bit of tea, love." Morsels of rosemary pork plucked from a dish, still juicy. "Oh yeah." Gnawing, chomping. Block of fromage. He took it out—a gourmand, a man of distinction. Crusty bread. Life of Reilly.

Like other virile animal species, once fed, he wished to cavort, range as if across a veldt, conquer. "Why should I?" he said to the door that gave access onto his estate grounds. He seemed to have been provoked. But then he recalled that the grounds were unavailable due to maintenance. Installing additional croquet courts. "Let them work!" he declared. "The bastards."

He exercised his itinerant urges upon the stairs, rising above the kitchen in all its white-tiled impressiveness. Mussolini had a balcony but the records failed to prove it was superior to this one. He tried a bit of Italian, unleashed upon the thronging square. Quattro formaggio and so on. "And so, in conclusion!" The echoes of the statesman. "That's one... meatball sub!" Light years it takes to reach those at the back. "And a lemonade!" He laughed, pretending to fall off his balcony into the many loving arms.

"What this place needs is a fountain," he observed dryly, turning to the door newly discovered beside him.

His captors had mostly stopped shouting and pleading from the pantry a half hour ago, when Monti stopped answering them. But now Jerome weakly yelled, "Il Duce!

You're going down, Il Duce!"

"Everyone's a critic." Exploring further his palatial inheritance, Monti opened the door to the attic.

It was a decrepit place. Not nice at all. Dusty, unfurnished. Across the creaking floorboards to a light switch. And now the seraphim sing and the dust motes dance and stillness abounds. "The fuck?" Taylor whispered, approaching the trophy. "Alasht, they have thought to see me as I..."

He set his wine glass down and fell to the floor beside the golden spectacle, taking in his hands the tri-pillared splendor and looking tearfully upon the fit bird topping the thing, holding the crown of thorns. Or halo as the case may be. With a tilt toward himself, he kissed her breasts. Then he found the inscribed brass plate at the bottom of the trophy. The inscription read Mark Leyner, but to Monti's intoxicated eyes, it read Monti Taylor. Imagine, if you will, a filmic CGI rendering of this on screen. Very few characters would require changing to get the correct name to blur into the incorrect but tantalizing one. He gleefully lurched to his feet, trophy in hand. If only he had his jumpsuit on, they could get those photos like the Formula 1 drivers atop the pedestal. He would spray champagne on his pit crew. He moved to the window, where moonlight fell flatteringly upon him and his prize. Holding it aloft, hot tears streamed down his cheeks, and was stilled, for once, in thought and in body, though swaying. "I wanna say fuck you to everyone," Monti said, in the cadence of the esteemed tributary. He thought of Gail, as he always thought of her now, the only image of her he hadn't eradicated from his mind: topless, wrapped in the white bedsheets of a New York City hotel, beside her friend Karen and Karen's foot with the painted toenails. "To my ex, Gail: fuck you." He thought of his father, leaning under the hood of a Peugeot 504, senselessly cursing its fan belt. Why in God's name would there be a replacement Peugeot 504 fan belt anywhere near Adelaide, Australia? Such was his affliction. "To my old man, for teaching me that everything you have no control over is your own fault: fuck you as well."

—37—

A rather sallow looking white man with styled hair edged in the door and into the party. Hair teased into a kind of canopy, adding fullness, not allowed to sit or fall. Dressed in black jeans, a black t-shirt (crew neck), and wearing necklaces and jewelry holding small stones, like turquoise, and inscriptions from dead lovers. He was Phil McBroom, 61, and he had played keyboard, sang, and been chief songwriter in a new-wave band of medium repute in the early '80s. In fitness centers and oil-change waiting rooms around the country, TVs tuned to a channel in the upper reaches of most cable providers' docket—a mix of scrolling headlines, weather, ads and music videos—flashed McBroom's face daily, stroking a synthesizer, vamping at the camera, singing (lip-syncing really) his band's 1983 megahit "You For a Day." In the video he wore a white sleeveless shirt showcasing his boyish chest and arms. To some degree, McBroom still saw himself as that thin, exuberant young man, though touring, fame, and its attendant hazards had ravaged his body. Walking, he crept over the floor in evident fragility. When he saw himself in the mirror shirtless, he saw sagging breasts and gray chest hair. He maintained in his face, however, everything that the rock-n-roll attitude required: determined rebelliousness, rugged handsomeness, a deep soul, outrage at his insufficient recognition.

It was well-known, in the mid-Hudson Valley, New York, where McBroom lived, that despite the acoustic sets that he continued to play in smallish clubs both upstate and in "the city" (featuring his solo-record material and the obligatory re-hash of "You For a Day,"); and despite the fact that McBroom retained his musical verve and entertainer's panache, he was barely eking by, the chief concern being not the cost of living itself, but the cost of dying—that is, health care. He'd become a proverbial poster man for universal health care, appearing on W-AMC and WNYC radio discussion panels on the topic, organizing benefit concerts with other '80s and present-day bands, raising funds for local charities that helped with health care expenses, and so on. Stumping for liberal politicians. Of course, he was denounced as a socialist by a certain segment of his fan base, and abandoned. This was the reality of 2018: everything is political. In the old days, if someone thought you sucked, they yelled "You suck" and walked out of the club.

McBroom arrived so very late to the fete because he'd fallen asleep in the afternoon—his usual bedtime.

Christine Wong recognized him. McBroom slipped into the fete, receiving her deceptively placid but nonetheless female attention, talking to her, becoming part of the clamor. A bunch of women's bodies forcibly close to his—the highlight of the week.

In the center of the room, Chief S. and Merrill Roselli spoke of the insensible pressure they felt to maintain bodily solidarity even when it was a losing proposition, such as now. "How precious we think our personal space is!" Chief S. observed. "It's not even our space. Whatever space we take up on this planet is just borrowed."

"I know, right?" Merrill enthused.

"This isn't *my* space. I'm just borrowing it. I can't own this space. Americans are very into ownership."

"So true," Merrill enthused. "I've had people apologize to me when I'm standing in line for a movie or something, and someone shifts their weight, steps back, and they don't know I'm there. They've come to within six inches of me, and they're like, *Sorry.* I'm like, you didn't *do* anything. It's no big deal."

"We're all in this room, but we're all trying to believe that we have the room to ourselves, with tons of space around us. We should just give it up and embrace our closeness," Chief S. said.

Merrill threw his arm around Chief S.'s shoulder, and Chief S. reciprocated.

"Yeah, man!" Chief S. said. "Just give in to it. It's so much easier. We're close, everybody! Deal with it! Love it!"

"Ha ha! Chief S., you're so extra!"

"Extra what?"

"Just extra!"

"Oh okay!"

They laughed and smiled and danced up and down, bumping into Santos Gougoutris and Ronald Worthington behind them.

Some other people, however, began to feel subdued—weary though not dispirited; they simply had been standing a long time—and to speak reflectively, their minds ranging wistfully from impression to impression. Hermann Donskoy said, "I remember the feeling of dialing a telephone. A rotary phone, they called it. I am not a nostalgic person, but the dialing of a phone...that I miss."

Petra Barnhouse (she and Andrew Knuthe had remained side by side for nearly 2 hours now, connected by their budding romance) said, "Do you think you'd be a different person if you'd been born somewhere else? I mean, obviously you would. A different country, a different language, culture. I don't mean that. I think of the beach, the ocean whenever I visit someplace like the Oregon coast. I could stand on the beach for hours and hours. And I have. But then I've lived all my life inland. Pennsylvania. If I'd grown up beside the beach, would I be bored by it now? You see what I mean? If the beach bored me, I'd be an entirely different person."

Some of them began to experience a kind of clarity and easefulness, almost a full-body and full-conscience insouciance, or an encroaching peace. Lamond P. Jackson was pressed up against a bookshelf, which though hardly padded and not at all horizontal, seemed to support and cradle him as well as any sumptuous recliner. Abagail Dahl had made a bee-line to the hulking, towering Jackson upon her arrival, chatting with him ever since, and now stood directly flanking him, as required by the occasion, incredibly close, so close in fact that her breasts touched Jackson's marble-esque chest. Perhaps some of Jackson's languor was the necessity to appear unaware of this interpersonal contact, which allowed him to continue to enjoy the feeling of Dahl's breasts pressing and brushing against his body—a thing otherwise pronouncedly improper in a crowded room. At the same time, he found himself saying things that might impress a lady. "Award, no award. It doesn't matter," he said. "I've got a Purple Heart. I've got a Medal of Honor. Am I proud of them? Yes. Did I deserve them? Absolutely. But, you know, life goes on. They don't make my bed in the morning."

"Uh-huh," Dahl said, gazing up into Jackson's eyes, brown like a dusty planet more exotic than Mars.

—38—

It was a cheerless mood in the pantry. Canace and Joyce Winslow, Evonne Sorenstam-Finch, Juan Ramirez, Tara Voss, Michael Dulka, and Jerome Ardizzone each sat on the floor, their backs against the wall, shelving, or the door. Dulka was slumped, his head on Voss' shoulder. Ramirez really wanted to cuddle with Sorenstam-Finch (and cash in on a BJ), but resisted for the sake of propriety. Ardizzone and Joyce sat at opposite ends of the room. After listening to the rock music selections and senseless party gibberish of a very wasted Monti Taylor for an hour, silence had fallen. Which was worse, their captor being drunkenly oblivious or just absent? Whereas before, Monti might have craved company, or succumbed to euphoric feelings and thus opened the door, now they were really stuck.

"Clean-up on this is going to be unbelievable," Candace said to no one in particular, staring at the floor.

"Premier will help," Jerome said.

"Damn right you will."

"I'm already crafting a message," Jerome said.

"We'll need a statement from Rajani. That won't be a problem."

"Mom," Joyce said. "Maybe let's not worry about it right now." With a nod and a beseeching look, she indicated the others.

"They key to this was, treating the lout on-site was the safest option *for him.*"

"Gabe is a master at damage control," Jerome said. "He worked for the Clinton campaign." Everyone ignored him.

"What about us?" Sorenstam-Finch said. "I'm the one who unlocked the door."

"Don't worry," Candace said. "We're not going to throw you guys under the bus. *Mr. Taylor became unruly...* yada yada yada. *History of mental illness....drug addict...*"

Sorenstam-Finch sighed in relief, wanly smiled at Ramirez.

A few minutes' silence.

"How are we going to get out of here?" Michael Dulka posed, his tone signaling the obviousness of his concern.

"In time someone will come," Ramirez said.

"What are they doing out there, that's the question," Candace said. "Don't they know something's wrong?"

"Yeah, you'd think someone would notice," Sorenstam-Finch said.

"You'd be surprised how little people think of others," Candace said. "Ironically, I'm afraid to say, in our line of work especially."

"You shouldn't have bolted the kitchen door, mother," Joyce said.

"That door needed to be bolted."

"Do you think there'll even *be* an award again at this point?" Tara Voss asked.

It was an audacious question.

"I mean, it'll be a tough rebound," Voss added.

"It's true," Candace reflected. "It could be the end of the Foundation altogether."

—39—

Francisco "Isko" Bautista arrived, essentially inching through the door, closing it behind him. Jeong-Hwa Pak welcomed him. Bautista stood blinking in confusion and fear, his ears overwhelmed with the sound of conversation, his eyes unable to believe the quantity of people. He'd been told it was a nice party full of nice people and would be a nice time. There would be some kind of lottery or raffle, with twenty-five grand that he could win. But this—this was a lot like the shipping container he'd been put in, with his brother Danilo, in Manila, Philippines, where he sat inside for three hideous weeks, reeking, nearly starving to death, rocking on the seas, sitting in their own shit and piss and vomit, sweating and shaking with a fever and chills, not knowing where he'd end up.

Bautista and his brother had been promised jobs and new life in America by a Chinese man they knew named Chaing. They'd paid him $1,500 each—their life savings. But they'd been sold into domestic and commercial slavery. They'd lived to see Boston harbor, then were carted to western Massachusetts somewhere. At God's mercy, he and Danilo had been rescued after someone reported suspicious activity to the National Human Trafficking Resource Hotline. Some local authorities and the feds got involved, raided the home where he and Danilo were held and made to manufacture garments in the basement. An agency set them up with housing, counselling, food assistance, and all kinds of shit. They were working on the papers that would grant them citizenship. Some of the people in the neighborhood where this happened nominated Danilo and Isko. Danilo had since left and gone back home to the Philippines.

Bautista stood there absolutely mortified. At least they looked like okay people, dressed nicely and enjoying themselves—not evil predators. He wore a cool new suit, black, he bought at Burlington on a credit card. It was Nautica brand, and he felt pretty fancy. When he saw the bar, he took a deep breath and started to cram his way through the crowd to reach it, feeling an airy kind of dissociation take over him, as the smell of close bodies and recycled breath overtook him. By the time he reached the bar, he saw himself arrive as if from the room's highest point. A body washing to the shores of alcohol.

The heat grew and grew, and oxygen seemed to be thin. Lewis Bradley-Brown had developed a headache that he couldn't account for: A headache from one small glass of Pinot Grigio? Balooja Inamdar was breathing rapidly, a kind of involuntary panting; instinctively, she kept lifting her chin to draw air from above the height of the crowd, where it might be clearer. She found herself wondering, *Am I being a snoot?* Her nose was raised, and it just made her body feel like she was expressing something distasteful. Johan Damgaard, in conversation with Rosalind Duffy, was unable to focus as he noticed even the basic physical movements of shifting his weight and transferring a drink from hand to hand became difficult. His balance was off, as if there were ball bearings on the floor. Duffy noticed beads of sweat on Damgaard's upper lip, like dew on a peach.

Many people, on the other hand, became filled with a pleasing sensation of accreting bliss. They felt like flowers opening petals on a spring morning. They lost awareness of the displeasures of the body—their sweating, prickling skin, their clinging clothes, the inability to move freely or see farther than six inches or so, past the person before them, past the many faces and bodies on all sides forming the outer reaches of their visual landscape. They became comfortable with this conscription, and their attentions turned to even more esoteric matters within themselves, speaking with a tranquil conviction that their personal sentiments would be heard and appreciated, were valuable, even essential to the moment, essential to their existence. The ataractic ambiance worked like a wedge, freeing their most private, sometimes inconsequential thoughts, yet they feared no reprisal for any perceived vapidity.

Claire Raney had been speaking to Phil McBroom about the last Mars rover to reach the planet. Just that morning,

McBroom had listened online to audio posted by NASA, of the howling winds on the surface of Mars. He'd expressed wonder and gratitude to live at a time when he could, from the privacy of his home, hears sounds from millions of light years away, recorded only a few days ago.

"Yes, that is amazing," Raney said. "It is a time of stupendous advancement. I get scientific articles in my morning news aggregator. We're launching rockets all the time. They put a vehicle on an asteroid passing by Earth. We have new photos of the surface of Jupiter. There's also a preponderance of esoteric scientific reporting. You know, the way algorithms work, once you read one of these, they give you more and more. I did that, and now I get summations of the most arcane studies. I read them with morning coffee. I treat it like a challenge. There I am, sitting in my kitchen, trying in vain to understand what dark matter might be, how scientists know what it is but cannot quite define it or confirm its existence. Some days, there are announcements about new prehistoric rock tools discovered in Ethiopia that change the entire timeline of human history as we understand it. Some days, new galaxies are discovered right in our back yard. Astounding stuff. Inexplicable waves detected coming through the cosmos. Theta waves, gamma waves. Whatever they might be. And yet, no matter what I read in the morning with my coffee, no matter whether I comprehend it or not, my day remains the same. I get dressed and drive to the office and work. What I've found is that the universe beyond my kitchen seems like a place entirely separate, even though I know it's the same universe that my kitchen is *in*, is contained by. I might look up to the sky in wonder at times, but even then, what I see is a either a blue slate, or a blackboard dotted with white light. I don't entirely believe, or recognize, that the cosmos discussed at science.com, is *right there*. I think of it as being elsewhere—somewhere I'll never be and that doesn't pertain to me directly. This is an incorrect believe system, I know, and I believe the blame lies with me— it's my shortcomings that keep my perspective as limited as it is. But at the same time, I find myself somewhat angry with the scientists, and with humans in general. What does it matter that we can measure the way light bends and compute the mass of stars, or that we know how radiation for solar flares works or how to put a robot on Mars? How does it help us? Every day, no matter what, I get dressed and go to the office. The California hills blaze. The ice shelf melts. We could find out tomorrow that every computation about deep space is entirely wrong, our understanding of every planet and galaxy off by some margin. Nothing would be lost. Not a single person on Earth would do anything differently that day or the next, except the men and women themselves and the numbers on their scratch pads, the variables in their algorithms. The authors who put out these reports would revise them, correcting what is essentially unverifiable stuff to the majority of humanity. Some people would notice and some people wouldn't. And that would be the end of it."

"You make good points," McBroom said. He was an old-school rock-n-roller who believed women were made for dancing in music videos. All four of his marriages had ended. When it came to women, the female perspective, he had never really been "her for a day," as his hit song professed a desire to do.

Abdullah Sethwi came in, sliding in side-style through the door, which clipped the heels of Cheng Liu and Abagail Dahl upon being opened. Sethwi, 24, was dressed in khakis and short-sleeve madras pattern shirt. Huge brown eyes, big ears, neatly combed black hair and rather beguiling mustache; a slightly bemused smirk on his lips. An ethnic Hazara, he and his family had been driven out his home town Quetta, where the Hazara were persecuted, humiliated, beaten and killed. They found refuge in Indonesia, aided by the UNHCR, but were mired there for three years, unable to work, study, or attain permanent housing. When they did get out, it was to Lebanon, where they were placed in a Syrian refugee camp—a huge compound of tents on the Syrian border, teaming with tens of thousands forced to feel al-Assad's tyranny. Only because of fate and charity were Sethwi and his wife and daughter able to reach the U.S., where they've been three years now. Their plight is too awful to recount, too harrowing to state in any way other than factually. If everyone at the fete knew of the profundities of such ongoing and pernicious displacement, forced to go to the other side of the world under threat of death, they would swallow hard and withdraw their nominations to the award.

Sethwi had fretted for hours at home over the prospect of coming to the fete. Once he did work up the will, he biked from a distant suburb, afraid to take a cab or bus or light rail, because he could not afford the fees, and was not entirely convinced that all these means would keep him free of persecution, abduction or arrest and deportation. At least on a bike, if someone strange approached, he could haul ass down the alley. The crowd, he noted, moving into the town home, was not unlike those that formed behind the UN food trucks that pulled into the camp at Halba—only better dressed, smiling more—desperate for something, just not food and a chance to live.

Everyone who saw Mr. Sethwi intuited that his was a face of someone who had travelled far and endured the torments and hardships of the wider world, who clung nobly to his dignity. They welcomed him. They moved into the room farther, as much as was possible, feeling that contorting mix of gratitude and threat that was their lot.

The air was very close now and growing more and stultifying and acrid. Andrew Knuthe tried to force open the windows along the east wall, those that looked onto Washington Avenue. But they would not budge. Nearly everyone's body was in constant contact with someone else's. The occasional nudges that had persisted for a while, the infrequent bumps of arm against arm, of backside to backside, had all stopped their annoying stuttering, their pestering stop-starts, and settled into permanent, predictable pressure. (If you tried to move off someone, you moved onto someone else.) It created a sense of solidarity. Everyone was, in a sense, a facet of a single mass of connected persons, like certain vegetables that when grown in clumps sometimes mesh their material with another instance branching from the same root, becoming an indistinguishable mass.

Some people began to feel disoriented. Gabrielle Rauch suggested to George Opfell that they find today's paper and check the movie showtimes. George chuckled uncertainly, smiled; his hearing was not so good, and he figured he'd mis-understood what Gabrielle had said. Wendy Friedmann thought she'd been asked something about her children, and she told an anecdote that she believed answered the query, from Charles Knott. She said, "Oh, yes, just this morning, I was making toast in the kitchen. My son Regis, he's 11, was sitting at the counter. The kitchen island. I noticed that the ceiling fan was turning, though I didn't have it on. I said, 'Now, what the heck. Is there a ghost in here?' The fan was not switched on, you see. Regis understood immediately. 'The hot air is making it spin,' he said. And he was right. It was just like the Christmas thing with the bells, he said. We have this little brass decoration where you light a candle, and cherubs circle over the baby Jesus in the manger." After a pause, she concluded, in a way that was meaningful to only her: "So: yes, very much so."

—41—

Monti Taylor lay on the attic floor, arm draped across the 2018 FAIR award trophy, snoring. A pool of urine spreads around him like a golden halo worn around the waist (waste).

The pool of guests in the parlor was now very much like a pool—a single mass, reaching from wall to wall. The density of the place rendered most everyone immobile. If someone wanted a drink, it was passed from person to person. Drinks had largely been abandoned, however. No one could hardly raise their arms to their lips. Many waves of doubt had washed through the populace. There would be no award. There was a debacle afoot. They'd been *had* somehow—victims of a con. But as if climbing through a cloud line, they passed through those doubts, and now breathed the elucidating air of certainty. Redemption was at hand. Any moment, they'd be ushered through the doors. The wait had been orchestrated to provide enhanced contrast; to be awarded now would be an added thrill, the physical and psychic release becoming one. Paradoxically, the arrival of figures such as Abdullah Sethwi and Isko Bautista, who bore such weighty burdens, only increased the dizzying thrill of anticipation. I will have won *despite* other such deserving people being nominated. My plight is equal to that of dissidents, the displaced, the persecuted. Global-scale worthiness.

On the precipice of victory, they found it difficult to discuss anything but the qualities in themselves which had yielded the impending result, which now felt more inevitable than miraculous.

"I fought tooth and nail," Barnhouse said. To conserve space, and embracing fully the strength of their budding fondness for each other, she and Knuthe had assumed the pose of a diffident teenage couple on a street corner: she with her back against his chest, he with his arms around her waist. All they needed was a couple cigarettes and feathered hair. "And I never lashed out, even as they fed us straight-up bullshit. It's nothing, probably just minerals in the water, they said. I behaved like a Christian. My mother would have been proud."

"The playing field is *not* level," Christine Wong said. The people pressed up against her had grown tired of trying to discern when she was addressing them, and when she was just speaking aloud; and anyway, they were lost in their own reveries and struggling for air. "I saw that from the start. I didn't *look* like an American. I didn't *think* like an American. I've shown what second-generation Chinese immigrants can do. And I didn't feel like an American *girl*, either. But I stayed true to myself. My *vision*. Ironic, because of my eyes, which people mocked endlessly."

"We've got to empower youth, that's all there is to it," Merrill Roselli said. He had been pushed down onto the love seat where previously Johan Damgaard had sat weaving stories. Roselli was no more comfortable than anyone else, however, because one, the air was thicker at the lower altitude, and, two, people were forced so close to the love seat that they toppled onto it, onto Roselli. At the moment, Jóhanna Sturludóttir lay across his lap. "But young people have to empower themselves, as I have. My parents said I was crazy for sleeping out in Grant Park. But I did it. And I got arrested. And I've been speaking out ever since. I have a platform now. But it's a platform I built myself. Not literally but you know."

"Dots and dashes, dots and dashes," said Hermann Donskoy, his back against a wall near where the food tables had stood earlier. The wall acted like a vertical gurney and he gazed into the crowd blankly as one would gaze at the ceiling when strapped to a horizontal gurney. "It turns you into a kind of automaton. A computer. But that's what the armed forces do. It's what they're required to do to you, to get the results they need. I was one of the lucky ones, I came out of it all right. Most of my buddies were basket cases. I don't know what you'd call that extra layer of protection against madness, but I seem to have had it."

"I knew it wasn't right," said Joseph Hector Depace, speaking of the way his wife died, without receiving adequate medical care, because they had shit health care coverage, because they were poor, because they were immigrants. Depace stood in the center of the room, held upright like a pretzel rod stabbed into a jar of jelly beans. That is, pressured on all sides, but otherwise limp and able to enjoy the carelessness of his predicament. "We worked in this country 40 years. We paid our taxes. We never broke the law. Then, when we need help, we don't have no pension. We don't have no savings. And they call it a preexisting condition. I knew it wasn't right."

"I saw it as an extension of the current administration, for sure," Andrew Knuthe said, his knotted hands feeling the rise and fall of breath in Barnhouse's abdomen. "Fake news accusations spreading into science. That's where I put my foot down. It's one thing to refute truths about yourself. But, sorry, you don't get to refute empirical data. We're not giving you that power." Barnhouse's hair stuck to his moist face; craning and twisting his neck did not create adequate tension to draw it off, and so he left it. He had not been entangled in a woman's hair since his wife had died, and it wasn't bad.

"I'll let you in on a secret," said Darla Emmenberg, to Avi Sobol, who had become her bodyguard, of sorts, keeping people from collapsing into her wheelchair, crushing her. "On page 76 of the hardcover edition of Mark Leyner's novel *The Sugar-Frosted Nutsack* some online comments are shown. It's during this section where one of the gods is trying to corrupt everything. There's one comment from a user called **BeachGirl** where she says, 'I hate people who just laugh at everything. Do you think spina bifida is funny or the Holocaust?' I remember reading that for the first time, and being like, Yeah! Asshole gods! But now I'm thinking, What are the odds of that? I have spina bifida, and you... well, you probably weren't at the Holocaust, but maybe your parents."

"I have always felt called," Santos Gougoutris said. "The

holy spirit touched me early. I gave my life over to God. Wanting nothing. Forsaking all but duty. Matthew 20:16, So the last shall be first, and the first last, for many be called, but few chosen." Gougoutris winced. His foot had been mostly squarely stepped on.

"The forces of tyranny and oppression will never win," said Jeong-Hwa Pak. "Tyrants can never silence everyone they need to silence, they'll never operate in peace, with to-tal impunity, because there will always be people like me who will resist. But resistance should not be a violent act. Resistance should be an expression of love. When I spoke out, I did it because the North Korean regime doesn't under-stand love. They only understand consolidation of power. That, to them, feels like love. And I feel sad for them." Pak was jostled and elbowed, bumped this way and that, con-densed. Someone's skull bashed his chin. He bore it sound-lessly, looking towards the ceiling. "That's a very sad way to live. I wish dear Leader could know .... *love*."

"I did everything I could," Balooja Inamdar mused. Hollis Fillmore stood near her—in close contact really—and she be-lieved he was listening to her, though he looked wan and dis-oriented, his pupils dilated. "God willing, I made my sister proud and did her memory justice. We cannot go on serving profits. Profit are why so many thousands worked at Rana Plaza. Profit are why the owners opened for business the next day even after the cracks were identified. Human life is more valuable than profit. What good are profits if we are all dead and cannot make use of them? That's what I believe, and, God willing, I convinced a few other persons to follow this belief as well."

"That is the irony of the information age," said Johan Damgaard, who was not entirely content to become immo-bilized by the crush of his worthy peers, and slithered rest-lessly between bodies, worming to no destination in partic-ular at a very slow rate of speed, meeting muscle and bone, meeting moist, smelly skin. "It's not information that we need." Worm, worm. "It's stories." Grunt, groan. "And when I say irony, I don't mean the kind of irony that you chuckle at. I mean, really, tragedy." He rested, breathing laboriously. Because of the thinness of the air, even moving these short distances felt extremely exerting. "The tragedy of the technological revolution..." Worm, worm. "... is that we communicate faster, everything's connected, but all we transmit is data. Data and selfies. Data isn't us at all. Data is just numbers. Selfies only tell us about ourselves in a single moment, from an arm's length. Only stories reveal to us who we really are from a perspective that we cannot reach with our arms. Nnnnnnnnn. Not even the longest selfie stick ever made can show us who are in the way that stories show us!"

"It's the last frontier of privacy," said Rosalind Duffy, leaning on her crutches. The loss of her right leg after the advancement of a foot ulcer had happened only months ago. Her law suit against her HMO had not gone to trial yet, and on the advice of her doctors, development and construction of a custom prosthesis was being deferred until the verdict, or settlement, of the suit. Her crutches kept the fete crowd from closing in on her as closely as they did to others—but only from Rosalind's sides. In fact because of the proximity of persons at her front and back, like Joseph Hector Depace, she was also being propped upright like a pretzel rod stabbed into a jar of jelly beans. Really, she was able to balance on her one good leg more easily than usual. "Our most private and sacred information is that about our bodies and what we do with them. It's a civil rights issue, and it's going to affect everyone soon. I'm a cynic about it, it's true. I don't trust these organizations, any of them. There's too much money at stake. I believe there will be a headline soon about a data breach with a health care company, and I don't believe it will be a breach. I believe it'll be a sale masquerading as a breach. Did you know there are transmitters small enough that they could be injected in you. They could give you a flu shot, and put in a device that reads your blood pressure. It's horrifying. And they won't stop unless they're *made to stop*. The R&D is happening right now. This morning in a meeting, some health care executive asked the question, How can get we get more data from patients? The question wasn't asked to help you. The question was asked to use it against you."

"I've raised hell in my way," said Denise Underhill. "I started a Facebook group. Sorry, not everyone can march up to capitol hill and make a speech to Congress. People have been called out, in the ballet community. They know who they are. There's a growing movement. There's a great fat-positive podcast now. I don't *totally* align with their message. I mean, I'm not fat, I'm large-breasted. But we support each other. I think things are changing."

J.B. Washburn entered. A former lineman for the NFL, J.B. had received a nasty concussion, and joined the players council and spoke out about NFL helmet safety, pensions, and how the league is failing to take care of those who sacrificed their minds for the game. Immediately after this he was traded away and traded away and eventually he quit. He came down on the Kaepernick side of the kneeling issue, and had seen some nasty shit done to a player who came out as gay. Now Washburn was running for state senate in Virginia and had a book in the works, being co-written with a sports journalist and radio personality. J.B. had been drinking at a bar just down Washington Avenue all night. He'd been stumping for months in Virginia, and the trip to the FAIR awards dinner was a welcome getaway. No one knew him here. He didn't have to be on his best behavior. He'd actually had an erotic escapade with a lady in his hotel room earlier in the evening, then returned to the bar/restaurant, called Manny's, for a porterhouse before coming here. Sex made him hungry. "It's really crowded," he said. Because of his height, he could see the entire room. Not that it wasn't obvious. "Maybe I should—"

"No, no, come in, come in," said Cassandra Mande. "We don't turn anyone away. *Everyone* is included."

Everyone moved an inch closer to each other, putting additional pounds of pressure on each other. In many areas, multiple bodies essentially occupied the same space, to the extent that that's possible.

Washburn spotted the bar and said to Mande, "Forward drive through the perimeter. On three."

In the far corner of the parlor, things grew quiet. Petra Barnhouse, who was the first person to arrive to the fete, was the first to succumb to syncope. Whether vasodepressor syncope or neurocardiogenic syncope was not clear. The last words from her mouth before the closing of her eyes the dropping of her chin to her chest pertained to the pineapple torte she had brought. Andrew Knuthe still held her in his arms and he detected the loosening of her body, its growing weight in his arms; but he was, himself, experiencing a mix of daydream-like visions, and surging intermittent thoughts of reassurance that he was not in physical peril, and acute phantosmia—olfactory hallucinations of his mother's lemon meringue pie baking. He was actually doing a counting breath, four pulses in, four out, and trying to focus on that. "I'm sure it was delicious," he whispered of the torte, but thinking of the pie. When Petra's body went limp, he believed she had taken his words as consoling.

A survivor of the Annapolis, Maryland, newsroom shooting arrived. She was pulled in. The people near the door forcibly leaned into the crowd, bracing, driving it back, to clear a spot for her. "Come on! Come on!" they said, until the door drew open wide enough for her to pass through, and she slipped inside.

"We have to hold space," said Merrill Roselli. "Right? We have to hold space."

"Yes, yes," several said, wincing, feeling roughed-up.

"No one else is going to hold space!" Merrill chimed. One of the most idealistic of the entire group, one of the most positive and affirming personalities of all, Merrill nonetheless experienced a terrifying flash. It looked like a cube in his mind, one of those three-dimensional cubes you see on a Geometry worksheet. What if there was in fact a finite volume of space within each of us? His nerves flared as if he'd stuck his finger in a socket. The cube was sanctity, the cube was boundary. An enclosed interior within a very broad and expansive exterior. What if people who weren't activists, people who appeared to be indifferent to important causes, were in fact managing the finite space available to them in their emotional and psychological cubes? It dawned on Merrill that keeping some things out rather than bringing them smack into the center might actually be a protective measure, not apathy, not hatred, not ignorance, not a sign that the person is a troglodyte (as Merrill had been known to yell at, for example, people sneering at him and his Occupy Chicago encampment, or people commenting on his Happy Meal Medium.com stories that they would buy Happy Meals if they damn well pleased).

"Oh, fuck," Merrill said.

Merrill had always been first in line when the Red Cross Bloodmobile truck came to campus. He donated every time, and often he fainted when the nurse nailed his median nerve, hurriedly attempting venipuncture of his median cubital vein. Merrill passed out now as well. He'd been so animated all night, the people nearest him thought he was doing something like a performance, a toy solider whose mechanism winds down. A marionette whose strings are cut.

For the first time in hours, the din that had resounded throughout the parlor and the adjacent room began to subside. The place grew quieter. People no longer had the breath and strength to hold forth and issue assertive statements or parlay reflective soliloquys. A lot of incoherent, disconnected shit was being muttered quite lowly. Christine Wong whispered of the play she would write, which she now conceptualized as perhaps being multifarious, like August Wilson's ten-play "Century Cycle." The theme of Wong's opus remained death as a commodity; it still would be set, at times, in a courtroom; but now it had expanded. She wanted to incorporate concepts from quantum physics, such as the notion of time being not linear but geometrically spacial, able to be navigated like any other geographic place. She would bring together a character from different time periods. Maybe her name would be Ann. 80-year-old Ann, 40-year-old Ann, 20-year-old Ann, and 5-year-old Ann would all share the stage, which for this scene was the set of a talk show. All these Anns would share with each other the perspectives of their age. "The oldest Ann is wisest..." Wong said. "The youngest Ann ... is wise too...but in a different way." Wong was having a good time. She enjoyed authoring, and in her hypnagogic state her ideas were very accessible to her, which created the illusion of mastery. Even as her eyes closed and her head fell back, a smile remained on her face.

Quieter. Ever quieter.

The mother of a victim entered, her hand appearing first, waving to get someone's attention. Someone near the door peered out through the crack.

"The door won't open," the victim's mother said. "Is it stuck?"

"Who are you?" a guest-candidate asked.

"My daughter was mown down by a racist during a Black Lives Matters peaceful march."

"Oh, god, let's get you in here."

There was a rallying effort by a half dozen people to form a human compactor and drive the parlor's contents further in. Not to liken them to trash—not at all, not even facetiously. But the physical effects were similar to a trash compactor, the back wall of the parlor being the compactor's bottom. Thus, as space was cleared, the door was opened, and the woman entered.

She was a woman of dignity and character. Late because she'd travelled by Greyhound bus from across the country, and we all know Greyhound buses are always extremely late. She wore a colorful blouse. It was kind of sad that she'd come here. The driver's, the killer's, trial had concluded only last week. The man had been convicted of first-degree murder and eight other lesser crimes attached. He'd be in for life plus 400 years. In other words, dunzo. What good would this award do? She didn't know. Not as much as her pastor had done for her. Not as much as her family had done for her. Not as much as her community had done for her, and her friends. But the people wanted her here, and she felt it was rude to decline, so she came.

"Wildlife," George Opfell said very quietly. His face was drenched in sweat, and he reeked of perspiration laced with the curious pharmacological residue of the many medications he regularly ingested to stabilize his blood sugars and thin his blood and provide pain relief and combat acid reflux. Stale mittens in a winter closet was the smell. Or the ancient grain amaranth soaked in shallow bowl until all the moisture evaporates and mildew forms. "Landscapes...west Texas..." George's chin crashed to his chest.

Hermann Donskoy had succeeded in decoding the latest intercepted message from the Viet Cong. "Sarge," he said. "They're pushing into Khe Sanh." His eyes closed.

Quieter. Ever quieter.

Lamond P. Jackson didn't think he was going to go. He rallied his inner strength, marshalled his senses to battle encroaching fatigue, warring against the urge to close his eyes. In Afghanistan, he'd stayed awake on night watch dozens of times, steeling himself against the desert cold, alert to nearly imperceptible sounds, the lives of his brothers in his hands. But this wasn't Marjah. This was the FAIR awards. Suffocating forces overcame him. It took about five jelly beans to prop up the substantial, muscled pretzel rod of Jackson's body. But it was a tight seal, fortified by the layers of people around him in concentric rings, expanding outward. His eyes dropped, his chin hit his chest. People assumed it was a military exercise of some kind—a tactical maneuver. The prospect of this man conking out was too frightful to entertain.

As the room grow quieter and more still and serene, the sense grew within those still conscious and living, not of panic, not of alarm, but of pride. The assured repose of the victorious and steadfast. As a group, they had shown valiant ethics. They had demonstrated principles. They had turned no one away. So many worthy and deserving people had been invited, and each had been welcomed. The bounty had been shared. Even now, as rumpledness settled over them, they looked winning, in their suits and dresses. In expiration, their contented dignity shone.

"Abreme la puerta," sang Joseph Hector Depace—a song of his youth, a song of hope and loneliness. Open the door,

I'm on the street. The tune of his life. It came to him as if across time.

Abreme la puerta,

que estoy en la calle y dirá la gente...

And now the saddest part. The people will say that this is a snub.

Que esto es un desaire...

His voice grew tearful. He felt the heat of a hundred bodies enter his nose and see it wash a field of black across his eyes. "Don't play those numbers, homey." In his mind, he pressed the TOTAL button on the cash register in his shop, the button in the lower right that he'd pressed a hundred thousand times. The bell dinged, and the drawer popped open. He had the money in his hand. Finally, he rested.

Quieter now than ever. An almost perfect quiet.

Part 2

The Aftermath

—42—

The two security men in black polo shirts who had confiscated mobile phones throughout the evening began to notice at about 2:00 AM that the party had grown quieter and quieter. From the front entrance on the first floor, they kept turning their ears towards the stairwell, hearing nothing—a silence alarmingly absent of the one hundred fifty-five people they'd admitted.

"When was the last time you even heard any noise from up there?" Kendall asked. He was the shorter of the two, with a low widow's peak, a man who can easily throw two 45-lb plates on each side of a 40-lb bar, step under it, and with the weight across the shoulders, give you ten or twenty reps—however many you wanted.

"Like fifteen minutes ago," the Egyptian-born Amasis Abboud said. He had been twisting a gold ring on his left ring finger since the eerie silence had begun. He continued to do so with butterfly-like nervous energy.

"Hmm." Kendall's mouth made a figure eight. It was a very faint Sri Lankan nod, which has a bit of sideways to it.

Around 2:10 they went up to check things out.

"At this one bachelor party, everyone had just passed out," Kendall said, climbing the stairs ahead of Abboud.

"Whatever. We're on the clock until 5:00 AM no matter what. Malone showed me the work order," answered Abboud.

"Wait a second, hold on, hold on, hold on. Go back. We gotta check the locks on those cases," Kendall said, turning around, and pressing Abboud's chest with his closed fist.

Back in the lobby, they tested the locks on two steel security cases and put the iPad in a third case—the iPad that tracked guest's Programmable Phone Reclaim chips, or as Premier Events Management calls them in their Client Services trifold brochures (printed out of Ithaca, New York, birthplace of David Forster Wallace), PPRs.

"Malone will have my ass," Kendall said. "Better safe than sorry."

Upstairs.

No one answered the door when they knocked. Even when they knocked and yelled. Abboud remarked that their knocking, then rapping, then pounding, sound muted.

"What do you mean?" Kendal asked.

"There's no echo," he said. "I don't hear the knock against the walls of the place. It's like knocking on a sandbag."

"Hmm."

Just then they both heard a sound. Abboud moved away from the front door and crept farther down the hall. Around the corner, he put his ear flush against the wall. "People yelling," he whispered, his brow creased with curiosity and growing fright.

"Lemme see," Kendal said. "Holy shit." He grabbed Abboud by the shoulder. "Okay, we gotta call Malone."

"Ah, Christ," groaned Kendal. Yeah, they would have to call the A-hole.

Gabe Malone ran a tight ship. That was his thing. His business was insured. He hired reliable men who don't drink. Muslims were great: tall, strong, good-looking Egyptian men were among his best security guys. And thank God he started doing his own in-house security rather than continuing to subcontract it. Once the licensing issues had been taken care of, it turned out to be one of Malone's best moves. On a given job, the cooks, servers, hosts, chef, and sommeliers could all do their thing knowing that if a fight broke out, it was security's responsibility one hundred percent. Step aside. We got this. The guys didn't have to be rocket scientists; they just had to possess the brain power to follow some protocols. Of course Malone passed the costs on to the customer. Which is all to say he did things by the books, so as soon as he picked up the phone and heard Abboud spouting about suspicious activity, Malone called 911. Not long after that, he was into the garage himself in some flipflops and baggy jeans, falling into his Mercedes E550, tightening a

leather belt around the jiggers of well-aged bourbon slosh-
ing inside his gut.

EMTs, firemen and cops galore had Washington Avenue
blocked off before long. When the doors to the Winslow
townhome wouldn't budge, they raised Fire Chief Stan Popovich to a window in a "bucket." There he saw bodies
mashed against the glass, not a soul moving. The windows
were tall, and the ceilings of the townhome high, with bright
chandeliers still burning. "Christ almighty," he said, motor-
ing up to take in the magnitude. He estimated over a hundred bodies. All his best men waited below Popovich with
their heart monitors, paddles, and CPR kits, gazing expect-
antly up at him. He drove the motorized bucket southward
to the kitchen window and saw it empty. There—he spotted
a steel door that likely opened in a stairwell.

Police Chief Pagliacci radioed at that exact moment. He
and a team were in the interior and had found the posted
building diagram.

"There's kitchen access from a stairwell on the south
side," Popovich said.

"Affirmative, we've got ID on the door" rang back
Pagliacci.

Popovich waved to Gertz to bring him down.

Using rams, they got in and established contact with
people in the pantry. Hearing they were police, Candace slid
the key, which she had the whole time, under the door.

Candace Winslow, Joyce Winslow, Jerome Ardizzone,
Evonne Sorenstam-Finch and Juan Ramirez were all alive.
Exhausted, dehydrated, and hypoxic, but alive.

"They stopped talking," Candace said, while an EMT
struggled to administer oxygen to her. She pushed the mask
away. "What happened? We heard them go quiet."

"Let's not worry about that now," the EMT pleaded. "Let
me put this on you." She fell back, and a muffled protest
came from underneath the hiss of oxygen. "This is my house,
god damn it! My foundation! I'm responsible!"

"Just stay calm, ma'am. Please."

Ramirez and Sorenstam-Finch were taken out standing,

blankets draped over their shoulders. Joyce and Ardizzone went on wheelchairs, and Candace, lastly, on a gurney. They were all kept from going to the parlor by a blockade of police officers and medics, and their questions were rebuffed. In the time it had taken to administer oxygen and stabilize each of them, Popovich had concluded that everyone in the other room was likely dead. Firemen in full suits and helmets began scanning, with digital wands and sensors, the kitchen stove, doors, and pipes, looking for propane, argon, carbon monoxide, radon, any other deadly gasses.

All those locked in the pantry were safely sedated in emergency rooms when they threw the ground stop and the carriage bolt on the door to the parlor and George Opfell's lifeless body popped into the room like a champagne cork.

"Watch out!"

"Jesus!"

Several other bodies tumbled at Opfell's feet. A hot, sour wind wafted in.

Amid the bustle of triage that ensued after access to the parlor was attained, one Hennepin County sheriff's officer, Trent Soobill, wandered up the stairwell and inspected the attic, which he thought looked conspicuously unexplored. In the dusty, barren room behind the unlocked door he found a lump on the floor which turned into a leprechaun-like dark-skinned dude sawing logs and cuddling a trophy.

If you want to reverse course to the arrival of Officer Soobill on the scene, and instead have Monti wake during the night and abscond, never to be discovered by authorities, turn to page - 243 -.

_____

To continue, just continue.

—43—

It was a conservative pundit at a cable network who stopped calling it "The 2018 FAIR Massacre," and instead referred to the night at the Winslow's townhome as "the democratic party's exploding fete."

All the news outlets covered the event. They had a lot to talk about for many months, starting with the death count, which was topped out at one hundred fifty-five. "Justice for #FAIR155" was a slogan that grew out of the super lengthy investigation, which—what do you know?—was derided, by certain officials in the state and federal governments, as being mishandled.

The Winslows stood accused of 155 counts of murder in the second degree. "Stood accused," that is, by U.S. citizenry on social media. In the public court, they were to be hung. Much was owed to their grandiose act of self-flagellation, some felt, vanity being one of the seven deadly sins, no? Never mind the explanations; it was not characteristic of the times. Memes abounded. There was one of Candace Winslow's face atop the body of Pol Pot, the Cambodian dictator responsible for the deaths of millions. A very popular and widespread one was of Ardizzone and Joyce Winslow as Han Solo and Princess Leia. Their lines from a scene in which they're held captive aboard The Death Star are written atop them.

I love you.

I know.

Han's crooked grin makes him so devilishly handsome— like a handsome devilled ham.

In the real world, however, there was no conviction. No, no, no. Strings were pulled. You don't have to sit very long in the parking lot of the Eden Prairie Country Club with your binoculars and your plate registration records in order to understand that the judges and lawyers and county clerks and construction company owners and so on mingling on the back deck are not giving each other plumbing tips.

The bonds between donors are tight. Tight as Metallica's snare drums. Or, as they would say, Success just has a way of begetting more success. It goes to the deserving. That was, broadly speaking, their observation. It was a core belief that they regarded to be a congealing tenet of their community. That's why they worked hard and went to church on Sunday.

Only the good people with their family values who were sensible enough to stay away from social media entirely were doing any hobbies in their Fiberglas-lined basements. Why? Because they had the time, and owned their lives.

Unfortunate for the rest.

It wasn't long before long-widowed Candace and newly married Joyce both had their charges overturned, and these two fine women went back to so-called normal life. Of course, it was no longer normal, but it was the same as before in the sense of no significant recourse. They performed the requisite community service, started a foundation and so on, but were otherwise restored to society unburdened by the legal system. Only their own consciences demanded anything of them.

Ardizzone, Premier Events Management, and Grand Soir Gourmands went back to hosting gala gigs. Many of their gigs were around election affairs—fundraisers not even typically but invariably. As for Gabe Malone, some said he'd moved to the mid-Hudson Valley and was buying up properties in the dear old capitol (or as the locals called it "Ol' Cap') of Kingston, NY, as well as in the dumpier neighborhoods of towns like Catskill and Hudson. He was opening two boutique hotels and had a handshake deal with Kingston's mayor to get a shop in the upcoming mega-residential/commercial development—you know, the one with the ten mil from the state's coffers. As luck would have it, they didn't have to run it all by the historical society at all. Or do an environmental review! What a boon!

Malone was encouraged by the locals to thank Mr.

Cuomo in a Tweet, showing a photo of the new bridge. So he did, showing its spans all lit up tangerine and delicate sky blue. "Beautiful!" #nypride, etc.

While most everyone agreed that Gabe Malone had sold Premier Enterprise Group and all its subsidiaries, not everyone believed he'd upped and bailed on his beloved Minneapolis, the town where he grew up raging in the mosh pits of First Avenue to The Replacements and Fugazi, The Dead Kennedys, Hüsker Dü, and the like. Some said he'd bought a place out on Lake Victoria, out past Chaska, and was living there collecting art, serving cocktails from a mid-century modern cocktail cabinet, and entertaining the young corporate types.

Joyce Winslow actually got a book deal out of it all, so she was working on that. It wasn't just a book deal, either; it was the beginnings of a "personality empire" that would start, she was told by her new agent, with a health and fitness how-to book complete with plenty of glossy color photos of Joyce doing physical routines with kettle bells. (She looked fantastic. Never better.) Later, they'd partner with someone like Clinique and do a scent or maybe a custom line of natural foods in convenient snack sizes, low-cal and yet filling, full of omega-3s.

Candace struggled. Seclusion. Withdrawal from society. That was fine. She felt ready to retire from public life. After all, this had all come after 40 years in the role of wife of Mr. Winslow, a prominent CEO and benefactor/philanthropist. It was a life of functions and appearances, and she'd had enough.

She had a new role: prideful victim. It was all Monti Taylor's fault. That's what she told everyone who would listen. He was a lunatic, a depraved lunatic. Just ask Roger and Frances Hanwell—they knew. The guy ravaged their business, a family business they'd slaved for decades to build up, and in the course of a couple years he bled it dry with his impossible shenanigans. Custom furniture? Only a dopehead would think that would be profitable.

From the crime scene, the authorities wisely took Taylor

to Hennepin County Medical Center, while the others were taken to the University hospital at Cedar-Riverside. No cross-talk or other threats to safety. Investigators didn't know what had exactly transpired yet, but they knew it wasn't good.

The first time Candace saw Taylor after the tragedy was on television, for Taylor's arraignment. Taylor plead not guilty; Candace guffawed.

The punditry sector got a nice shot in the arm. Hours and hours of legal experts running the numbers on likely defenses. If your vision improved every time someone uttered the word "optics," you'd have been one sharpshooter after a few weeks of this. Online news articles, opinion pieces, hashtag campaigns, all the usual stuff. Jury selection was scrutinized over, and several camps were outraged at different points. A lot of new advertisers came on board at the networks during this whole unfortunate tragedy.

Monti was held without bail until the trial, a few months later. The charges were reckless endangerment in the second degree, a felony. Taylor appeared in a navy blue jumpsuit, hair shaved to a millimeter. He looked disturbingly more African-American than ever, but also more serene in the visage, a certain practiced remorsefulness in his eyes. Actually, maybe making his skin color more prominent through additional scalp exposure was tactical.

Duke and La Hanwell each testified for the defense—excoriating lies of the most preposterous kind, their specialty. Gail was a key player from the stand. She came across as a kind of Anna Nicole Smith for the millennial set with a dash of Tonya Harding thrown in. In the end, Taylor's state-appointed attorney, a woman named Heath, capably argued that the terms for serious physical injury of the reckless endangerment statute were not met. None of the plaintiffs whom Taylor locked in the pantry suffered organ impairment; none of them suffered protracted health impairment or serious disfigurement or any impairment at all, in fact, that increased their risk of death. Heath went further: "Your honor, the Winslow kitchen pantry is spacious, comfortable, and well-stocked."

Larry Blackwell was back on the scene—the Hanwell shyster in chief who'd put the squeeze on Monti. (Taylor flipped him the bird once from across the courtroom). "Objection!" Blackwell exclaimed, standing up, "Your honor, uncooked rice makes birds stomachs explode; that's why it's not allowed to be tossed around at weddings."

"Your honor, the plaintiffs are all humanoid in form," Heath said, wearing her smart taupe skirt-suit. "They're not birds."

"Objection overruled. Mr. Blackwell, perhaps you should take a biology class."

The judge—it was Lance Fucking Ito himself; he was back—awarded three years' probation and court-ordered substance abuse treatment! Smack went the gavel. Taylor stood and smiled.

Yet, Candace managed to patently misconstrue in her conception of things the fact that Taylor wasn't in the parlor and had no direct hand in the deaths of the FAIR155. Not a single one of them. In her mind, however, he remained directly responsible, and she continued to spout this line of reasoning and deride the legal system that allowed for such atrocious miscarriages of justice. It gave a her a lot to brood on, and under different circumstances might have roused her to civic action—this problem in society of crime and fair sentencing, it needed to be solved. But for now she wouldn't be the one solving it.

More painful to her than even this was the lingering question of whether, when it was all over, she might be decreed by future generations as having fallen "on the wrong side of history."

Thusly, with these concerns she holed up firmly in the townhome on Washington Avenue (an avenue named, by the way, for our America's very first president), systematically redecorating, replacing every carpet, cabinet, table and credenza until the place no longer resembled the site of the 2018 FAIR Award dinner. She gutted the Louis Quatorze, from the floorboards to the yellow poplar built-ins to the egg and dart molding, and kitted it all anew in austere Danish modern. Charles Knott led the design phase.

Candace was civil with the decorators and laborers shuffling around her home and making a royal dustheap of it. Her heart remained guarded, however.

From the get-go, Candace never spoke the word massacre, and she never would. There would never be another FAIR award awarded, and that pained her. *She was* the FAIR award after all, and it was her. It was her baby. They'd had nine marvelous years—Candace having started the foundation in 2010. But, as wig banks face infestations, so do the pillars of society crumble in changing weather.

During those long afternoons inside the 6-bedroom house, often it all came back to Candace, despite the association-free sleekness of the decor. Any time she closed her eyes, really, and so her days often were "bolstered by pills," to borrow a phrase. These pills were supplied by Dr. Rajani, who after enduring his testimony, cross-examination, and subsequent investigation by the state medical ethics committee (Clean as a whistle!), took up classic cars as a hobby. Basically just buying them, knowing what's under the hood, storing them properly, occasionally driving them, and then of course showing them off. The first car he added to his collection was a green Aston Martin DB4.

Whenever he held dinner parties, he continued to perfect his recipe for pasta fazoula.

About a year after the event, once the verdict backlash had fizzled down to embers, and the street protests and marches stopped, once the whole tragedy was well buried in people's consciences by other tragedies, their attentions thoroughly snagged by corporate malfeasance, legal injustices, political scandals, celebrity wrong-doings, additional school shootings, class action suits, and the usual electioneering scrums (2020 was an election year after all), Candace kind of felt left out or otherwise ready to take additional steps towards healing the community, and so she came up with the idea of a monument—a memorial. With the right donations to the Minneapolis Parks Commission and to the

Guthrie Theater, who co-owned the land, space was allotted in Minneapolis' Gold Medal Park. Gold Medal was a brand of flour made by Pillsbury in the huge flour mill that used to be *the* major economic driver of Minneapolis in its early days. Candace's donations were sizeable enough to make Gold Medal Park into FAIR155 Park.

Corporations are people these days, so what's the difference?

For the curious, yes, as it happens Candace *did* know several women on the Guthrie Theater's board of directors—they'd been going to one another's balls and galas and dinner cruises since 1960 or so, back when you could get good chintz by the yard.

An 8-ton granite sculpture honoring the victims was dropped by a Terex crane at the top of the 32-foot-high mound at the center of the grassy park, even though the mound had been made in honor of the shape of ancient Native American burial mounds that used to dot the landscape of Minnesota's prairies. Oh, well. There was symmetry in the fact that just across the street was Remembrance Garden, in tribute to victims of a 2007 highway bridge collapse. In this sense, from a chamber of commerce perspective, the Gold Medal park redesign was a good thing because the Grief & Tragedy segment of the tourism market was really booming, and the second memorial would really make Minneapolis' "East Downtown" area a huge draw. They would also do a bust of Joseph Hector Depace, on a nice tall pedestal.

You have chosen to let Monti get away.

—44—

Darkness. A very unsettling kind of darkness that Monti was accustomed to. If you waited a while you could typically remember drinking with someone at some point the night before. Oh, yes, those bastard rich fucks, circle-jerkers of the Hanwells. He remembered the incredible throng, the goddamn *rager* that was going on in their place, and he remembered feeling dehydrated and stoned as all hell and quite happy-numb for a while, but also knowing that the Oxy had done him in. Yeah, that happened. Where was he now, though? He rolled onto his back to begin the detective work, uncoiling his arms from some unshapely metal contraption.

The trophy! Fuck's sake. He shoved the thing aside.

There was light in a nearby window. Getting onto his knees, he peered out. Street lamps. Bar La Grasse! Christ, he was at the Winslow's still, in their attic!

You're a dead man, Il Duce! Taylor recalled hearing. Who had said that?

Parched, mouth cakey, eyes crusted, still drunk, he stood and took some rejuvenating breaths. All right—options? Across the room, he found the door he'd come in, but remembered the pantry, having forced those stiff pricks in there. *Shit!*

Oh, additional *shit*: he had been playing around with a knife at one point.

Back at the window, he peered out. It was a shed-style dormer, roof tiles just outside it. The paint cracked when he forced the widow up. There was no screen. Okay, here we go. He patted his jeans pockets like any upstanding working man headed out the door to the office. Gigantic iPhone 6, unmistakably present. Weed pen—present. Small key fob for the Grand Cherokee—miraculously also present! Things were looking up.

Monti took one last look behind him, lunged back and snagged the trophy. Why not? A memento.

Out on the tiles (Zeppelin III, track 5) it would be nice to say that all Taylor's expertise and experience from bridge-work welding, that his climbing of girders and hanging from precarious ledges, as well as the sign-hanging up in the rafters of Hanwell Mercantile, came in handy. It did not. He wasn't wearing any type of harness, for one thing, and the clay tiles were dewy-moist, and the pitch must have been 60 degrees. His first move was to sit, trying to keep his center of gravity low, but his shoe gave out and he tumbled onto his back to keep his patella from exploding against the hard tile. As he barrel-rolled off the roof, he saw his life—no wait, that was only the vaguely seraphic figure, the golden lady, of the trophy, which he still clutched. The branches of a massive Northern Catalpa tree in full flower, how nice, broke his fall. After a succession of sharp jabs about the ribs, back and head, and a painful scraping across the face, the ground walloped his entire body at once.

Stillness. Ears ringing.

There are walks of shame, and then there are walks of grace. Taylor was immune to shame. He was shameless—somewhat like the name of some Irish poets. He'd been battered before. Bar fights—sure. Sleeping in strange places, like cars, that'll do it too. But he knew how to carry himself in a way that revealed neither pain nor misgivings, or really anything untoward about one's dire condition. This was his special gift of grace. It only required a forward thrust of his animal nature—a move Taylor saw as not obnoxious, in fact defensible, because it's naturalistic, by nature. On Washington Ave., he empowered the essential creature within. Essential creatures have a right to walk around town at any hour, irregardless [sic] of alleged prior doings, no? Cloaked in this unassuming air, he left the grounds of the Winslow's huge neo-Gothic building, (it was neo-Gothic, right?) he found Washington Avenue and strolled along the sidewalk, holding the trophy in one hand as one holds a bag of groceries. He might have whistled, if he didn't fear discovering his teeth had been loosened in the fall. Again and again he clicked the key fob in his pocket.

Bwip-bwip!

"Fuck yeah," Taylor said, spotting the blinking tail lights of his vehicle.

A '78 Chevrolet Caprice Classic rolled by and honked at him. Monti tipped his hat, which was not there.

At Ked and Olivia's place, Dingo had shit on the living room couch. That was fine.

"Oops. Have a little accident there, Dingo?"

Dingo was springing from the floor to Monti's chest again and again. Excitable pooch.

Leash, found in a drawer. Taylor had bought a leash since the run-away incident of Day 1. He put dingo on it now. Then he disposed of the turds using paper towels, added food and water to Dingo's bowls, and climbed the stairs to the master bath, where he inspected himself in the mirror.

A red scrape down his cheek and neck. Shirt off—ow!—a big reddish irritation of the skin at the right lateral deltoid, extremely tender to the touch, and upon closer inspection yellowing quickly subcutaneously. Profound soreness of a hip, no visible marks. A gash on a thigh, not deep, and a knot on a shin. Creaky pain in an ankle. All in all, Taylor figured he probably would survive without treatment. He rotated the shoulder, working the delt. Not good. The delt was the only question mark.

He slept the sleep of the dispossessed, ailing delt toward the ceiling.

Daylight, sometime on the functional side of noon. Taylor emerged from the bathroom in a cloud of steam, a towel wrapped around his waist. From his duffle bag, he fetched fresh-ish jeans and his favorite top: a red Queens of the Stone Age shirt from the *Era Vulgaris* tour. Sitting on the bed to clip his toenails, he flipped on the 40-inch 4K strapped to the wall of Ked and Olivia's bedroom. From it, the unfurling horrors danced toward his eyes in multi-layered forms: scrolling text about a body count; the chillingly familiar sight of the Gothic spires, the filials and tile shingles of the Winslow townhome, even in the foreground some boughs of the flowering catalpa tree!; and finally, as Taylor juiced the volume, the somber/piqued tone of the news anchor's voiceover reciting the gruesome, fresh-as-cut-earth facts.

"...first responders on the scene. Fire Chief Popovich is scheduled to make a statement this afternoon. In the meantime, multiple deaths, as many as *one hundred* or more, that is the tragic scene on Washington Avenue in Minneapolis this morning. Again, if you're just joining us..."

In the kitchen Taylor rhythmically gulped a giant glass of tap water, washing down four 200-mg tablets of Aleve. Hands shaking, he ripped open cupboards to piece together a pot of coffee, while CNN played on his phone.

"...and Director Candace Winslow all taken to Cedar-Riverside Hospital, where they are undergoing treatment and reported to be in stable condition."

He dashed to the sink, feeling protestations from the gut-full of water. Spitting and coughing, he fought a hurl. Dingo (he'd let the mutt back in) stared up at him, actually twisting his head in the eerie simulation of human curiosity that was Dingo's principle charm. The Pekinese in him really shone at these moments; this look of apparent canine compassion had garnered many Insta likes back in the days when Dingo was Gail's constant companion and served as "resident beast" of Hanwell Mercantile. Now he wanted to kick the animal in the face.

Taylor gazed out the kitchen window at the back alley, without much of its contents really registering upon his brain. "Well," he said. He sighed heavily and pushed himself away from the counter as a boatman shoves himself off a dock.

He put on shades and ball cap, slipped out to the garage, where he violently shoved and tossed the belongings he'd so carefully brought from Tania's place—shoved them to the back and sides of the garage, making just enough space to pull the Cherokee in. The garage door lowered with loud finality.

Dingo still sat in the kitchen, no longer curious but a touch judgy in the eyes and snout. "Fuck you, Dingo," Taylor said, returning into the house and going with a heavy step to the rear of the house and descending the stairwell to the basement. At the bottom of the stairs, he faced the sign Ked had drawn by hand: **Gurmukhi Studios.** Taylor grabbed and twisted the handle.

With all the cold deliberation he could muster, he lifted down the red Fender telecaster with the rosewood body—the entire body was rosewood, not just the fretboard—from the wall mount, found the Fender hard case, put it in, and snapped the latches. Then the same with the limited edition Randy Rhoads Jackson Flying V (white polka dots on black paint job). The gold of its pickups gleamed with promises of glory—damn it, he looked!

With one guitar case in each hand, Taylor climbed the stairs like a pallbearer doing double duty, a knot in his throat, through which he hummed a warbled version of the Ozzy Osborn classic "Crazy Train."

Good times, he said to Dingo at the top of the stairs. Dingo perked up.

At Twin Town Guitars on Lyndale Avenue, where they dealt in new and used instruments, the guy was appropriately inquisitive about the cause for sale. "Why you letting these beauties go, man?"

"Need the money, you know," Taylor managed to choke out. He kept his shades on in the shop, hiding his guilty eyes. He prayed to ...something... that the guy didn't ask him to play so much as "Smoke on the Water."

The sale required showing his ID—couldn't be helped. While the guy scribbled out a receipt ticket, the incriminating peal of police sirens wailing Dopplered past.

"Jesus," Monti said aloud, then mentally facepalmed his nose into the rear wall of his skull. Lyndale Avenue was a main thoroughfare leading to downtown, but that's not what it sounded like.

"Can you believe this with the FAIR awards, man?" the shop guy said.

"Fucking unbelievable," Taylor grumbled.

A sweat-inducing half hour later, he walked out with a check for $5,100. He pulled the Cherokee calmly away, and swore up a fucking storm for a solid half-mile—just letting off tension, just cursing his life. Dingo barked along. He sat in his wool-lined bed on the passenger seat.

Bank drive-thru in ballcap and shades. He didn't risk going into the lobby to cash it. He could just pull cash from the road—the bank was national. He'd leave a transactional trail, unfortunately, but what could he do?

Deposit. Punching buttons. Whistling. Mumbling, *Come on, come on, come on.* God damn ambulances screaming up the road—cut the sirens already! Nothing to be done about the cameras everywhere. Receipt like a tongue.

And out of here.

Thirty-five W is the interstate that leads south of Minneapolis. There are about one hundred and forty-four spots you can get on it in the Twin Cities. It's a commuter's town. Convenient travel is a civic priority. Heading to the first, at 31st Street E., he and Gail's old dealer leapt to mind—Ross. How easy it would be to contact him. Imagine the shit-ton of little round white innocuous-looking Oxy pills one could obtain with five grand. No, no, no, just get your ass out of town. Out of town, there wouldn't be anyone Taylor knew to score from—not that he couldn't figure it out using Craigslist or trolling the parks of whatever town he ended up in.

Just go, just go, just go. Gas, gas, brake. He looked at his weed pen. Just wait, just wait, just wait.

The 31st Street ramp was closed, all busted up by a back hoe. "Fuck!" Getting to the next at 36th Street was a god damn nightmare. He went the wrong way down 1st Avenue, a one-way avenue going north. Jumping off there to avoid accident or arrest put him on something else that made the 46th street ramp the better option. His phone beckoned. Weaving down Lyndale, he thumbed into his contacts and deleted Ross, tossed the phone back in the center console face down.

"God damnit!"

Still, he knew where the guy lived, and it seemed like his hands might yank the wheel in that direction any second. Around 40th Street, he passed through a commercial corridor overrun by geriatrics, stroller-pushing pedestrians, and idiot drivers. Again the Cherokee was filled with throat-strained cursing and Dingo's sharp yips. By the time Taylor gunned it up to highway speed, he was nearly in tears, and felt 80 percent out of his mind.

Two songs later, though, the cabin of the Cherokee was thick with weed vapor and thrumming with the rhythms of Queens of the Stone Age's "Misfit Love." He'd passed through the last of Minneapolis' southern suburbs, Burnsville. Ahead of him lay the flat-ass landscape of southern Minnesota. All the silos one would ever care to behold. The corn was only knee-high this time of year, yet its rows still strafed in the eyes of the passing road-warrior. Five hours to Des Moines. Somewhere between here and there, he hoped to trade the Cherokee for a conveyance of a different provenance, while eating as little into the $5100 as possible. A dead swap would be ideal.

Taylor felt more cheerful.

"What do you say, Dingo?" In all the movies Taylor had seen, the canine companion offered shows of support, even if it was just a bleary lifting of the head.

Dingo said nothing.

"That's so like you, buddy," Taylor said, patting Dingo's head.

—45—

Evonne Sorenstam-Finch sat in rock pose on her yoga mat at the front of Studio A, the room in the Center for Healing & Emotional and Spiritual Safety dedicated to yoga and meditation. There was also a library, a youth center, Studios B & C, a media room, a kitchen, several private talking spaces, and some outdoor facilities in the back yard. She was demonstrating a breath and posture for her one student who sat before her, a light-skinned black man in his early thirties, a filmmaker named Paul Treeley.

The events of the 2018 FAIR Awards dinner were behind her. Ironic how her previous traumas of being kidnapped and held captive and being married to a controlling, psychopathic closeted gay Christian had prepared her for the relatively breezy trauma of being shut in a kitchen pantry for 5 hours or so. Of course she had Dr. Martin as well. They brought somatic cognition therapy to her experience of the 2018 FAIR awards dinner as soon as Sorenstam-Finch got back to Pittsburgh—well before the trial began, which required her presence to testify.

It was difficult to comprehend that 155 people had died in a nearby room all the while that she sat there bored and guiltily wondering if she was the winner selected for the award. But it was enlightening to see that, not incidentally, it was her sexual motivation that had gotten her in the bind to begin with. Residual misinformed thinking from the Dudzic affair: believing Ramirez would only like her if she serviced him sexually.

That was then. Sorenstam-Finch did the work and recovered fast. All in all, she did not feel terrorized by the event— just as stable as before, practically; it was just a case of another element to add to the regime she already had in place: of not suppressing, hiding from, ignoring, belittling, judging, or transfiguring her feelings into false or more comfortable feelings. She was getting on pretty well.

No question, the settlement helped. Tara Voss had reached out to Evonne and Juan Ramirez to join her and Michael Dulka in a lawsuit against the Winslows and the foundation. Sorenstam-Finch didn't want to make waves or offend Candace. It took some convincing—done by Dr. Martin, who identified Sorenstam-Finch's latent desire to have the Foundation belatedly announce the winner who'd never been announced, and to have it—of course—be her. This was not likely to happen, she came to face. Eventually she signed on as a plaintiff, and the civil suit was settled out of court. Voss, Dulka, and she each received a sum, and Sorenstam-Finch used hers to upgrade her plans to *rent* a space for her dream center to *buying* a sumptuous three-story walkup not in Troy Hill, but, even better, in nearby Old Allegheny Rows Historic District.

"Arms are in the up position, like this, sixty degrees" Sorenstam-Finch said. Seeing Treeley mimic this: "Good. And it's a forceful inhale and exhale through the nose like this." She demonstrated the breath. "You've done this one."

This was S-F and Treeley's third session together. Yes, initially her target population was young adults, who are vulnerable. But she'd been advertising in local sources, and word was spreading through the Pittsburgh healing arts community that this new place, Anahata (the Sanskrit name of the fourth, or heart, chakra) offered just about everything yoga-wise at great prices.

"Breath of Fire, right?" Treeley said.

"That's the one. Eyes are closed down, fingertips curled to the palms, thumbs extended. Annnnd timer is on." Sorenstam-Finch turned up the music on the iPad connected to the in-house system.

Drums pounded. They both closed their eyes, rolled them in and up to look at their brow points. Their rhythmic breathing, *ff, ff, ff, ff, ff, ff, ff,* was all that could be heard other than the *tablas* and *dholaks.*

This was just a warm-up. Afterwards, they did a full set of postures, standing, sitting, kneeling, targeting the fifth chakra, the throat chakra.

When it was all over, and their mats rolled up and put back in the cubby, the music turned down, they sat in some giant beanbag chairs drinking tea.

"That was amazing once again, Evonne."

"Oh, thank you."

"I can feel ideas coming for my screenplay. How did you come up with this stuff?"

"Well, I didn't come up with it exactly. The practices are codified in books from a yogi who taught in the sixties in California."

"Right."

"But the idea to offer this class in particular, that came from a dream, actually."

"A dream?"

"A man came to me in a dream. He spoke to me. Artists, he said. Writers. These are the ones who need your guidance, your teachings. He himself was a storyteller. I just *knew* this—you know what I mean?"

"Mmm," Treeley assented.

"He showed me his own body, like the insides. It's hard to explain. He was just able to turn it inside-out. I saw a black mass, like a tumor maybe, which I understood to be ego. It was blocking everything, clinging to everything, mucking up his body, causing him great pain. Then he showed me pens and notepads, keyboard and books."

"Hmm. Interesting."

"Crazy, right?"

"Who do you supposed it was?"

"No idea. He seemed to be riding on an iceberg. He seemed to be speaking to me from the Arctic Circle. His hair was very contemporary. He reminded me of Benedict Cumberbatch."

"Huh."

Just then Sorenstam-Finch's phone buzzed. She glanced and saw it was Ramirez texting. He was gone. She'd kicked him out about two weeks past, and he wasn't coping well.

They regained contact about 45 days after the awards

dinner. He came to Pittsburgh from Minneapolis, where he lived, as soon as Sorenstam-Finch invited him, and he didn't go back. At first, it was lovely and romantic. With the Foundation disbanded, kaput, and his settlement money in hand, Ramirez started a poetry and photography journal, which was fine, though not lucrative. The problem was, he had no practices of his own. Initially respectful and curious of her many modalities, after a month or two, he started to complain about the cupboard space that her teas took up and generally to kid her about how gung-ho she was for all that is holistically medicinal. Then one day he ordered her to turn down her sitar music. It was a "Ajai Alai"—a beautiful mantra! Soon his handsomeness came to reflect more of an arrogant swagger, and he bought lots of new clothes, and when she was at the Center leading classes or writing curriculum or hiring staff, or counselling teens, he was drinking tequila with his poet friends, smoking cigarettes, and planning revolutions and crazy trips to the gravesites of poets Federico García Lorca and Rainer Maria Rilke.

She made it clear that if this is what his lifestyle was going to be, it wasn't going to work. Ramirez pretended to change his ways for a few weeks, cashing in on the sex, trying to converse about spiritual well-being. But he failed miserably at that because Sorenstam-Finch was no dunce. "Strike two" was enough for her—the last straw. When he came home at 4 in the morning stumbling drunk, toting a bag of fried chicken, she sent him packing.

He'd been texting his regrets ever since; she'd been ignoring the texts.

This Treeley character was nice. He was divorced from a woman named Pamela, dabbled in documentary film and creative writing and amateur philosophy. He lived in up in the boonies in New York but made the pilgrimage to her studio on a gut-shot whim after his browser mysteriously redirected him to a google news story about the Center for Healing & Emotional Safety, in which Sorenstam talked about the new series of workshops she was running on ego. He called it a "total rando." He said it he was in the shower on morning with music blasting through his PC, a song called "Superunknown." When he got out, the page was open. Sorenstam-Finch didn't blink at this cosmic happening.

The two stood and looked out on Old Allegheny Rows. The evening was early but it seemed promising.

—46—

A mellow summer night at Nordhaus Lofts, where Jerome Ardizzone and Joyce Winslow bought a top-floor penthouse together after Jerome received his recent raise. He lounged on low-slung piece of padded deck furniture on the balcony with a glass of Mezcal on the rocks in his hand. Slices of the sky peeking between downtown's skyscrapers appeared to him to be a color he knew as Yale Blue. In 15 minutes, night would be total, a daily achievement that Jerome had been meeting with a touch of unease ever since the night of the FAIR awards dinner. He had his consolations, however.

Just behind the glass door where he sat was the kitchen: its quartz countertops, its undermounted sinks, its in-wall USB ports, all of which he cherished. These were the finishings of the resilient. They signified Jerome's not-only-continued but increased relevance to the elite professionals of the Twin Cities. He was still a striking figure on the social landscape—and still wore 33-inch waist pants, and was still gluten-free. In six days, he'd be hosting a 300-head, 12-hour party aboard the two-decked, 130-foot *Catherine*, a yacht owned by the CEO of one of Minneapolis' professional sports teams. His schedule for the remainder of the summer looked just as prestigious, right up until August's trip to Morocco.

"Gorka tonight, babe?" Ardizzone called. A single star, he noticed, winked white in the sky.

Joyce was changing clothes in the bedroom. She'd done some press interviews about the workout/recipe/lifestyle book in the afternoon, after which she endured a long commute home from the studios in St. Paul. The interstate was always a bitch crossing the river. "Mmm," she moaned skeptically. "What about Alma?"

"Alma," Jerome mused, getting up. "Alma'd be okay." He stepped inside, his bare feet on the living room's cool bamboo floor.

"They have that watercress and truffle thing," Joyce said, walking in, flipping her hair out of her blouse collar.

"Yeah, sure."

"And you like the duck."

"I *do* like the duck."

They met in the middle of the room to exchange a kiss and a pat. "Lemme just have a glass of blanc."

"No hurry." Jerome plopped on the couch and flipped on the TV. He liked to get the latest poll numbers on the up-coming election. Instead of that however—

"Oh boy."

"What?"

"Something on Damgaard."

"*Damgaard?*" As in—Was it dirt? As in—His estate has been raking in millions in posthumous sales. Is the guy's shit not air-tight?

Speaking of enduring, worse than rush-hour traffic was enduring what Jerome and Joyce had already endured: a full 12 months of post-FAIR media blitz. Legal analysts ballpark-ing what a reparations package should total (in USD). Panels discussing what safety inspections should be required of properties and facilities used by nonprofits. All manner of feel-good remembrance pieces on the victims, replete with shots of empty garages, empty barstools, empty coatrack pegs. Ardizzone and Joyce were compassionate people, but there were limits. They personally were no longer dwelling on the event—it was in the past.

Was that was easier to do when you hadn't managed to lose a loved one? Perhaps, Jerome would have said. Never-theless, there were limits, and often the best thing with a tragedy was to just move on.

Joyce came over with her wine and sat, legs tucked under her. She raised the flute to her lips. "Hardline?" she said skeptically, reading the show's title watermark in the corner. "I thought they were off the air."

There was a whiff of the Trumpian about her remark; Je-rome chose to ignore it. He juiced the volume.

Male voice, clearly of a journalist: "He wasn't?"

Female voice, Danish accent: "No, he grew up in Roskilde, a town outside Copenhagen."

Candid home photos of the Danish storyteller flowed across the screen. His youthful, somewhat goofy face and fluffy blond hair. Then video showing the adult Damgaard, the stylized story-teller/guru gesticulating profoundly on a stage, the giant TED logo on a screen behind him.

Male journalist: "Do you think he's a fraud?"

Female, Danish accent, now on screen, a dour looking woman in her thirties in a bizarre plum-colored blouse: "...Yes, I do think he was a fraud. He never climbed any *gerlaap* trees. I mean, maybe once or twice. But I'm certain he wasn't even from Aalborg, like he said."

In the *Hardline* studio, the *Hardline* reporter, a handsome man in a dark suit, steps ever-so-slowly towards the camera. "With the help of Johan Damgaard's cousin Signe Damgaard, *Hardline* retrieved records from Danish government offices showing that," (the journalist lifts the single sheet of white paper in his hand) "indeed, Johan Oscar Damgaard lived in *this* brick home at 78 Vestergrade, in one of Roskilde's charmingest neighborhoods."

A cute little red-brick house with a red tile roof is shown.

Next *Hardline* showed various excerpts from Damgaard's writings, reproduced on screen, all of them citing an upbringing in a rustic cabin deep in the Denmark's Gribskov Forest, in Central Jutland. The cousin debunked several other of Damgaard's top-selling inspirational yarns.

"People will still buy his books," Jerome said.

"And listen to the podcast," said Joyce.

"And enroll in his retreats."

They watched a bit more, which indeed featured media bigwigs looking into the crystal stock ticker, kicking around the question of Damgaard Enterprises' future earnings potential.

Announcer tease: "When we come back...Damgaard's publisher distances themselves from the author."

"Ah, they'll be fine," Jerome said at last. He stood up and killed the power to the 54-inch Samsung. "Now let's go get me that duck."

On his way out, he stopped in the prized kitchen that he never used. His tumbler of Mezcal was sweaty on the outside, a phenomenon he found to be one of the eternal charms of summer. Draining it of Mezcal, pleasantly water-down and nicely chilled, he set down the rattling glass on the quartz countertop. He knew no matter how many nights he left it to sit, the quartz would never stain.

www.ingramcontent.com/pod-product-compliance
Lightning Source LLC
Chambersburg PA
CBHW031940010726
47493CB00007B/2009